The Soldier's Trainer

The Caregivers, Volume 6

Rose Fresquez

Published by Rose Fresquez, 2022.

Copyright © 2022 by Rose Fresquez.
ISBN: 978-1-961159-05-1

All rights reserved. Except for use in any review, the reproduction or utilization of this work in whole or in part in any form by any electronic, mechanical or other means, now known or hereafter invented, including photocopying and recording, or in any information storage retrieval system, is forbidden without the written permission of the publisher.

The Soldier's Trainer is a work of fiction. Names, characters, places, and incidents are either the product of the author's imagination or are used fictitiously, and any resemblance to actual persons, living or dead, business establishments, events or locales is entirely coincidental.

To my editor, Deirdre Lockhart. You're a true blessing from God. Your insights and wisdom have helped shape this story.

To all men and women who make sacrifices to fight for our freedom. Thank you!

To my children Isaiah, Caleb, Abigail and Micah, you fill my heart with joy. Thanks for the giggles, laughter and encouragement.

And to GOD, Who makes everything possible. Without God's wisdom and creativity, this story wouldn't be in existence.

ACKNOWLEDGEMENTS

I WANT TO THANK THE Lord, my Savior. Without you, Father, there's no point in trying to do anything at all. It's my prayer that I can honor you with my words. I thank you for connecting me with an amazing group of people who helped support me in accomplishing this novel.

To my husband Joel, who works so hard to provide for our family, so that I can stay home and take care of the kids. I'm so blessed that we get to journey through life together.

To my insider team, thanks for always suggesting the coolest ideas.

Anna Bottoms, Melissa Levert and Brandi Bryant (A veteran), thank you for helping me with my research for the Hero in the Soldier's Trainer.

Jerri Hall, Thanks for your support and encouragement always. You're such an inspiration

To Nicole, Deb, Melissa, Marie, Nancy, Linda, Katherine, Elizabeth and Trudy. You ladies are so amazing for the time you invested to brainstorm, beta read and critique my manuscript. Thank you from the bottom of my heart.

CHAPTER 1

Chad Whitlock shifted in his seat when a woman not much older than him adjusted her hand to dominate the armrest. He repositioned his arm oddly, felt a pop in his right shoulder, then winced at the faint pain that lingered from minor shrapnel injuries three months ago. He intended to keep his pain to himself.

His hip was better now, which should make him grateful. But how could he feel anything other than horror when he was alive and his friends had died? They'd almost made it through the sixty-two days left in their company's rotation.

His chest tightened with a searing loss as he fought memories of that tragic day.

Stifling a yawn, he peered through the window to the white clouds the plane floated over. He had no idea how long the flight from Virginia had been, but he'd stay awake until he landed in Pleasant View.

He didn't need a raid of nightmares planting IED explosives in his brain among the other horrifying images that taunted him in his moments of stillness. But he *did* need a clear mind when he met Tessa Richardson.

Not that he was confident Tessa was waiting for him at the airport. If by some miracle she showed up to pick him up, how long before she realized her mistake in inviting him to stay with her family?

He let out a slow breath. As long as he kept his demons under control, everything should work out. Thank goodness he had a triathlon to train for.

His army paycheck was minimal, mainly because he'd enlisted in a voluntary position. Financially secure, he didn't need to work, although he intended to get a job after the triathlon and jump right into civilian life. Boredom wasn't an enemy he'd ever surrender to.

He shuddered, cringing at the thought of the unknown. What was life like after combat? Having enlisted at seventeen, he'd never had a career outside the army. Now, after twenty years of friendship and brotherhood, he could only hope he'd fit into the new lifestyle—a beginning with the girl he'd met a year ago through the mail before progressing to emails and FaceTime.

Their friendship started when she sent packages to his unit. They'd opened two big boxes with nuts, beef jerky, energy bars, and everything that reminded him of America. Then her simple note opened his heart.

Dear soldiers,

Thank you for your sacrifices for our nation. If I could thank you in person, I would in a heartbeat. Please know you're not forgotten. My church and I pray for your safety often.

Tessa Richardson.

While everyone was fascinated with their snacks and swapping for treats, he'd reread the note. Who wrote letters these days?

Never one to get packages, he'd been touched by the stranger's kindness. Compelled to thank her, he sent his letter to the return address. She'd written him back almost three weeks later, and he'd responded, beginning their friendship.

Whether Tessa showed up today or not, she'd given him a reason to survive the last mission while he waited alone to die after his companions. He'd struggled to dig his wallet from his pants pockets, just to stare at her face one more time. Her kind smile triggered a memory of their conversation before they'd been called to detonate a possible Improvised Explosive Device (IED).

With his strength renewed, he saw her smile while her words echoed—*"I can't wait to meet you in person!"*

Words that gave him hope he could survive and have a new start with a friend like her. Or at least he'd convinced himself she'd be a friend and nothing more.

After hours of Chad yawning and shifting, the pilot announced their landing and reminded them to fasten their seat belts. Once they landed in Pleasant View, Chad flung his duffel bag over his left shoulder and walked through the terminal, barely registering the activity as he scanned over the heads of people in the small airport.

He hoped to see one face—the refreshing face that had roamed in his mind for months.

By the baggage claim entrance, people held up signs with names. He didn't see his name. But Tessa would surely recognize him from hours of FaceTime and the photo he'd emailed her the month they'd met. Several yards away, people hugged their loved ones. Just as his gaze dragged further, he saw her.

His heart quickened the way it had whenever they spoke on the phone. But they were just friends—he couldn't offer her anything more.

She peered in his direction. Her eyes squinted, probably in search of him. Her long hair cascaded in waves over her yellow sundress.

She was here, waiting for him. His insides warmed, and he swallowed hard, unsure if he *could* settle for friendship. Unable to contain his patience, he cupped his hands around his mouth. "Tess!"

She turned. Her gaze found him. When she smiled and her hand flew to her mouth, his breath whooshed from his body, and his legs struggled to shuffle through the crowd.

She started toward him, and he lengthened his stride to meet up, ignoring the twinge in the hip he'd thought had recovered. Those long hours of sitting didn't help. Grinding his teeth, he fought the urge to shove everyone out of his way.

Wow! Even more beautiful in person, her flawless brown skin glowed, and her subtle curves softened her athletic build. Her long legs stirred up thoughts he had no business thinking.

"Chad!" She leaped forward when she neared, and his doubts and fears vanished as she threw her arms around his waist. The soft weight of her melted into him, and he swooped her up and twirled her around. Her giggles echoed a sweet melody that blocked out the chattering people and droning PA announcements.

While the world shrank to just the two of them, he set her down and cupped her exquisite face. Her eyes, so soft and shiny, rendered him speechless. Were those tears? For him? Had *anyone* ever cried for him?

Overcome, he leaned in, and captured her mouth with his.

She gasped, hesitant at first, but then kissed him back. His hands cradled her face, and his lips moved against hers. He held her close, relishing the taste of her and the softness of her skin as he supported her head. Then, somehow, he separated his lips from hers and peered into her face.

She fluttered dilated brown eyes, then stepped on tiptoe, and trailed her hands to the healing scar on his cheek. His muscles quivered beneath her fingertips.

"Does this hurt when—?"

"Negative." It had been so long since anyone showed concern for him. But a man who'd lost men under his watch didn't deserve sympathy.

Not wanting to dwell on his lingering battle scars, he wrapped his arms around her slender waist and closed his eyes. He then buried his nose in her hair and soaked in the subtle scent of rain and wildflowers. As her chest rose and fell against his, she smelled and looked far better than in his fantasies.

He wanted to say something, thank her for the warm welcome, but his throat clogged like he'd swallowed metal.

When he eased out of their embrace, tears fell from the side of her eyes, and his heart constricted, though, surely, they were tears of joy. He wiped them away with his thumb. "Hey, I don't want you to cry."

"I'm sorry. I don't cry often." She sniffed, blew out a breath, and started walking.

"I hope I didn't create a new habit for you." He fell in step as they strolled toward the exit. "I don't need my trainer to fall apart."

He tried to keep his voice light, but deep down, he felt like a torn ligament—unstable. He needed the multisport race now more than ever. Needed a legit distraction while he figured out what to do with his life.

While she drove him in her blue Trailblazer, a force of awareness hovered between them, and the car closed him in, the air almost stifling. She could probably feel it too, as she tried for small talk, different from their cozy FaceTime chats. She talked about the hot day, yet the temperature felt perfect when they'd walked toward her car in the parking lot. Although it could be hot for her since he was comparing the mountain weather to the Middle East, where he'd spent the last eighteen months.

"Your flight was good?" she asked, her posture stiff and her gaze intent on the road.

"Not so bad." How he hated this small talk! He tinkered with the chain on his neck. The dog tag beneath his T-shirt brushed his chest. "What did you do today?"

She cleared her throat. "I came to pick you up from the airport."

It was almost seven thirty, and she couldn't have been at the airport the entire day. He was done with small talk. He already knew the music she liked, gospel and folk-pop, but he wasn't sure what to talk about either. So he reached to push the dial on the sound system.

"Let's see what music you listen to."

A contemporary song erupted, no doubt a Christian song as it mentioned Jesus. He leaned back. The sun, sinking down the horizon, almost disappeared behind the mountains. They were driving past a farmhouse with horses grazing in the lush grass of the pasture. The wildflowers scattered along the roadside offered a promise to the kind of life awaiting him.

"We should be there in twenty minutes." She spoke over the music as the song came to a climax and another song started.

He rubbed his palms over his joggers, then grabbed his knees. *Think, Chad!* How could he fix the awkwardness? He hadn't planned to kiss her, but since things had gotten out of hand, they needed to talk, really talk, like they used to. He turned off the radio. "Would you like to grab a bite?"

That was all he could manage. Asking her on a date on day one would be like skipping elementary and leaping for middle school. So he'd done things backward, but he needed to go back to kindergarten level now.

"My mom made us dinner."

Tension tightened his shoulder muscles, then spread down his back and arms. He shuffled his feet, wanting to spring up and walk away, every bit of his body urging him to address the kiss. They'd both agreed over the course of the year to be friends and nothing more. Given his failed marriage, he wouldn't consider marrying again. He and Tessa had been friends until he'd lost control. And right now, he needed a friend.

He cleared his throat. "Listen, you probably need an explanation for what happened back there, but I have none."

Her lips curled into a ghost of a smile.

"I don't kiss my friends." He couldn't give her false hope. Well, maybe he had already. He'd sensed a deep affection and desire in her kiss as if she'd been planning on kissing him too. "I can assure you it will not happen again."

"Glad to know." Her voice was a whisper, and her response almost bothered him. Shouldn't she be upset that he wasn't planning to kiss her again? "If it's of any comfort, I don't kiss or date my clients."

"Good." He meant that. Really, he did. He'd feared for her safety and been jealous thinking she might fall for one of her clients. "Given that you go to client homes, there's consolation in your response."

A frown pinched the center of her forehead as she made a right turn to a bumpy road. "I don't understand."

And she'd better not understand how she affected him. He wasn't capable of handling relationships. Which led him to another question.

"The people you give free therapy to, do you consider them clients?"

"Not exactly." She glanced at him, her frown deeper before she refocused on the road. "Why?"

In case he lost control and kissed her again, he'd stay a charity case and pay for his training later.

"You should know you shouldn't take everything I say to heart." He rubbed his clean-shaven jaw. "I have brain damage, you know."

"What?" She whipped her head his way before she pulled her car to the side of the steep road. He jerked in his seat when she slammed her foot on the brake. "Do I need to take you to the doctor?"

He winced at her panicky voice. Bad on him for pulling such a terrible stunt. He stared at the distant mountains as he urged her to resume driving. "I thought I'd try for a joke, but it didn't work."

Her smile wobbled. Then she rolled her eyes. "I'm glad you're okay."

He was far from okay. Just being here with her flashed images of combat soldiers vanishing in the explosion, only leaving clouds of dust and shards of metal. Guilt, sharper than any shrapnel, gnawed at him. He sat there at a loss of words for the rest of the drive.

Then gravel bounced under their tires. They drove into a rustic mountain property where two cabins nestled up beside each other in the woods beyond the main house. He breathed out. The spacious property offered the perfect place to lay low and forget his last tour.

Or maybe not laying low, he realized when Tessa parked before a two-story stone house. A woman stood on the porch. Dressed in a plaid shirt, she crossed her arms and leaned against one of the support posts. It had to be Tessa's mom, but the photo Tessa shared with him had a cheerful woman. Did Tessa's mom have a twin?

The woman's gaze was intent on the car, staring at him through the windshield. More deadly things never terrified Chad, but this woman's frown sent his heart into hyperdrive.

In case she was staring into space, he lifted his hand to wave and make sure his eyes weren't foggy.

She didn't wave back. Maybe she wasn't staring at him after all. But why the stern look and pressed lips?

"I forgot to tell you—Mom has a love-hate relationship with soldiers."

"No kidding."

The woman appeared ready to send him back from where he'd come. He didn't mind staying at the hotel, but Tessa had been enthusiastic about him staying here. How could she have not disclosed her mom's reaction to soldiers? Did her mom even know he was staying here?

Tessa swung open her door, something he should've done for her, but he didn't have time to think while frozen in place. Soon, he'd find out if he was staying or looking for a hotel tonight.

CHAPTER 2

Dim evening light streamed through the east-facing dining room window, warming Mom's plants on the sill. As Mom served dinner, the tangy garlic roasted chicken scented the house. Tessa would have settled for grilling and eating outside, but Mom wanted to make the meal special—a traditional oven-baked dinner. Something different from what Chad likely ate while stationed for combat.

Still scorched by memories of the unexpected airport kiss, Tessa moved the fork in her mashed potatoes, smearing the gravy around and keeping her face tipped toward her plate. How was she supposed to ignore that heated kiss while her lips still tingled with the aftermath?

Now and then, she managed to glance at Chad. Mom kept him occupied answering her questions. While Tessa should be coming to his rescue, her tongue remained too frozen to form a coherent sentence.

She'd hoped they'd transition from friendship at some point—but not today. Not so fast.

"What are your plans after the triathlon?" Mom leaned back in her ladder-back chair, worry evident in her frown, her food forgotten. More gray strands shimmered in her short hair over the seven years since Dad died. While her skin was as dark as Tessa's, wrinkle marks acquired from days of worry and hard work creased the edges of her eyes and lips and puckered up the middle of her forehead.

"I haven't thought beyond that, ma'am." Chad forked another chicken bite and lifted it to his mouth.

Unlike their plates, his was almost empty. He was either hungry or using food to shield himself against the discomfort Mom created. Silence passed as he finished his green beans and chicken. He then reached for the bowl of mashed potatoes and scooped two spoonfuls onto his plate.

"Are you thinking of going back to active duty?" Mom asked again.

Chad's chiseled jaw moved, working on the food in his mouth. His gaze roamed to the piano, a few feet away, and the close-up portrait propped above it. Dad dressed in his uniform, the corners of his mouth folded into a tight smile.

Needing to answer for Chad, Tessa used her big brother as an example. "Elias has been home for four years." Her brother was always second-guessing his career choices. "Doesn't seem like he has all the answers yet."

Chad shrugged, and his Adam's apple bobbled when he swallowed. "I completed my years of active service, but it'll be an honor to serve my country if they need me." His face fell, green eyes darkening as he tipped his chin to the piano. "I'm so sorry for your loss."

Mom glanced at Tessa as if wondering how Chad knew about Dad.

"I told Chad about Dad." In their year of communicating, besides sending him photos of her family, she'd told him a lot about them.

Still needing to get through the list of her questions, Mom asked, "What did you do in the army?"

Chad's jaw twitched, and his fork clattered against his plate as he set it down and pushed it away a bit. "EOD Specialist," he responded in a low voice. "I mean Explosive Ordnance Disposal."

Mom arched her brow. "You disable bombs?"

"That sort of thing." He pressed his lips together before nodding.

Knowing Mom's struggle to get attached to soldiers on active duty, Tessa hadn't bothered to tell her about Chad's role. Then he'd gone silent on her for an extended time before he'd called her from the hospital in the early spring.

The terror that something had happened to him chilled her again. He could've died while putting out one of the explosives. She shivered, hoping he never had to go back.

When she raised her head, he was staring at her across the table. She forced a smile and tried to keep the panic out of her voice. "You're very brave."

All American troops would be out of the Middle East by the end of the year, but they might need Chad's skill in another war zone.

Keeping his chin tucked down, Chad moved his fork through the mashed potatoes he'd added to his plate. With the way his fork clicked against Mom's best china, he must be uncomfortable.

"Thanks for serving." Tessa sipped her water, needing to say something, anything to eliminate the stretched-out silence.

Mom's chest rose and fell when she blew out a slow breath. She then reached for her fork and stabbed a piece of white meat, lifting it to her mouth.

When Chad resumed eating, Tessa forked a green bean. Forks clinked against the porcelain as they ate. Then he thanked Mom for the delicious dinner, stood, and started gathering the empty plates from the table.

Tessa touched his arm to stop him. "I got it."

"You're our guest." Mom stood as well.

"I don't mind KP duty." He stacked the used plates and picked them up.

So Tessa faced her mom. "You made a delicious meal. You should relax while we clear the table."

Mom opened her mouth, seeming to think about it before she sat and sipped her water.

Chad's footsteps thudded on the hardwood floor as he followed Tessa into the kitchen. The worn floors needed new polish, but she hadn't gotten around to hiring a professional. Everything in Pleasant View was overpriced.

With Mom relying on the income from her job as a hardware associate and the vegetables she produced, Tessa moved into the basement so she could pay half the bills, instead of paying rent somewhere else. They still had four more years to pay off the three-acre property. Then perhaps Tessa could start entertaining the things on her list. Things like expanding her care packages to the troop ministry. With word about the ministry getting out, she had more soldiers on the list to ship packages to. Her priority remained the Middle East since Dad died there. With increasing donations filling the church's spare storage room, she'd soon need a bigger location.

The kitchen felt small with just her and Chad. After stacking the dishes in the dishwasher, he leaned against the green-tiled counter and crossed his ankles. She stood against the opposite counter, tucked her hands behind her, and grasped one of the maple cabinet drawer's porcelain handles. Her heart raced as the air swirled between them.

"Dinner was good."

"Yeah." She twisted her fingers tighter, the handle smooth against them. Wow. His broad shoulders stretched out that light-gray T-shirt, and his ripped arms bulged up the tattoo on his left biceps as he crossed his arms. No doubt the trace of scarring on his cheek and forehead had everything to do with the injuries that landed him in the hospital.

Bandages had been wrapped around his head in March, but it didn't seem like his brain was damaged. The lacerations, although healed on his face, had left thin red traces that would fade with more time.

His lips twitched upward, and Chad cleared his throat. Perhaps reading into her thoughts.

Oops. She'd been caught staring. Heat tingled up her neck, but the fluffy white frosted cake beside him offered a perfect change of topic.

"Mom made you a cake." At least, she said something logical while looking at him.

He winced, then touched his flat stomach. "I don't think I have room for dessert."

Too warm, she fought to look him straight in the eyes. He'd eaten so fast. "You seemed a bit stressed."

He tucked his head and rubbed the back of his neck. His fingers rasped against the razor-cut hair he'd likely had trimmed recently. "Is it obvious that I stress eat?"

With Mom's unfriendly reception, anyone could end up stress eating. "I'm not judging."

"If it's not a problem, can you show me to my room? I'll call it a day."

Beyond the window behind him, they probably had another thirty minutes of daylight. The stove clock showed almost eight thirty, and she relished these long summer days. But she'd better not force him to stay for dessert where Mom might hound him.

Tessa still wanted to know why he'd been in the VA hospital, why he had those slim red scars on his forehead and cheek, but Mom had asked enough questions already.

"You're staying in the cabin across the yard. I'll escort you."

He lifted his right hand to the side of his head and saluted her, a playful grin quirking the corners of his mouth.

How could he seem so unaffected after he'd kissed her breathlessly at the airport?

She started from the kitchen, certain he'd follow, then waited while he apologized to Mom for not staying for dessert.

"It'll be here tomorrow." Mom shrugged. "Unless you're planning to leave tonight."

"I can go to the—"

"That's not what she meant." Grabbing and tugging at Chad's arm, Tessa frowned at Mom. Just why was she acting as if Chad's visit was a surprise? What did she mean, though? Tessa gave her a look, a warning to mind her manners.

"You're welcome to stay." Mom raised her chin and folded her hands on the maple dining table Dad built while on convalescent leave. "But I'm sure you still need to figure out whether you want to stay or not."

What was wrong with her?

Obviously, she was still bent out of shape after Tessa's ex ended things. Kanon had been in the reserves then, and his PTSD kept him from pursuing a relationship. While some people worked through it, the depression and anxiety hindered others from doing anything else.

Could Chad be different from Kanon?

A twinge pinched her heart, and she half smiled at Chad, giving his arm another tug before releasing him. "I'll show you to your place."

He wished Mom good night, then followed Tessa to the driveway, the porch light bright as he retrieved his navy duffel bag from the car. Slinging his bag over his shoulder, he fell in step with her.

The sun had sunk below the mountains, the birds were singing out their good nights, and the shadows were deepening as they crossed the yard.

"You have several structures on your property." Chad nodded to Mom's greenhouses visible in the dusk east of the main house.

"Mom likes to garden. She grows vegetables for the local farmers market."

"It's good to have a job you enjoy."

If only Mom didn't have to work at the hardware store, but Mom insisted they needed the money. Tessa had made a decent amount working as a full-time therapist and wanted her mom to have a break, but Mom preferred to keep herself busy.

Wildflowers pushing their way through the flagstone pathway brushed against her strappy sandals and tickled her toes.

"I like your mom."

She almost choked on her saliva. Could he be sincere in that compliment? He kept walking, and she didn't dare study him to discern his sincerity. Not when she didn't want him thinking she was gawking. He'd made it clear he wouldn't kiss her again, and she had to respect that. After all, he was her client.

But since he was here, he needed to know Mom wasn't a mean person. Although seven years later, Dad's absence left scars on Mom's once outgoing personality. "She's been quite sensitive since Dad died."

Chad chuckled. The low rumble almost reverberated through her body, making it tingle.

"Her sensitivity is different."

"It is?" Mom's tone always changed whenever a soldier who joined them for dinner flirted with Tessa or showed any interest in her. Her grieving compelled her to protect Tessa from the same fate.

"Looks like she'd be heartbroken if you left."

Tessa breathed in deep, savoring the pine-scented dew-dampened air. Who could consider leaving this? "I'm not eager to move out, but Mom's busy enough and has plenty of friends to keep her company if I wanted to. For now, though, I don't want to pay rent while there's room here. I'd rather save up for a gym someday."

She was thirty-two, too old not to be sure when someday would be. But the soldier ministry had become a priority. She'd fallen behind him and skipped a few steps to catch up. "I hope Mom didn't scare you with her questions."

He stopped walking, and the cabin's porch light revealed the challenge on his face. "Depends what kind of scaring we're talking about."

His stare weakened her knees, so she resumed walking. The chirping crickets, croaking tree toads, and trickling creek behind the cabin added peace to a perfect evening.

"As long as you're still my trainer, I'm not scared."

At the cabin, she stopped on the lower step, then tipped her head for him to go ahead, but he waved her to lead the way. So she took the three steps to the door. The potted red geraniums alongside it wafted a sweet fragrance in the air. She'd been busy preparing for his arrival and rearranged her schedule to accommodate his training sessions. Good thing none of her clients needed immediate therapy like they'd required before.

After pushing open the heavy wooden door, she reached to turn on the switch, and warm light illuminated the spacious room.

"You don't lock the cabin?"

"It's pretty safe up here, except for bears showing up looking for food."

"I'll keep that in mind when I cook."

The cabin only had a microwave, but him hovering over her at the doorway, his spicy scent mingling with flowers and cedar, made it impossible for her to relax enough to say so. Her heart rate escalating, she entered the one-room cabin and stopped halfway to the queen-size bed.

"Someone put a lot of love into this room." Chad dropped his duffel by the door before winking.

"It wasn't much work." Only a few touches here and there. Far easier than figuring out what to do with her hands now. She clasped them behind her, then felt silly standing there like that, and pretended to smooth her hair for an excuse to move them. "My brother lived here when he returned home. We hired a contractor to fix up the cabin for him."

"I can't wait to meet him." Shadows darkened the skin under Chad's eyes. They looked even darker now than when she'd noticed them in her car at the airport. How many days and hours of sleepless nights had he endured?

"What's the mat for?" He nodded toward the corner by the end of his bed.

"In case you need to do push-ups or something."

He thrust his hands in his jogger pockets. "I'm not doing any exercises without my trainer."

"I'm all yours for the next twelve weeks."

"I have a feeling this bill is going to cost me an arm and a leg."

With the way his eyebrow lifted, he was joking. But just in case... She smirked back. "Seems you think you can afford it. After all, you're the one who keeps turning down my offer to train you for free."

"You're running a business, not a charity." He shrugged. The floorboards creaked when he moved to the bed, dropped onto it, and bounced a bit, testing it out. He then fingered a white heart on the red bedsheets beneath the royal-blue comforter. "Hmm, someone likes hearts, I see."

Her face heated at the rhetorical statement. He'd better not think she was hinting at romance. "Those were the only ones at the store the day I went shopping."

Not entirely true. They'd had black bedsheets as well. But those seemed grim, like dressing the place for mourning. Maybe she should've bought the depressing things. She didn't regret buying the rustic rug beneath his tennis shoes. Although from a consignment store, its earthy braided beiges, browns, and reds complemented the wooden walls and rustic furniture.

"Thank you." He saluted her. "I don't want to take up any more of your time. I assume we start training tomorrow?"

They hadn't discussed his schedule yet. She hadn't been sure how he'd feel after his injury, the injury he'd refused to talk about since March. "We'll go shopping tomorrow, then go through your routine. I already have a printout for you."

She tapped her chin, searching the room for any instructions she might need to relay. Then she nodded to the window above his bed. "It can get hot in here, so feel free to open the window."

She didn't need to look through the curtain on the glass back door to remember the wicker table and chairs she'd positioned on the back deck or the hammock she'd strung in the trees, in case he needed to rest between training.

Sensing his gaze on her, she tried to keep her focal point on the nightstand. Another rustic piece she'd bought from the consignment store. "You can use the dresser to store your clothes. And call or text if you need anything." She spun around and pointed toward the open bathroom doorway. "Extra towels are in the bathroom cabinet."

No need to point out to the kitchenette with its cozy table and single chair nestled by a window or its microwave and coffee pot.

So she faced him, but to avoid staring at him, she fixed her gaze on the three paintings surrounding the TV. What else would he need to know? Shoes!

"Slides are in the drawer below the bed."

Without permission from her brain, her gaze flitted to him. He'd crossed his arms. His green gaze on her, his grin unapologetic.

She shouldn't have taken out the fan above his bed. But the fan blades triggered Elias's nightmares. She hadn't considered putting it back for Chad.

Curiosity over his smile had her narrowing her eyes. "What's so funny?"

"I've been thinking what an amazing teacher you are." He uncrossed his arms and rubbed his hands over his pants. "I'm pumped for my training."

With his compliment warming her to the core, the room shrank below its fifteen hundred square feet. Her teeth dug into her lower lip. She clasped her hands in front of her, then gave a gentle roll of her eyes. "Did you even listen to anything I said?"

"Everything." His smirk deepened. "Would you like to quiz me?"

If she were the teacher and he the student, she'd fail at assessing him. Swallowing, she managed to speak. "Training you is going to be harder than wrestling a bear."

"It's been a while since I wrestled." He sat taller, his green eyes glinting, his lips quirking. "I'm game whenever you'd like to wrestle."

He was so impossible, yet thrilling!

At a loss for words, she clasped her hands behind her again. What had they even been talking about?

Nothing. Okay. Something about a workout since she was a trainer.

"We'll talk about training, um, expectations... tomorrow."

She needed to leave because she was talking about expectations rather than their workout routine. Taking a step backward, she pointed at him. "Training." Or was it expectations? "Make sense?"

"Totally."

That amusement in his eyes was going to undo her. She took a few more steps backward, forgetting to turn around until she ran into the wall.

"I'm okay." Oh! Her voice sounded so weak, and she was so breathless. She spun to face the half-open door. "Good night."

"See you in the morning." Chad's voice bounced off her back as she closed the door without turning to give him another glance.

The night breeze had never felt so refreshing. Finally able to breathe, she pressed a hand over her heart and took in the darkened sky. It was going to be the longest three months of her career. They hadn't even started training, and she was having a hard time holding a normal conversation. Maybe if he hadn't kissed her, things could've been different. Either way, she needed to get a better handle on herself. Chad was a client, no different from the other clients. As long as she could assure herself of that, she'd make it through training. Right?

CHAPTER 3

Lying atop that royal-blue comforter, Chad fought combat images overlaid with the smiles of the guys he'd been with in the field that day. "I should be home in time for my daughter's birth," Tommy had beamed as Chad slid on the blast suit.

Although he met a new crew on most of his company's rotations, it only took one day together in the field to form an unforgettable bond.

Shaking off the memories, he yawned and willed himself to rest despite the bright light on the nightstand. Perhaps the brightness would drive out his nightmares. Perhaps tonight would be different.

The shower had refreshed him, and he'd left off his shirt since Tessa said the cabin could get hot. Now, he moved his hand, his chest hair pricking his fingers as he touched the raw tattoo he'd had inked to his skin. It had stopped weeping two days ago, and the skin was no longer puffy. But the shaved hair growing back in the area felt odd.

He turned toward the wall. Then, not liking the way his right shoulder carried the weight of his head, he rolled to face the front door. Finding it hard to settle into a comfortable position, he flopped to his back, folded his hands behind his head, and stared at the wooden ceiling beams.

A smile twitched his lips as he thought of his arrival. Tessa's genuine smile when she saw him, the warmth of her embrace, and oh, what a kiss!

His entire body jerked at the sweet memory. It was the best kiss he'd ever had. Raw and vulnerable, no doubt Tessa felt the chemistry and explosion just as much.

She was adorable when flustered. She'd been out of sorts instructing him where to find certain things in the cabin. He'd had a hard time not staring at her heart-shaped face, her fluttering long eyelashes, and those kissable lips that he shouldn't know tasted like fruit.

Suddenly warm, maybe he needed to open the window. He sprang up and thrust it wide before flopping back atop the covers.

Thinking of Tessa's kiss only served to torture him and break his promise. He'd do whatever it took to keep from kissing her again, especially since her mom didn't trust him. Bettina was smart to see right through him. She clearly didn't want her daughter dating a soldier, but she could probably smell the wrong soldier when she saw one.

It was for the best anyway. He needed a trainer, not a girlfriend.

There was a reason Nelly left him twelve years ago for his best friend from high school. The same unknown reason terrified Chad about starting a relationship he wasn't capable of nurturing.

His eyes explored the abstract paintings on the log wall. The first resembled the log cabin he was in. Another depicted a dog. It was cute, but who knew what type of dog it was? He'd always wanted a dog, but his ex had taken his when she left.

The third painting, a deer drinking from a stream, relaxed him, quenching his thirst. The vivid details captured his interest until his heavy eyelids slid closed. He let himself drift to a peaceful scenery. The gentle stream burbled beyond his window. He woke to birds singing outside and took in his new surroundings. He'd slept all night.

The soft breeze moved the curtains, its cool air chilling him. He patted at the covers beneath him, but he didn't feel like moving. He was at the cabin—his temporary new home. A peacefulness swept through him when Tessa came to mind. He was here because of her invitation.

Okay, he was also here with the desire to cling to her like family in any kind of form. They were only friends—so when would his mind get that all-important memo?

A gentle rap sounded on the door, and he ran a hand over his face, too lazy to leap out of bed. Another tap sounded. He hadn't locked the door after Tessa left last night. She'd said it was safe, except for hungry bears. If a bear were tapping on the door, it wouldn't understand his invite.

"Come in."

The door creaked and edged inward. His heart quickened as Tessa walked in with a tray of something smelling savory. He sat up, sucking in a breath when she stayed close to the door, her gaze intent on him. "Hi."

"Good morning." She half smiled before she tore her gaze from him to her tray.

When did she have time to make breakfast? "You're up early."

She peered at the curtained door beyond his bed. "You slept in. I brought you breakfast."

Should he ask why Bettina wasn't joining them? No. He'd rather not start his day answering any questions if she'd come up with a new list in the middle of the night.

"I'm going to leave this here for you." Tessa walked to the counter next to the microwave, the gentle sway of her curves hypnotic beneath the teal leggings she'd worn with a snug white and blue print top. She was so fit.

She started toward the door. Leaving already. He didn't mind eating alone, but he could use the company, her company.

"Will you join me for breakfast?"

"Um..." She half faced him, staring above his head. "If you get dressed, maybe?"

"Oh." He glanced at his hairy chest, then his duffel bag on the floor. Of course, she was uncomfortable with his bare chest. "I'll get dressed, then."

"I'll be back in a few." She left, the door closing behind her.

After pulling on his sports shorts and a T-shirt, Chad walked to the bathroom, washed his face, and brushed his teeth even though he would brush again after breakfast. If he was sitting across from her, he'd better not reek of morning breath.

When she returned with a smoothie, they sat on the back deck, the stream trickling under its rear supports. After she prayed, she sipped her berry smoothie while he ate an omelet stuffed with sausage and vegetables.

Although he'd slept in, he had to tease her for being such an early bird. "It's only seven, and you think I slept in?"

"You missed the sunrise at six."

"I would've been up if you'd given me a heads-up last night."

"Let's try tomorrow."

"It's a da—" Whew, he stopped himself from saying date! "Deal."

He then reached for his smoothie. He tasted the bananas sweetening up the tangy berries, then rested the glass beside his plate. "Why are you only having a smoothie?"

"I'm not big on breakfast."

He didn't know what her morning routine was, but he didn't want her to change anything for him. "Is it odd that we're having breakfast without your mom?"

"On Wednesdays, she takes her vegetables to the market." Tessa wrapped both her hands around the frosted glass. "She also has to be at work early. Even when home, she spends hours in the greenhouse gardening. Then late June, she transplants some of the vegetables to the garden."

Yesterday's awkwardness vanished as Tessa relaxed, laughing now. "I have such terrible gardening skills—Mom never lets me near her garden. Plants just hate me, but that's okay." She sank back in her chair and sipped her drink through a metal straw. "I like sleeping in on Saturday mornings, but Mom used to need my help in the garden before she gave up on me. I think I lost interest in gardening altogether."

"The flowers on the front porch are thriving just fine."

"I planted those two days ago." She leaned closer to his chair, wafting her shampoo's subtle wildflower scent. "I hope you take better care of them than I could."

"I can't guarantee their livelihood in my care. But I'll try."

He forked his eggs, eating while she talked about their mountain property. Her company soothed him as pleasantly as the gentle lap of water trickling below the deck. Two deer traipsed in the green grass between the tall aspens beyond the hammock.

Everything felt surreal, this moment alongside a beautiful woman more like some kind of a dream. Could it last forever?

ON THEIR DRIVE INTO town, Tessa's flowery scent dominated the car as Chad craned his neck toward the mountains. Wasn't she driving *away* from Pleasant View? "I did some research on your town, and it looks like we're missing all the shops."

"You did?" She beamed. "They charge way too much here. Plus, with the variety of shops where I'm taking you, we're more likely to find what we need."

"Let me see." He tapped his knee. "Woody Creek, Snowmass Village, or Basalt?"

Her smile spread wider. "Wow, you did your research, I see."

His chest puffed. Memorizing the nearby towns had been worth it.

In Snowmass Village, she led him into a sports equipment store. The wonderful scent of leather from baseball gloves and other gear beckoned him as they walked past before the rubber coming from the bicycles lined against the wall overtook it.

He'd done triathlons before, but he'd never taken time to research a perfect bike, like Tessa must have when she pointed out which bikes he should consider for the Ironman Triathlon.

Chad picked out a green bike, his favorite color, rolled it away from the other bikes, and tested the seat and leg length to ensure it was the right size. Then he tried out two other bikes. He wasn't much of a biker, except for the times he'd ridden in and trained for previous triathlons. Or when he returned to the Virginia base. He also selected a helmet as well as a handful of cycling jerseys, shorts, and shoes.

But Tessa better not plan on him biking back all the way to Pleasant View today.

"How are we going to transport the bike in your car?" he asked before paying for the items.

"I brought a bike rack."

He hadn't paid attention to notice a rack hitched on her car. "You're prepared."

"I'm sure there's many things I don't have ready."

They drove to another sporting goods store she claimed would have the right swim gear. There, she slid a piece of blue paper from her royal-blue handbag, then skimmed it.

"You made a list?"

"I did some research. I want you to have the right gear for your race."

She had plenty of questions for the associate before Chad chose one of the tri suits and a cap and goggles. He also bought two extra pairs of shorts and zip-up long-sleeved tri shirts. He'd need gear for training anyway.

Same with running shoes. Tessa had details of the perfect shoe he needed. He got cycling shoes and two pairs of running shoes, as well as a new pair of tennis shoes.

By the time they finished shopping, his stomach growled for another meal.

"Someone is hungry." She chuckled as she drove past a handful of mountain shops and a gas station.

He shrugged. "It is twelve thirty."

"What do you feel like eating?"

All food was better than his lack of options in deployment. "Surprise me."

They stopped for lunch at a burger joint where umbrellas shaded the red patio tables, and the smell of onions and grilled meat made his stomach rumble even louder. Tessa ordered sweet potato fries, a grilled chicken sandwich with no bread, and iced tea mixed with lemonade. He ordered a burger, french fries, and the same drink. Although he'd made it clear he was paying for lunch, she put up a fight, stepping in front of him to pay. So he slid his hands around her waist and scooped her aside.

She shuddered, clearly affected by his touch. Her eyes widened while she peered around the joint as if to see if anyone was watching. Except everyone was minding their own business.

Good, his distraction tactic worked. Chad handed his card to the skinny man behind the counter.

After paying for their order, they carried their drinks to the patio, taking the only empty table at the end.

"That tactic back there?" She shook her head.

The breeze blew wisps of dark hair into her face. His fingers twitched to reach out and brush the glossy strands away from her forehead. She was stunning. This was going to be the hardest twelve or so weeks of training he'd ever had. Trying not to fall in love with her? Hmm! May God help him.

Forgetting what she'd said, he focused on the creamy drink in front of him. "I've never had tea mixed with lemonade before."

"Seriously?" She plucked the lemon wedge from the rim of her glass and squeezed it into her drink.

"It's a first for me." Just like having an irresistible female trainer. Somehow, he forced himself to focus on the lemon wedged on his glass. "Should I squeeze the lemon?"

The ice clinked when Tessa stirred her drink with a paper straw. "First, drink it. If you like it, you can then squeeze the lemon and see if it gets better."

The way she sipped her drink convinced him he'd like it.

A pair of crows landed on the railing and cawed for attention. As they settled and preened, a lady at a nearby table tossed them some fries.

Chad reached for his glass, pulled out the straw, and chugged the tart liquid. Oh man! He winced, then set it down. "I assume you like tart drinks?"

Tessa's soft laugh whispered over him as she slipped a sugar packet from the bowl on their table. She ripped it open and poured it into his glass. "It will taste better sweetened up, but I usually avoid sugar."

He tested the drink, and his shoulders relaxed. "You're right. It tastes better when sweet." Just like her kiss.

"So..." She swallowed as if sensing his unclean thoughts. "We need to go through your routine."

"Okay." He sat taller, his heartbeat quickening as her gaze held his. He braced a hand on the nearby patio railing, needing to do something other than focus on the electricity charging between them.

"You're the captain. Tell me what to do, and I'll obey."

She gave her eyes a gentle roll, then huffed out a breath. "We only have eleven weeks to train, even if we need twelve to thirteen."

Did she forget he was a soldier? Despite the mild injury she didn't know about, he could train in four weeks or less if needed. "I don't need eleven weeks."

"You'll need some recovery days between training." She brought out her tablet.

Chad gave it a cursory glance, not long enough to read anything, before swigging more of his drink.

"I'm going to email you the schedule. I didn't want to send it until you got home."

"Why not?"

She shrugged, resting her hands on the table edge. "I wasn't sure you'd come."

He hadn't had any doubts about coming to Pleasant View. The only doubts he'd had were whether she'd been serious about her invitation. "I wasn't sure you'd be at the airport waiting for me."

Her soft smile warmed his insides. "I'm glad we both kept our word."

So was he.

When the server brought their food, Tessa prayed and gave thanks for it, his safety, and their reunion. Through their virtual conversations, he'd witnessed her faith and begun to see things through a different lens. In war zones, God made so much sense, especially when she explained that God was the only one present in the darkest moments when no one knew the battle raging in your mind. She'd encouraged him to cling to God during battle. Yes, he still struggled to understand the whole relationship with a God who wasn't visible, but he had nothing to lose by believing in the unknown. After all, his life had few constants, so he could use a God who was always with him, visible or not.

"Amen," he said in agreement to her prayer, then bit into his hamburger, downing the swallow with the tea and lemonade mix. "I can't believe you'd order a chicken patty and sweet potatoes at a burger-and-fries joint."

She paused from slicing her chicken, then made a face at him. "I'm only letting you off the hook today and tomorrow."

Right. She'd warned him about making diet changes when they started training. He wagged a ketchup-sticky fry at her. "I remember hiring a trainer, not a dietician."

"Afraid you hired the entire package."

It wasn't what she said, but it was the intimate tone she said it in, that sent his blood rushing and warming his entire body. Tessa was the whole package.

CHAPTER 4

Even if Chad was eager to start training the next day, Tessa needed to perform a fitness assessment. He was physically fit, but hiding the extent of his injuries and pain. He hadn't talked about his hospital visit. She'd never have known he'd been admitted if he hadn't called her from the bed with his head bandaged, but his scars stamped a reminder of whatever accident he'd survived.

Twice during their virtual calls, she'd asked about it. Each time though, he'd changed the subject, clearly not interested, and she couldn't do anything about that.

When he was still overseas, she'd almost talked him out of the triathlon in case he needed more time to recover, but he'd said the triathlon was the one thing he was looking forward to doing after combat. A triathlon was one thing, but the Ironman was no picnic.

While she couldn't keep him from doing something he wanted to do, she didn't want him to get hurt during training.

So, that morning, after watching the sunrise, she'd made oatmeal muffins and a smoothie—her ideal breakfast. But he considered it a snack. She then had him join her in her gym, the nearby cabin. Although impractical for a therapy practice or a gym, it served for her to work with clients who didn't mind the drive. Someday, she'd save up enough to rent a realistic gym close to Main Street.

As Chad stepped on the exercise mat, morning light streamed through the rustic wood-framed glass door and window, glinting his brown hair with a golden hue.

She swiped a finger on her tablet as she asked him to stand still and close his eyes.

His brow lifted, and he crossed his arms. "What does closing my eyes have to do with your assessment?"

He was a distraction without trying, but if he protested, her job would be cut out for her. She moved a step back, braced a hand on the log wall, and hoped the slight distance would enable her to speak without his charm sidetracking her.

"It will be easier for you to relax when you have your eyes closed."

"You think?" He cocked his head, looking at her too intently. Then, without complicating her job any further, he uncrossed his arms, lowered them to his sides, and closed his eyes.

"Try to breathe naturally."

"Is there any other way to breathe?" His chest rose, then fell. His broad shoulders stretched out the navy-blue word *Army* on his gray T-shirt, its print matching his sports shorts.

She stared at his bare feet, then dragged her gaze up all the way to his head and the rumpled brown hair that looked so fun to touch. Chad was athletically built. After running into him shirtless yesterday, she'd fought not to think about the details of his broad chest. Even before she'd jerked her gaze away, she'd glimpsed an inked section on his hair-dusted skin, though she hadn't looked long enough to read it. Still curious to know what the word was, she'd have to put the matter to rest.

Shaking her head to focus, she noted his spine, pelvis, and hips lined up vertically. As far as body alignment went, his posture was neutral which was good.

His jaw twitched, and his arm muscles strained. He'd balled his hands into fists. She hoped having him close his eyes hadn't stirred up any bad unwanted memories.

"All right, trainer." He opened his eyes, finding her staring at him. The earlier lightness in his tone fell away. "I expected you to tell me when to open my eyes."

"Good thing you read my mind. I was about to..."

She trailed off, losing her focus. So she checked the tablet. Right, the posture assessment form.

"What are you looking at now?" He left the mat and crossed the hardwood floor to her side, his hair barely brushing her forehead when he tried to peek at her tablet.

Tessa punched the power button with shaky hands to close the screen. She then rested it on the press bench next to the weights. "If it's okay, can you step back on the mat, please?"

He did as asked. Now, the detailed postural assessment was going to be slightly uncomfortable since she had to touch him, and she told him so. "I'm not sure how you feel about that."

"I'll make an exception." His playful tone returned. "With you being my trainer and all."

Closing the gap between them, she itched to touch his hair, but she didn't have to touch his head to know it had a neutral posture, just like his back.

Her fingers twitched. She wiped her damp palms on her leggings, then reached to check his shoulders. But heat climbed up her neck as her fingertips connected with his hard muscles.

"So tell me about your gym and why you switched from being a physical therapist to training."

Her discomfort fled, and the warmth touching her heart now had everything to do with her love for her job and nothing to do with her previous awkwardness.

"A few reasons. One being that I liked the flexibility of being my own boss."

Then she frowned. One of his shoulders was slightly elevated over the other. It could be nothing of concern, but she couldn't take that risk. "You're one of my first clients to train. The exception." He'd be good practice, her trial "run."

"Who is the other exception?" Something sharp clipped off the ends of his words. Why?

"My brother." Elias had been the reason she'd expanded her career. "Can you move a bit?"

She tipped her head, urging him to scoot to the wall so his hips and shoulders touched the logs.

He moved, and she hesitated to touch below his waist to his pelvis. But she'd have to. Using both hands, she placed one on each side of his pelvis. Her hands were shaking, and Chad shivered.

"Sorry." She held her breath and avoided looking at his face. "I have no way to evaluate your hips without touching you."

He said nothing.

Stepping back to glance at him, she sensed his gaze and fought for her eyes to sweep everywhere on his body except his face.

His hips and shoulders were level. She made a mental note of it and the Q angle, knees, and feet.

Her heart thrummed against her ribs louder than his rapid breathing when she stepped further away. With the posture assessment done, she'd hold off on the movement and flexibility assessment.

The twenty-minute assessment felt like an hour. She wiped her damp palms on her thighs again, then nodded to the window. "Why don't we take a hike?"

That would give her the perfect opportunity to make her final assessments.

Raising one brow, she cocked her head at him. "Are you up for the task?"

"Affirmative."

He sounded so much like her father and brother, like he fit into her life. She clasped her hands behind her back to keep from swiping them on her leggings again. "Let's head back to the main house to eat snacks and make a picnic lunch before we leave."

TO MAKE IT MORE THAN an assessment, Tessa took him on a technical hike rather than a walk to the Dagon waterfall.

On the trail, Chad talked about the tasks in the triathlon. "It's been a long time since I went mountain biking."

"We'll start slow." She slowed to climb over a curved boulder in their path, and he sped ahead, climbed up, then took her hand to help her climb up and down.

"I should be the one to assist you with the climb." She pointed to his backpack with their lunches on his back. "I'm walking light."

"You won't walk light as long as you have a problematic client."

"Tell me about it."

It was odd that he considered himself problematic, but if he meant being a temptation to Tessa, then he was right. With his good looks and charm, he was going to be another heartbreaker. Obviously, he meant something else entirely, but she'd be carrying the weight of keeping things professional.

The perfect temperature, high sixties, made their ascent easier. Pine needles cushioned their path as they climbed over the rocks and kept a steady pace. Since it wasn't a designated trail, they were the only people on the so-called path. But out of the eight or so nearby waterfalls, Dagon was the closest to her house. They wouldn't make it to the falls today but could get to the hilltop and take in the breathtaking view while they ate lunch.

She slowed to let him walk ahead when she remembered her purpose. Did he rotate through the torso while walking? Check. Did his arms swing consistently from side to side?

Hmm. The arms were slightly off, but trekking an uneven path made getting accurate results harder.

Chad turned, his brow creasing. "Tired already?"

"Just taking in the scenery." Given that he'd suddenly become part of the magnificent view.

She lengthened her stride to catch up, their shoes crunched against fallen limbs and last autumn's leaves. Blue warblers sang in the trees, their color bright against the greens, and small critters scattered from their path.

Chad kept turning and looking in all directions, taking in the view, until he stopped under a pine-branch canopy and closed his eyes. He inhaled, then exhaled before opening his eyes. "Please tell me you come here often."

"Only in the summer and early fall." *If* it didn't start snowing in September. "Sometimes we miss fall because winter starts in September."

He rested a hand on his hip and peered down the valley, the towering waterfall tumbling into a lake just visible. He pointed. "Is that our destination?"

The awe and wonder tinting his voice urged her on. But the last thing she needed was to have him injured in her care. Most people didn't know about Dagon Falls because few daring people loved the challenge of getting to it. Her curiosity had compelled her to make it there.

"It's dangerous."

His brow lifted.

Duh. Danger was his job description.

"How dangerous?"

There had once been a swinging rope bridge, but by the time she discovered the waterfall, only ripped ropes dangling between the two boulders gave evidence of that. "We have to swing on ropes to cross." Sturdy ropes she hoped, having no clue who was responsible for putting them there.

Chad scratched the lengthening stubble on his chin. "Have you been there?"

"Twice." An adrenaline rush flowed through her at the thought of the thrilling experience and the pristine scenery payoff.

"That smile makes the decision easy." Chad eased the backpack from his shoulders and lowered himself to one of the flat boulders. "Let's have lunch, then hit the ropes."

The ropes sounded good. "It's dangerous." But her weak protest wouldn't likely convince him to back out of the adventure.

He unzipped the bag and pulled out the Ziploc bags with their lunches. His was the sandwich and hers the lettuce wrap. "Did I tell you I live for danger?"

How could she argue?

While they ate, he stretched out, bracing one hand on the boulder behind him and kicking his long legs out as far as they could go. "What made you become a trainer and therapist? Why both?"

"You forget I'm a dietician and life coach too."

"When you told me on the phone, I had to see for myself." He plucked the alfalfa sprouts from his sandwich and tossed them in the empty Ziploc bag. "If you don't load me with all the veggies, I can put up with your diet."

"I'm not sure I can pull off all the great meals." She bit into her wrap. The avocado tasted so good.

"Is everything in that thing you're eating *green*?" He elbowed her. "Green's my favorite color, but eating it all day is pushing it. Seriously, why are you so conscious of what you eat?"

"Studying the effects of most ingredients they use in food led me to be more careful about what goes into my body." She huffed away the pout forming on her lips. It had also hindered her from enjoying her favorite junk food.

Chad nodded. "About your career." He lifted his sandwich to urge her to answer his earlier question.

"Liability like I said earlier." Insurance rates had gone up, so she had to contract with medical companies to work as a physical therapist. "If I'm training, I can be my own boss, and although I still need liability, it's affordable." For now, at least.

The pout threatened to slide back into place. She bit into her wrap to focus on something else.

"Are you covered now?"

What did he mean? As if reading her confusion, he clarified, "Do you have insurance for your job?"

"No."

He cocked his head with a quizzical brow. With him, everything was lighthearted, so she had no idea when he was serious.

She waved the wrap toward him. "Don't tell me you intend to find fault in my training and bring charges against me."

"You said you have three other clients."

Right. "It's not as consistent therapy for any of them, and one isn't a paying client."

"Let's get you insured."

"Not happening now." She bit into her wrap, savored the romaine lettuce crunch and the creamy avocado, then swallowed and licked a dollop of avocado from her lips. "I don't have money to start paying for insurance."

"I'll pay an advance for my training." He put his sandwich on his knee over his shorts and reached for his water bottle, uncapped it and took a sip, then set the water between his legs. "I like how your physical therapist in high school inspired you to go into the field."

Wow. He still remembered the high jump accident she'd told him about eight months ago.

"What motivated you to go for those other fields?"

"My brother."

"How?"

"He had PTSD after his last tour." The lingering ache at the memory resurfaced. She dipped her head and picked at a bit of moss on the boulder, sinking back into one of the darkest times in her family. "He stayed in the cabin for months, ate junk food he'd ordered online and had delivered to the cabin."

When she peeped up, sadness had seeped into Chad's mossy-green eyes, his full focus on her as he ignored the bee buzzing over his half-eaten sandwich.

"I took classes to help him get back on track, kicked up my therapy sessions with him, and battled every single day to have him do any of those things." She never wanted a repeat of that with a family member. Three years into their mourning Dad, Elias returned with an amputated leg.

Chad laid his hand over hers. "You became a trainer and dietician to help your brother?"

She nodded, fighting the tears now threatening to choke her.

"Where does he live now?"

She cleared the lump in her throat. "Three hours away. He wanted to stay far from home." Mom cried whenever she looked at his prosthetic leg. Tessa turned her hand beneath Chad's and returned his grip. "I was hoping we could do the 5K for veterans he helps organize on the last Saturday in June."

He squeezed her hand. "A 5K run would be good training for the 42K run in the Ironman. And when do I get to meet Iris, Liberty, and Myra?"

She'd not only talked about her friends but had also been babysitting Myra when he'd called her. Myra had bubbled her cuteness and showed her face through the phone. As for Iris, they'd have to wait until she came to town for her family reunion. "You'll meet Liberty and Myra soon."

Liberty had been bombarding her with texts to set up a dinner date for Tessa to bring Chad. "They are just as anxious to meet you."

When they finished eating their lunch and shoved the empty Ziploc bags and water bottles back in the backpack, Chad stood and reached for her hand. "Ready for our next adventure?"

She was always ready, but was he? Surely, he'd know what he could and couldn't handle.

"As long as you are."

His warm and strong hand wrapped around hers, his palm connected to hers, and an unfamiliar extra level of warmth surged through her. Adrenaline, and adventure with an attractive soldier, had never been better.

CHAPTER 5

Tessa promised they'd take today, his first day of training slowly, the same way his recovery days would go—days he wouldn't have training. Yesterday's hike had proven to Chad that his shoulder and pelvis hadn't recovered.

He could only hope she hadn't noticed. Whatever her assessment entailed, he'd ignored the dull ache that shot through his thigh during the hike.

Hardcore, Tessa continued to tempt him in every way. She'd swung effortlessly on the ropes while he'd gasped for air as the muscles in his right shoulder gave way to a strain that stirred up remnants of pain.

So much for taking on a challenge, as if impressing Tessa would do either of them any good. What had done him some good was when they'd landed in the frigid lake, squealing in excitement. Her eyes had sparkled, and she appeared carefree, as if diving in a cold lake was something she did often.

They'd had to get out and climb on boulders to the rope to swing their way back. Then they'd hiked home in wet clothes.

By the time he'd gone to bed, he was restless despite his exhaustion, barely sleeping which only resurrected combat memories.

At some point, he'd given up on sleeping when he felt the onset of a headache. He'd taken a couple of Advils, the medicine he'd brought with him just in case. Knowing Tessa's punctuality, Chad showered and dressed well before she showed up with their breakfast.

Afterward, he hadn't wanted her to leave yet, so he asked her to stay put while he cleared the table. He wanted her to show him how she normally started her day.

Now seated in the wicker chair to his left with a wicker table separating them, she read from her Bible. Something about running the race with endurance.

The morning breeze wisped her hair across her face, and he tried to listen while he took her in. She'd worn dark leggings with a blue exercise tank top under a white shirt. Goose bumps scattered over her bare arms. With the air still slightly crisp, the coolness seeped through his white T-shirt. They could both use another layer of clothing, but he didn't want to move or interfere. The perfect morning stillness seemed almost sacred, something he'd never truly experienced.

Now, the giant orange ball of the sun emerged from behind the mountains, creating a sight worth not blinking.

Peace permeated him, its physical presence almost tangible as the gentle stream coursed below the deck. Pink and blue wildflowers along the bank swayed in the morning breeze, bringing a sense of satisfaction. It almost felt like home. That was if he remembered what a home outside a military base was supposed to be. Okay, so he'd had a home with his aunt, uncle, and cousins, then his ex. But he'd barely stayed home long enough to get a feel for it between his deployments.

"'We do it with a crown that lasts forever.'"

At her gentle voice, he blinked to refocus and give her his full attention. She closed the Bible on the table. "Just that brief. And then I pray."

He rubbed his hands against his sports shorts. "Let's pray, then."

She clasped her hands. "You want me to lead us?"

He nodded and imitated her by clasping his hands. Her faith, depicted in her emails and letters, inspired him. Her love for God came across through her actions to the soldiers who received her care packages inside and outside of his unit.

So he'd sought out the army chaplain when he needed spiritual guidance.

"And for Your mercy…" As she continued, her prayer, like rain in the desert, quenched a thirst he hadn't even known was crying out in his parched soul. When he joined her with a clear amen, she pressed her lips together. Then her brown eyes searched his.

As if she knew how he felt physically, she said, "If I push you to do this training and you get hurt, I'd be the worst trainer and physical therapist. I'd never forgive myself."

Unease chilled his heart. He rubbed at his chest. Maybe he should tell her the extent of his injury. He hadn't had a major injury, nor had he been left with serious damage. But he couldn't talk about it without bringing up the *how* of it all. And he couldn't talk about *that*.

He caught a falling pine needle, then crushed it between his fingers, emitting a soothing scent. "Even if I had an injury, I wouldn't blame you if I got hurt. Besides"—he winked—"you're getting insured."

Undeterred, her eyes searched his, perhaps trying to see through his heart. He swallowed.

"Please, tell me now if there's anything I need to know. I can help you with the right exercises before we train."

He flinched at her sincerity. With her looking so sweet, and concern etching her brows, he could imagine himself her worst nightmare if he lied.

Still, he flashed his cheekiest grin. "I thought that was the point of your assessment."

Rolling her eyes, she blew out a heavy breath. "I want to hear it from you."

She couldn't have figured anything out by staring at him yesterday. Her shaky hands as she touched his hip during the assessment still made him shiver with desire—a longing he hadn't felt in ages.

"Now that you've seen me face-to-face"—she narrowed her gaze, determined to wrest his secrets from him—"I thought we could start opening up to each other."

"I don't want you to worry about me."

"Don't you think it's too late for that?"

Ugh. Why did his problems have to be hers? His ex, Nelly, never pestered him for information he didn't volunteer. Which he hadn't minded after spending most of his life without being fussed over. But again, Tessa was different, and she cared for him.

He'd seen sheer panic on her tear-streaked face when he'd FaceTimed her from the hospital three months ago. How he'd regretted calling and making her sad! But he'd needed to see her, hear her....

The water flowing below them rippled into the silence, and he tilted his face to the quivery aspen trees. Saplings and mature trees shivered in the breeze, their lush green leaves happy for this season, although they'd die off in the fall.

As much as he longed for a full life with Tessa, deep down he was just like the aspens. He'd never be able to hold onto a relationship any more than those trees could hold onto their leaves. Try with all his might, the outcome was as inevitable as a changing season. Or so he'd thought after their kiss at the airport.

"Ahem." She cleared her throat.

Right. She wanted answers. Deserved them, really. As a friend and trainer. "The injury I had a few months ago... Remember, I didn't call you for a while?"

He managed to look at her, determined to talk about the injury and leave the gory details out. "That mission didn't, um..."

Tessa closed her eyes as if holding her breath as he told her about the IEDs they'd gone to disable on the roadside. He'd disabled the reported ones, or so he'd thought until he sighted a wire connected to three other bombs almost thirty yards away.

Deactivating those extras should have been his cue to get back like his friends had suggested. His corporal's words rang through his head as if crackling through the walkie-talkie now: "There's a few eyes on us, sergeant. We'd better let the engineers handle the rest."

He closed his eyes. His mind whirled him back into the parched land. A blast echoed, the explosion booming, and he covered his ears with his hands. He was back to that tragic day, running. The gear was too heavy as he yanked off his helmet, his feet struggling toward the swirling dust of shrapnel, the only remains of his team vanishing right in front of him.

He should've died with them. What right did he have to be the only survivor?

He felt hot, then cold. His body trembled as dark memories engulfed him. The unconsciousness in desolation, the gasping for breath while his shoulder bled and his head throbbed. His forehead must have bled too. He couldn't remember, but he'd ended up with a shrapnel cut to his forehead.

"I'm so sorry, Chad." A soft hand touched his shoulder, and he jerked, unworthy of sympathy. "We don't have to talk about it."

"Too late!" An unexpected heat seared him, blinded him, and he stood. He didn't find Tessa's hand as comforting as it should be. "I shouldn't have come here!"

"I'm glad you're here. Training for a triathlon."

He raked a hand through his hair and stomped across the deck, then clutched the hard metal doorknob. He'd planned the triathlon before the explosion that had snatched three men. A cold fist squeezed his chest. How had he thought he could ignore their loss? Go on with his plans? He'd never felt so unhinged—like he was the bomb waiting to explode.

"I need to leave."

"Stay."

He yanked the door open, and she followed him inside the cabin.

"I didn't mean to ask about your injuries." Her voice shook, but he couldn't look at her. He just gathered the two shirts strewn on his bed and shoved them in his duffel bag.

"You can't leave."

"I can do whatever I want!"

Liar! He couldn't even look at her. One peek at those deep brown eyes, and he'd do whatever she asked. He should be at a base somewhere or wherever soldiers went after finishing their tours.

The army would take him back since his injuries were minimal. *If* they were in need of more techs. Maybe they weren't now that they'd withdrawn from the Middle East.

"Please, Chad." Tessa touched his back to get his attention before moving to stand in front of him and looking him square in the eye. "Soldiers don't just quit."

"At their post, they don't." Unlike him, who'd failed when he insisted on following the wire to disable one more IED—costing him three men under his leadership. He'd led many and gone on many more dangerous missions over the years, but he'd never lost the entire team.

Maybe one man or two would get injured or die. But all three dead?

And now he was lounging at some cabin with a beautiful woman for a trainer. A woman staring at him now without blinking. Her care and passion burned with a golden fire in those eyes. Her sweet scent of spring and wildflowers stirred something in him, feelings he shouldn't be experiencing, feelings he had no right to.

Those feelings only surged a ripple of anger that stiffened his every muscle. He ground his teeth. "Soldiers don't have to answer to anyone with details about their lives."

Perhaps she'd stop asking. Good thing he hadn't bothered putting his belongings in the chest of drawers and didn't need to pack now. He tossed his bag on his back and marched for the door.

"It was a pleasure meeting you." He didn't bother looking at her. "Tell your mom thanks." He opened the door, stepped out, and closed it behind him.

The door creaked open as he stepped onto the lower step.

"I'll drive you," she said, her voice resigned. "That's the least I can do."

He performed an about-face—stupid! Those brown eyes shiny with tears flooded him with regret. Grinding his jaw, he hardened himself against all emotion. "I'll be fine walking. Thanks anyway."

She shook her head. "I can help you."

Physically, maybe. But emotionally? "I don't need help."

"Hmm." She let out a mirthless laugh. "I'd expected you to react like this, but I'd convinced myself I was wrong to think that way."

"What's that supposed to mean?" Ouch. Too late to take it back, he winced at his sharp tone.

Tessa's shoulders fell. God forgive him. He had no right to cause her such pain.

She lifted her hand to wave. "Be careful."

He snorted and spun around. Even the worst that could happen to him could never even out the loss of the people under his care. He started his march down the flagstone path. Gray clouds covered the sky he'd earlier hoped would be sunny. God had decided to paint the sky gray to match Chad's mood.

At least he had plenty of time to make it into town, and if he got a hotel, he'd stay tonight, then book a flight back to Virginia. As he followed the rugged road Tessa had driven on his arrival Tuesday and again on Wednesday for their shopping trip, a family of deer meandered in the pasture. How would it feel to be like them, having no care in the world? Could he ever go back to that point in his life, with no melancholy or dejection?

He continued his journey, stopping from time to time to sit and give his achy legs a break. Perched now on a fallen log, he rubbed his forehead and took slow breaths of heady pine-scented air, and the silence around him faded beneath his howling thoughts. The red-hot anger, followed by his icy reaction toward Tessa, hadn't been necessary. How had all that come about, anyway? He rarely got angry. When had he become so low that he could lose it on someone he admired?

He pushed to his feet, slung his bag over his good shoulder, and sidestepped a patch of daisies growing alongside the road. One hand strayed to the phone in his pocket.

As soon as he'd settled in, he'd intended to call his cousin, Liam, and inform him of his arrival. Maybe he'd head there instead. It was high time he visited his cousins. Liam, being the stable one, could help Chad get a grip on his life.

The cloud cover was godsent, and although he could walk ten miles, carrying his duffel bag didn't make it easier. But he'd reached some sort of civilization again, and more homes peeked through the trees the further he went.

Stopping again to catch a breath, he pulled out the phone he hadn't used since arriving in Pleasant View. With minimal lodging options in town, he called the motel closest to Tessa's home—apparently, only ten miles away. They had availability, and he made a reservation.

Almost two miles away from the hotel, a raindrop landed on his arm. Groaning, he lengthened his stride. Sure, he might encounter rain during a triathlon, but not with everything he owned carried on his back.

He broke out into a sprint when more drops pelted, barely registering the random cars as he raced alongside the road like a crazy man.

By the time he entered the two-story adobe motel just before three, his hip hurt from walking, his shoulder hurt from carrying the duffel bag, and his head hurt from arguing with Tessa. And his clothes were damp from the drizzle.

After the girl with a pierced tongue handed him his key, he headed to his second-floor room. Many times smaller than the cabin, the room smelled slightly musky. Or maybe the smell was a combination of his sweat and dampness from the rain.

He showered and hung his wet clothes on the chair in the corner. After unzipping the bag he'd set on the table, he rummaged for his cleanest shorts and a white T-shirt. Despite not being in a waterproofed bag, the clothes had stayed dry. More importantly, so were his harmonica, the foldable fan, and Tessa's letters all tucked in the Ziploc bag.

He massaged his throbbing temples, then reached for the jingling container to take a couple of Advils. Oops! Remembering two things about meds, he ran to the bathroom to retch the medicine. Rule number one—always drink a beverage to down the pills. Rule number two—never take this medicine on an empty stomach.

The oatmeal breakfast had been short-lived, and he was starving. So he called a number from one of the flyers on the coffee table, then ordered pizza.

He tried not to think of anything or anyone, Tessa in particular, as he massaged his temples as if he could soothe his head without the meds.

By the time they delivered his pizza twenty minutes later, his headache had subsided. He gobbled a few slices before reaching for the remote and blasting the TV to a sports channel to keep his thoughts from interfering. He was almost out of clean clothes and had meant to ask Tessa where to wash his laundry that morning. Instead, he'd lost it on her.

He couldn't care less about clean clothes. He shifted on the vinyl sofa, rested his feet on the coffee table, and slid a photo of Tessa from his wallet. He'd cut it to fit his wallet. The same photo had gotten him through the horrific hours in the desert.

He touched her small face captured now in his hand, his finger tracing the outline of delicate cheeks and sweet lips. She was the reason he'd come to Pleasant View. The reason he'd woken up every day over the last months with renewed hope. The reason he'd lived through the desolate hours when no one knew he'd survived the IED. For hours, it had just been him, pressing his hand to his bleeding shoulder and praying to God for his survival. When he'd thought he was going to die, Tessa had come to mind. Then he'd struggled to pull out his wallet and stare at her dear face, weighed down that, although they hadn't met in person, she'd be shattered if she learned of his death.

And he'd survived. Then he used her as his inspiration while he busted himself through physical therapy and challenging strengthening exercises for his muscles to regain full mobility. Now, like the quitter Tessa had just witnessed him to be, he was giving up before he started.

Sliding the photo back into his wallet, he crossed his feet on the table and reached for one of the folded papers, their first letters, before they'd begun using email and virtual communication. His hand shook as he unfolded the paper to reveal cursive writing as dainty and dear as she was.

> Dear Chad, thank you for the note. It's odd that I'm thanking you for thanking me, but your note surprised me. No one has ever written to thank me before. I'm glad I now know your name so I can mention it when I pray.

> I'll be sure to send more beef jerky now that I know it's a favorite for you and your friends. You asked why I sent packages to strangers, but I don't consider you strangers. You see, I do this to honor my dad.
>
> Do you miss home? How long are you stationed there?
>
> I don't expect you to answer those questions, but I couldn't help it. I'm sure you have more important things to do, but it was a pleasure meeting you through your letter.

He traced the line he'd read, his heart quickening with the memory of the night he'd opened her letter in his bunk. He hadn't even known he'd been smiling until one of the guys poked his head into the door and asked what made him grin so wide.

> I'll leave you with one of the Bible verses that comes to mind when I pray for you and the rest of the soldiers.
>
> "Greater love has no one than this: to lay down one's life for one's friends" John 15:13.
>
> Be careful,
>
> Tessa

He'd had to respond after reading that letter. Especially after reading about her dad. Plus, who could just not answer her questions? So he'd written another letter.

Folding the paper and sliding it back into the bag, he stared at the empty room.

A horrible sickness rose inside him over his parting from her. Those had been tears in her eyes when she'd offered to help. Thinking of them and her words—*"Soldiers don't quit"*—choked him up.

Hmm. Soldiers, yes, that should be him, but it wasn't. He wasn't a qualified soldier after all. Not when he'd compromised the safety of those under his leadership.

Gripped by such melancholy, he didn't desire anything, not even the harmonica he played whenever he felt sad. Not up to moving to the twin bed, he shifted his feet from the coffee table and stretched out on the couch. Then he stared at the spinning fan casting shadows over the popcorn ceiling.

Calling his cousin would have to wait until he felt like socializing. He just wanted to be alone—alone in his thoughts. He didn't feel the strength to tinker with browsing for flights on his tiny phone screen. Virginia would only remind him of the wife who'd left him because he didn't have what it took to be a husband. Where would he stay in Virginia anyway? Another motel and for how long?

Soda Creek, Virginia had plenty of memories, his childhood being one of them. He shuddered, a sick emptiness swallowing him up.

More than the silence in Tessa's cabin made him feel at home. If silence was all it took, he'd buy a mountain cabin and seclude himself from the world.

When he closed his eyes, images of Tessa swirled behind his lids. Her smile, her daring adventure, and her teasing all emboldened him to swing on the ropes and ignore his pain—both the physical and emotional wounds. His cheeks lifted with his smile. The cabin was only fun as long as she was there to keep him company.

Exhausted, he closed his eyes. Sometime later—he had no idea how much later—all he could hear and see were the bomb blasts and raw images of people being swept up in the dust of an explosion.

He woke with a start, panting, perspiration drenching his shirt. He touched his racing heart. Good thing he'd kept the light on.

"I can help you." Tessa's promise rang clear in his head as if she was whispering to him, touching his shoulder to comfort him. How he longed for her touch! How had he not found it appealing earlier when she'd tried to comfort him?

Ugh. He'd ignored her and stalked off like a rebellious teen running away from home.

The nightstand clock lit one a.m. What was he supposed to do until sunrise?

He sat up and moved to the bed, unzipped his duffel bag, and pulled the manila envelope of Tessa's letters from the Ziploc bag. Then he retrieved his harmonica. It was going to be a long night.

He knew what he needed to do. He'd have to swallow his pride. Bettina would gloat since she'd guessed he was a wanderer. Although she hadn't warmed up to him, he'd managed to get through the dinners with minimal conversation, but now, there'd be a slight comfort even in Bettina's prickly personality.

The Reality wasn't about Bettina and what she thought about him, but about him making things right with a woman who cared for him, a woman he cared for in deeper ways than he dared to admit.

CHAPTER 6

Tessa didn't know what to do when she got up on Saturday, the day she'd planned to be Chad's second day of training. Unable to sleep normally, she'd woken early, dressed, and headed to the kitchen to make omelets while Mom was picking vegetables. With breakfast made, she wiped down the fridge handle for the third or fifth time.

Where had Chad gone? She hadn't expected him to stay away all day and night. Sure, he'd had an outburst, but why hadn't he come to his senses after the anger subsided? She'd regretted asking about his injury the moment he started talking. She'd felt useless as he stared into space, trembling, then covered his ears with his hands.

Way to go, Tessa. She opened the fridge, shuffled the contents, and scrubbed the top shelf. Being a physical therapist didn't mean she was also a counselor. She should've known better after dealing with her brother. Elias had never talked about what caused his injury. Why hadn't she thought of that *before* asking Chad to disclose any pain? Okay, knowing if he was in pain before she shoved him into a beastly race was critical. Still, she should've been careful about how she worded it, made sure he knew she wasn't pushing him to share the details of what happened.

The kitchen door opened. Mom stepped inside, set down another basket of fresh-picked vegetables ready for the Saturday farmers market, and shed her gloves. "The celery is gorgeous today, and my cukes are coming along. But, oh my, slugs got into the pumpkin patch. I'm going to have to come up with a better way to keep them out."

Tessa nodded. Maybe she could come up with something. She wouldn't exactly be focusing on a triathlon or training since Chad was gone. He'd seemed serious about leaving, and she'd better get her mind used to it.

"Smells good in here." Mom washed her hands, squeezed Tessa's shoulder, then carried the plate Tessa handed her to the dining room. "You may not be one for growing veggies, kiddo, but you sure know how to cook with them."

Tessa followed her. Sitting down for breakfast before Mom left to deliver her vegetables would keep her from thinking about Chad.

Mom eyed the lone plate in Tessa's hand. "You didn't make an omelet for Chad? Is he joining us for breakfast?"

Huh. Maybe she shouldn't have had breakfast with Mom today. Mom hadn't touched her omelet, and although Tessa considered her questions rhetorical, she sensed Mom's need for a response.

Pressing her lips tight, Tessa eyed the vertical blinds where morning light streamed into the dining room, highlighting the now-neglected floors Dad had kept varnished. It was easier not to look at Mom while she made up excuses for Chad.

"He wanted to check out the town." Tessa could hope he hadn't taken a flight to Virginia already. He'd left his bike leaning against the cabin where they'd put it the day he'd purchased it. He'd also left all the triathlon equipment in the chest of drawers. Yes, she'd checked after he stormed off without pulling out anything from the drawers. He probably hadn't unpacked his bag because he'd known he would leave suddenly.

He had to come back for his stuff, so she'd take consolation in that.

Mom was smart to have doubts about Chad. Although Tessa had her doubts too, apparently she couldn't keep from falling for the wrong soldiers.

Okay, they weren't even dating, and just because Chad kissed her senseless didn't mean she could cling to him. What bothered her most was that he was quitting and giving up on his training without even trying.

Forget the training! All she wanted was for him to feel better if he had an injury.

"Hmm." Mom tapped her fingers on the table, pulling Tessa from her thoughts. "Shouldn't he be concerned about starting his training?"

Having worked an extra shift last night, Mom wasn't around to notice Chad's absence at dinner. So Tessa hadn't had to explain why and how he'd left.

"I need to give him some time before we get into serious training."

Tessa forked her omelet and lifted it to her mouth. She usually loved the tomatoes and spinach in the eggs, but today, she didn't find them tasty or flavorful as her mind wandered to a man she had no business thinking about.

He'd been eager to start his training, but he must be dealing with trauma. Elias, the ever-quiet and sweet man, had returned from deployment with outbursts he'd never had before.

"As long as you don't fall in love with him." Mom reached for her glass of orange juice. "It's best to keep things professional."

She was right, but Tessa's reasons to avoid Chad stemmed from her experience, regardless of whether Chad was stable or not.

"We're just friends." Sure, they were.

Well, they *would* be if her heart could remain stable in his presence.

With Mom's knowing gaze on her, Tessa had better switch the topic. "So what are your plans for the day?" Not exactly a subtle question since she knew Mom's usual schedule.

"I just need to deliver those vegetables to the market." Mom tipped her chin toward the kitchen. Lettuce and broccoli among other vegetables lined the counter in baskets.

"I can't believe you picked all those vegetables this morning."

"Early to bed…" Mom shrugged, forked a bite, then took a sip of juice. "So, if you aren't training Chad today, what will you get up to?"

"I can go with you to the market if you want."

Mom chuckled. "I'm only dropping off vegetables before I go to work."

Oh. "I thought you worked afternoon shifts on Saturdays."

"I've been taking on extra shifts lately."

Not that she needed extra shifts. "You shouldn't be working so much, Mom. Just because I'm training Chad doesn't mean I can't keep up my end of the bills around here."

"You know how I like being busy."

Tessa nodded, understanding Mom's need to stay busy.

"How'll you keep busy, now that training is off your plate today?"

Today might be a good day to visit a friend. "I might go hang out with Liberty and her daughter later."

Now that her friend's husband was back in her life, Tessa couldn't just hang out with Liberty whenever she pleased. Liberty didn't work on Saturdays, but her weekends were probably best spent with her family.

But that didn't mean Tessa couldn't offer to babysit Liberty's daughter so her friend could go on a date with her husband. That'd be the best plan for the day. She needed a distraction, and rather than having an intense workout, which she resorted to when conflicted, hanging out with a busy toddler sounded appealing.

After helping her mom load the vegetables into the SUV, Tessa returned to her living quarters in the basement. She showered, then changed into shorts and a pleated green top. Its petal-design sleeves tickled her shoulders when she moved. Since she'd washed her hair last night, she didn't need to go through the ritual of drying her thick hair that morning.

In her bedroom's full-length mirror, she gathered her hair into a messy ponytail. Then she moved to her nightstand, and her fingers brushed against a lidded, clear cylinder vase when she grabbed her phone. The time on the screen was only seven.

Too early to text a married woman on her day off.

She'd already had her prayers before dawn and read her Bible while journaling her thoughts. She'd done all she'd normally do by now. She eyed the cylinder holding all the precious letters Chad had written her. Another cylinder on the other side of her dresser held Dad's letters. Elias never responded to any of her letters, but he'd called and emailed whenever he managed.

She twisted open the jar with Chad's letters, hoping to get closure in case she'd misunderstood the selfless man who'd taken the time to write to her.

Choosing a letter she'd wrapped in a tiny tube and labeled Number 2, she smiled and unrolled his slanted scribbly writing.

Dear Tess,

Did I say I hate writing? I feel too lazy to add the A to your name. I still had to answer your questions though. You asked how long I'm stationed here, but I'm afraid my company's rotation still has almost a year. As for missing home, this is home for me when I'm doing my job. Do I sound pathetic? If I do, then I'll change it up a bit. I miss the food in America, but I'll have plenty of time to catch up when our tour is over. We could use some air conditioning around here, but if I have to request that you ship that, then you may never send us snacks again.

Tessa chuckled, remembering how hard she'd laughed as his humor flowed through his words. Glancing at her reflection in the dresser mirror, she felt warm, the way she felt when Chad ended the letter with a request, saying he was already looking forward to another letter from her.

With her next letter, she'd included her email address and sent a care package with three foldable fans and lots of beef jerky.

Chad hadn't emailed but had written that he liked getting her letters since he'd never had a pen pal. He also asked for a photo of her so he could put a face to the letters. At that point, she'd felt there was no harm in sending him her photo, and he'd sent her his. Soon they were emailing, alternating with handwritten airmail letters, then FaceTime.

Tessa blew out a breath as she rolled the letter and fit it in the tube before setting it in the cylinder. She still had a lot to learn about him, even though he resided deep in the recesses of her heart.

Still not sure about what to do, she pulled out the two outfits from the laundry basket next to her dresser and carried them to the washer in the laundry room beside her bedroom. She could do laundry, but she needed to gather more clothes to run the cycle.

The wooden stairs creaked as she left the basement.

With Chad gone, she should strip off the cabin bedsheets and replace them with the extra set she'd kept in his chest of drawers. Whether he returned or not, the bed needed clean bedsheets. It would also give her a chance to think and pray for him while she sat on his bed.

As she crossed the yard, the sunshine, shooting light and color through the fluttery aspens, lifted her spirits. The air smelled fresh after yesterday's rain, and despite her hopeless plans for the day, having a promise of a sunny day in the mountains comforted her.

On the flagstone path to the cabin, strings of glittering music made her pause. It seemed like the music was coming from the cabin. Hmm?

She turned her head, leaning to the side and cupping her ear to make sure it wasn't the creek. No? It wasn't just the water rippling, but something metallic and cascading.

Curiosity urged her forward, lengthening her stride. Dew-misted wildflowers and grass that snuck close to the path brushed against her ankles, and crisp air filled her lungs.

Even if the cabin was unlocked, she knocked in case Chad had returned. Did he play an instrument? He'd never told her, but she'd never asked. She knocked again, and when there was no response, she pushed the door open into an empty room.

Chad's duffel bag was on the nicely laid-out bed. The dirty bedsheets were balled in a circle on the rug near the nightstand.

He was back! A smile lifted her cheeks. The music sounded louder, beckoning from the back porch.

Laughter slipped free, and she scooted across the room, then slid aside the curtain on the back door.

Hunched in a chair with his gaze to the creek, Chad gripped an instrument that fit in his palm as he blew through it, moving his lips from its left, then to its right.

Tessa's hand rested on the door, her moist palm forming a handprint on the glass.

The tune's sadness gripped her heart, tightening her chest. As if aware he was being watched, he stopped and shoved the instrument in his shorts pockets. Then his neck jerked, and his gaze met hers.

She dropped her hand to her side. Her stomach coiled into knots. He held her gaze, and she felt breathless, self-preservation urging her to look away. But she didn't. Chad's rumpled hair suggested he'd either just woken up or been wandering all night. The vulnerability and the dark circles around his green eyes made her ache.

Something was wrong with him. Something he'd almost shared yesterday. Something that had unleashed an outburst. He could have anger issues she hadn't learned about during their virtual conversations.

When he raised his hand in salute, she slid open the door and joined him, then turned the extra chair to face him.

"You look beautiful." He reached across the table and touched the leaflets of her blouse. A breakout of goose bumps shivered across her arm when his fingers brushed against her shoulder.

"Thank you."

She pointed at his shorts where he'd stashed the instrument. "I didn't know you play—"

"It's just a harmonica." He pulled it from his pocket. "Doesn't take much skill."

"It sounded professional." She tucked her hands into her lap. "The song was sad."

His soft chuckle didn't warm his green eyes. "I play sad songs to suit my mood."

A frown squeezed her brows. He must be struggling if he was playing sad songs. "Are you going to be okay?"

He set the harmonica on the table, his eyes searching hers. "I'm sorry about yesterday."

She nodded. "Where did you go?"

He rubbed the stubbled growth on his chin. "I walked into town, stayed in a motel, and entertained the idea of going to Virginia. But I took a cab back this morning, and I'm here now. When I thought of home, well..." He cleared his throat and pressed his lips together. Then his voice emerged low and serious. "You're the closest thing to home outside my combat life."

She gripped the chair arms, going dizzy. Wicker pinched her fingers. Something that felt like crushed ice clogged her throat, and her lips parted to ask a question. But she forgot what she wanted to say. Which was okay since her tongue was frozen anyway.

"You're very nice. I like you." His sheepish smile begged her to smile back. "I also know you don't date clients."

She could make an exception. "Okay."

"I wouldn't play by your rules on that one, but I'm a mess anyway."

She had her insecurities and doubts. "Aren't we all?"

He turned his gaze to the space ahead. Wildflowers swayed with the light breeze. The moment passed as smoothly as the water flowed below them.

Knowing how yesterday had ended, she'd ask about his family instead. He'd been orphaned at twelve—that much she knew. "Have you talked to your cousins since you returned?"

He shrugged. "I was going to call Liam when I got to the base, but I was in a hurry to get here."

Her heart swelled that he'd been as eager to see her as she had been to see him. "Tell me more about your cousins."

"Liam and Dylan Knight." He nodded, staring into space. "We're a few years apart from each other." A sad smile loosened his lips as if fond memories resurfaced. "Liam was always responsible, three years younger than me, and Dylan, five years younger." He shook his head, his face crumpling. "I'd be surprised if Dylan's alive."

Oh my! Even after his reaction yesterday, she couldn't keep from reaching over and touching his hand.

His fingers twitched beneath hers, and his gaze lowered to her hand. Then he turned his hand and gripped hers back. "It was nice having the boys and their family in my life. Like it's nice having you in my life. I never had much of a family of my own. I never knew my dad, and my mom traveled a lot for her career."

Made sense. He'd once said his mom was a singer.

"I spent most of my childhood with a nanny, but I could always count on my mom's love." His lips twitched, that soft-sad smile reappearing. "Mom called me every night before I went to bed."

Tessa's heart squeezed as she imagined a younger Chad. He must have been a fun little boy with a great sense of humor. "I can tell she was a wonderful mom."

"Yeah..." His voice shook. "That jet..." His Adam's apple bobbled as he swallowed hard and his grip on her hand tightened almost painfully. "When her jet crashed, I thought my life ended as well."

"I'm so sorry, Chad." She cupped her other hand to his face, turning him to look at her.

"It was a long time ago." He focused on the hammock strung between two aspens. "I moved in with my aunt and spent five years with my cousins."

Tessa scooted back in her chair, tucked her feet up beside her, and let him unload.

"Their dad had a temper and often beat their mom—right in front of us."

Tessa gasped.

And Chad turned heavy eyes on her. "She... my aunt... attempted suicide during a family vacation. She survived but spent years in rehab."

"Oh, Chad..." But what more could she say? How could words help such childhood trauma?

"It made me stronger. I joined the army at seventeen."

He'd needed an escape, a place to belong. No wonder this funny, strong man could have anger outbursts. Losing his mom and ending up with emotionally unstable relatives could leave a child scarred for life.

Add to that the possible trauma from his job...

Good grief, he might be in worse condition than her ex-boyfriend. Mom was right to suggest keeping things professional. Except Chad was opening up while Kanon never got to that point.

"I want to go through this training." He slid down the neck of his T-shirt to reveal his right shoulder. "I got hit right here."

She stood and moved close to him, her fingers trembling as she traced along the scar's still-red jagged edges, puckered where the stitches had been. "Just don't ask me the *how* of it. The blast suit saved me from intense shrapnel effects." His voice dropped to a fear-laced whisper. "I underwent rigorous physical therapy after the incident. I wanted to be in great shape when I got here."

Could she talk him out of the Ironman Triathlon? Would he settle for the half triathlon?

"On a scale of one to ten, how much does your shoulder hurt?" She cupped her hand on his shoulder, letting her fingertips leave butterfly kisses along the scar.

"Mildly, and the doctor thought I could pull off a triathlon if I got another week or more of therapy."

Yet he'd intended to keep his pain a secret? He didn't rate his pain like she'd asked, so it was probably a six and hurting more than he was letting on.

"I can help with therapy."

"I know." He looked at her, his sincerity seeping through his eyes. "Even if I said I don't need your help, I'm at your mercy."

He then lifted the corner of his shirt by his waist with one hand, his other hand tugging the elastic on his shorts, pulling down a section to reveal a red scar on his hip. "That's another one."

She lowered herself to take a good look. Cut sideways, the wound went above and below his waist, but she didn't dare touch or look longer. Concerned about his injuries, she pressed her hands on her heart. "I presume they took out the stitches?"

He nodded, covering the area when he dropped his shirt and gave her a knowing look. "It's been a long time since I've been fussed over. I may not respond well to that kind of attention."

With the kind of environment he'd grown up in, it made sense.

"You better get used to the attention." Caring for and cheering on her clients to achieve their goals came naturally to her. "I'll be giving you a lot of it."

"Just don't have mercy on me. I need to be ready for that race."

"You can try for the half triathlon instead—"

"No!" His chin jerked up. His jaw flexed. "I'll stick to the plan."

They didn't need a repeat of yesterday. "Then we have a lot of work to do." She moved back to stand next to her chair. "First, let's get you fed."

Then she'd need his updated imaging tests and doctor's report. "We might have to work on getting you a doctor in town too."

"With you, I'm in good hands." He stood, grinning sheepishly, his light tone warming her heart. "And you won't want to be near me if I don't get some laundry done. In the meantime, can I help you make breakfast?"

"Not today." She gave a wave, beckoning him to follow as she crossed the deck to the cabin. "Gather your laundry and follow me to the house. While you get your laundry done, I'll get your breakfast."

Chad was a distraction she didn't need in the kitchen. Plus, she needed to work on ways to squelch her feelings for him, and that meant creating some distance whenever she could manage.

Happy, Mom? This is me keeping things professional.

CHAPTER 7

After Chad's army doctor emailed the recent X-rays to the new doctor in Pleasant View the following week, Chad started a routine of physical therapy and exercises to improve mobility in his shoulder and hip. Tessa wanted to start with water aerobics to relieve pain and build muscle without causing more damage to his injuries.

Chad felt like he was in boot camp all over again when she took him to a lake five miles from their house.

"When I told you not to take it easy on me, I didn't mean you should freeze me to death." He winced as he joined her in the frigid lake.

"Consider this part of your training." She splashed water on him, and he grimaced. "You'll be swimming in a lake for your triathlon anyway."

"You're the worst trainer." He rolled his eyes, his tone light as he held his breath to train his mind to adapt to the water. With the swim shirt and shorts snug to him, he waded toward her. How were her teeth not chattering in this frigid water?

"Yet you chose me as your trainer." She moved closer, sliding a green pool noodle toward him before taking his right arm to ease the injured shoulder up. She eased it up, then down. "We're going to work on relaxing your arms using this noodle."

Goose bumps intensified throughout his body, and his nerves crumbled at her touch when she moved the noodle in front of his chest and stretched his arms forward for their upper body strengthening exercises.

"Move your hands forward a few times. Then we'll work on push-pull alternating." As he complied, she shoved the noodle aside.

He worked on sideways arm raises, forward arm raises, and figure eight arm rotations.

They then worked on the lower body for his hip, doing lunges, hip stretches, pool planks, and single leg balances. Silence abounded, their voices echoing across the water while birds skimmed the surface and a woodpecker hammered at a pine. Huh. No one else was anywhere nearby. "This lake doesn't seem public, and it's not on your property. So are we going to get in trouble here?"

"It belongs to our neighbors, the Johnsons." She lowered herself into the water, sinking until her head vanished under the surface before she emerged and wiped the water from her face. "We've used it since I was little."

His cheeks lifted as he imagined Tessa's childhood growing up in the mountains. He stretched his leg beneath him, no longer able to touch the rocky bottom. "What did you guys do for fun?"

Her smile beamed like the morning sun. "Dad took us fishing—at least when he wasn't on deployment."

It didn't sound like they'd fished often, but her fondest childhood memories seemed to be of the time she'd spent with her dad. Chad's chest squeezed, bittersweet with wondering what having a dad was like, but glad she'd had one who loved her.

"How did he die?"

"He got shot." Her lips thinned, and he stopped short of touching her face to comfort her. Touching her could lead to hugging her, then smelling her scent, and pushing back the hair now clinging to her face—an excuse to cup her chin and kiss her. That his mind had imagined it all out gave him a good reason not to trust himself around her. "We all have to die eventually."

"Doesn't take away the pain of missing a loved one." He knew. He'd never stopped missing his mom, and he'd only known her for a few years of his life. Hit by the sick emptiness of loss, he swallowed hard and pressed a hand to the hollowness in his chest. Not exactly how he wanted this day to play out as they dwelled on losses. So he'd better redirect the conversation. "What other activities did you guys do growing up?"

"We used to bike and play with kids from the area." Her lips quirked as she waved toward the woods. "As you can see, it's not exactly a tight-packed neighborhood, teeming with kids. There weren't a lot of girls nearby. I had my girlfriends at school, but after school, I hung out with my brother's friends. The Johnson boys were such brats! Elias always stood up for me, but the boys used to tease me, egging me on to try things I should know better than to do. And I didn't learn any better until I got injured in high school doing the high jumps."

She flicked water from her face. Dewdrops still clung to her luscious eyelashes. "That landed me in therapy and inspired my career, so I owe those jerks something."

She rolled her eyes as she called the boys jerks, her fondness evident in the twinkle in her eyes and the upward twitch of her lips.

He could well imagine her as a kid with an unstoppable adventuresome spirit. If only he had special memories to share! But he didn't. The revitalizing light in her eyes was evidence of what her hometown meant to her. What would it feel like to belong somewhere?

They continued with more water aerobics, gradual walks, and light weight lifting the following days, and he felt more strength in his arm muscles each passing day. Spending his days with Tessa was rewarding, especially now that they were back to their normal friendship.

With her being funny and lighthearted and sharing her love for the world around her, he felt lighthearted despite the shadows that taunted him in her absence at night.

Not only was Tessa passionate about her job as a physical therapist but also determined to have him meet his goals to recover and start his training. He hadn't expected to be ready for training earlier than two weeks, but by the tenth day of therapy, he didn't feel the lingering pain in his shoulder when he carried weights. And his hip and thigh didn't hurt when Tessa did a leg-roll test on him.

When he told her how well he felt, she had him get another set of X-rays and a new evaluation from his doctor at the Pleasant View Wellness Clinic.

Besides their walks and jogs in the last two weeks, Chad was ready for real training and thrilled when she took him to the recreation center to meet his swim trainer, Kinkaid.

The smell of chlorine clogged the air and burned the back of Chad's throat as Kinkaid talked to him. Tall with blond hair, probably in his early thirties, the guy stood there in shorts and a tight T-shirt. What kind of training was he going to offer if he wasn't in a swimsuit?

Chad had never had a trainer for his previous triathlons, but then he'd never done the Ironman. It was legit hard, and now more than ever, he needed the challenge, something to prepare his mind to endure the memory of the men he'd lost.

If Tessa wasn't his trainer, he may not have thought of hiring a coach. In one of their virtual conversations, she'd told him about her career change to a personal trainer, and he'd conjured up the idea of a triathlon and asked her to train him. That was before he'd been injured and before he'd registered for the race.

"Today, I just want to see the areas we can work on." Kinkaid's voice drew Chad from his wandering thoughts. The man's slow gaze lingered on Tessa. Seated on a poolside bench, she gave Kinkaid a curt smile, not genuine like she smiled for Chad, but enough to whip unease into Chad's heart.

"So, as I was saying—"

"I swim, you watch." Chad cut him off, needing to get this over with so he could whisk Tessa out of Kinkaid's sight. He ground his teeth to hold back the urge to tell the instructor to keep his focus on Chad, the student, not Tessa, the student's trainer.

Swimming wasn't Chad's favorite sport, and if Tessa was as poor a swimmer as he was, then he needed Kinkaid. But not at the cost of losing Tessa to the man. *Well played, Chad. If I can't have her, nobody else can.*

Without waiting for further instructions, he lowered himself to sit at the edge of the pool, wincing at the coolness as his legs sank into the chilly water. The swim shirt he'd worn over jammer tech swim shorts didn't shield him. His gaze shifted to Tessa, and she offered her soft and genuine smile. Their gazes held, and warmth replaced his unease over Kinkaid staring at her. His heart quickened. He let his cheeks lift and waved.

She gave him a thumbs-up and mouthed, "You've got this."

The wall clock above her showed six forty. The pool would be opening to the public in forty minutes. If Kinkaid wasn't waiting for him to settle into the pool, Chad would reach out and drag Tessa into the water. But this was only Day 1. There'd be plenty of days to mess around.

He would be lying if he said his attraction to Tessa wasn't growing stronger. He needed to save her from himself—he owed her that. But resisting her was harder than walking through a minefield.

As if reading his thoughts, she called his name, her brows lifting. "Your instructor is waiting to see your strokes."

"On it, captain." He plunged into the water. Today's lesson was more about getting comfortable than nailing the sport. Or so Tessa said as she drove them to the recreation center.

His body cut through the water with smooth, easy strokes as he waited for Kinkaid's next instructions. But was his instructor even paying any attention while making small talk with Tessa?

Chad felt his arms give way, more with tension and unease about leaving her with the guy. He swam back to the deep end where he'd started, raised himself out of the water enough to brace an arm on the cement deck, and wiped the water from his face. Seriously? Kinkaid had moved to stand by Tessa?

Chad's body jerked. He swung over, gripped the ladder, and climbed from the water. Then he stooped to scoop up his towel and bit the inside of his cheek—just because he was cold standing there, of course.

Tessa nodded to him as he stood by the pool.

"You're off to a great start." She beamed, but he couldn't force a smile. What was wrong with him?

"Is that all you can do today?" Kinkaid glanced at the timer in his hand.

Whoa. Chad hadn't realized he was going to be timed. In response, he dove back into the water determined to show Kinkaid he may not need his training.

When he'd had enough, he emerged, and Tessa ran to him, handing him a fresh towel.

"You forgot to bring your swim cap."

"Thanks for the towel." He had the swim cap in the mesh bag, but it wasn't necessary. "I'll remember tomorrow." He dried his hair, then his arms, and over his dripping suit.

"Tomorrow, we'll swim for forty minutes." Kinkaid crossed his arms, widened his stance, and nodded at Chad. "From observing your strokes, I've seen you're right-hand dominant and tend to pull to the right, your stronger side—even after your shoulder injury—when swimming. You can keep on track in a marked-up pool but could veer into a somewhat diagonal line during the race, wasting valuable time and energy as well as getting in other swimmers' way. We'll need to perfect your freestyle. The freestyle strokes are critical for crossing the lake in the triathlon."

"Who doesn't like swimming in lakes?" Chad mumbled under his breath. He was insane to think he'd pull this race off. He hated lake swimming, but he had a renewed purpose for doing the race. For his friends. Plus, he'd given Tessa his word. He wasn't quitting.

"Let's ease into it slowly." Tessa scooted between him and Kinkaid, clearly concerned that Chad could still get injured.

Chad rubbed the towel over his hair, raking it the wrong way and no doubt leaving clumps standing up. "I think I can swim for forty minutes."

"I know you can." She squeezed his shoulder, sending shock waves throughout his body like she did whenever she touched him. "Your first days of training are all about working on getting you comfortable so you don't dread it."

"Tessa is right." Kinkaid's fond gaze on Tessa and that slow smile he gave her made Chad want to shove him into the pool.

"See you tomorrow." Chad fought a growl before turning to Tessa and telling her he'd meet her at the car.

"I'll wait for you in the lobby."

"I wanted to talk to Tessa, actually." Kinkaid moved closer to her, stepping into the place Chad vacated.

If the army had taught Chad anything, he'd never appreciated the skill of preciseness as much as he did now when he took the fastest shower of his life. By the time he left the locker room and walked past the workout room and toward the lobby, he couldn't remember how he'd put on his clothes and what he was wearing since he hadn't paid attention.

Tension tightened his muscles when he saw Kinkaid's hand on Tessa's shoulder while the jerk grinned at whatever he was saying. Tessa stepped back to create some distance between her and the flirting man. Good.

"That was fast." Kinkaid spoke, being the first to see Chad.

Tessa's eyebrows rose.

"I have other things to do than spend time in the recreation center." Chad swung the mesh bag of his wet clothes in the other hand as he marched toward the sliding door. He thanked the tan-skinned woman behind the counter before he made his exit. Tessa would get the message and follow.

But he could hear Kinkaid call her name again, probably making another attempt at his alluring approach to things. Groaning, Chad ground his teeth. Whoever Tessa wanted to date shouldn't bother him. He'd flat-out told her he wouldn't kiss her again.

Outside, the morning breeze seeped through his damp hair, and goose bumps scattered on his arms. His tense muscles stiffened, a sense of defeat threatening to drown him. Just great. Like he needed to add this unexpected jealousy to his long list of issues.

He hated how Tessa was affecting him. Having been dumped by his ex-wife, Nelly, he should know relationships didn't last. Not for him anyway.

He wouldn't start a relationship that would blow up in his face. He. Would. Not.

He stomped to the end of the brick building. The words slammed into his head with each harsh step.

Then the sliding doors whooshed open and prancing footsteps followed him. So he slowed his steps. He didn't have to turn to know Tessa scooted up behind him.

"What's the rush?" She caught up, then fell in step.

Since she might've cut her conversation short, he'd better keep any sharpness out of his tone. "What was that about?"

"What do you mean?" She stopped walking by the crosswalk into the parking lot. Her big brown eyes searched his, so innocent and dear, and warmth rushed through him.

He didn't die in the desert, but he may undergo a slow death swooning over her. Another one of her snug exercise tops encased her slender frame, and the lime-green sleeveless blouse layered over it brought out the lighter flecks in her eyes.

"Please." He smirked, trying to get a hold of his feelings. "The guy was flirting, right in front of me. He couldn't have cared less if I drowned."

Tessa rolled her eyes and crossed her arms. "What gave you the impression he was flirting?"

No way did she miss Kinkaid's smoldering looks or lame excuses to touch her shoulder. "You're just messing with me."

He resumed walking, an idea spiraling. Next time he went in public with her, he'd stake his claim so admirers assumed they belonged together.

She snickered. "Don't tell me you're jealous."

He hadn't thought he would be either. "Why would I be?" He almost choked on his forced chuckle. "We're friends."

He managed to glance at the pink sky when he approached the car and Tessa pressed the fob to unlock it. He opened the driver's side for her and closed it once she took her seat. He wanted to be the one driving her and not the other way around. He'd need a vehicle again. He'd sold his after the divorce and had no reason to buy another one since he volunteered for the next mission.

"What time does the car lot open?" He sat and fastened his seat belt.

"Not so sure." She drove out of the parking lot. "Why?"

"I want to take you to breakfast. After that, I want to buy a car."

Her brows creased as she joined the morning traffic. "Why do you need your own car?"

"I want to start driving you places instead of the other way around." Plus, then she wouldn't need to tag along to his swim sessions. He couldn't deal with the jerk swooning over her in front of him.

"You can drive my car anytime. Cars are expensive right now."

She had no idea he had enough money for hundreds of cars, money he'd inherited from his mom. He still generated a stream of income from the companies Mom and her husband had willed to him. That was another conversation for another day, so he turned on the radio.

A familiar pop song erupted, and the rich voice had him looking between Tessa and the radio. She sang along to the tune. Did she know this song and artist?

His heart raced, and he pushed the button to turn off the radio. "Who's the artist?"

"Why did you turn it off? That's one of my favorite artists. Leora Crisp."

He turned on the music, hoping the song was over, but another song by the same artist played. "Is this a CD or something?"

"My car is one of the few that still uses CDs." She shrugged.

Tessa loved Leora Crisp's music enough to buy her album?

He ran a hand through his hair and peered through the side window. Unbelievable. Mom died years ago, and although he didn't have a physical collection of her music, royalties were sent to his account for another fifty-eight years.

"You okay?" Tessa pulled into the parking lot, near shotgun buildings that must form Pleasant View's downtown. Baskets overflowing with flowers hung on tree branches and quaint lampposts along the street.

"Leora Crisp, huh?" He shoved his hands beneath his thighs, surprised she'd never told him about her favorite artist. They'd had so much to talk about. They must've missed discussing music and artists.

Tessa turned off the engine and faced him. "Why do I get the feeling Leora Crisp brings back bad memories for you?"

Sort of. Sadness had blanketed him in his early years after Mom's death, but he'd been used to not having her around. Except, hearing her music made him ache for the mom he didn't have anymore and the life he could have had if she'd lived.

He swallowed. "She's my mother."

Tessa's eyes widened, and a gasp slid out. She frowned, opened and closed her mouth, then touched his shoulder.

Not wanting her to feel sad or cry, he reached up and squeezed her hand on his shoulder. "It's okay. I'm fine." He'd lived by that motto for as long as he could remember. "Let's go have some breakfast."

She nodded, but she'd have more questions about Leora Crisp, no doubt. Perhaps talking about Mom would give him too.

CHAPTER 8

Everything seemed different since Chad's arrival. Besides enduring the ongoing adrenaline surging through her, Tessa spent more time selecting her clothes. She didn't trust her feet, afraid she'd trip in front of him, or her voice, afraid she'd squeak when she talked to him.

In just over two weeks, she'd crammed more time with him into that space than she had with anyone other than Elias. Now, she could scarcely remember life before Chad.

So how was she still learning something new about him each passing day? Things she hadn't expected. Like Leora Crisp, one of her favorite eighties pop singers, being his mother.

Tessa had spent over an hour on the internet, searching and reading about Leora Crisp two nights ago. Chad had said her real name was Lenny Whitlock, but the search engine didn't know Lenny Whitlock. Leora Crisp had a handful of ex-spouses, but none were named Whitlock. The wealthy man she'd dated right before they'd both crashed had been almost twice Leora's age, but love had no age limitations.

No wonder Chad couldn't find his dad since she'd given him her maiden name. She probably hadn't named his father on Chad's birth certificate, either.

Too bad she'd died so young. He'd missed out on having a mom and dad.

As they continued to keep things professional, the tension and heat between them lingered. Knowing what would happen if they pursued a relationship helped them keep their distance, but having him be jealous about Kinkaid sure deepened Tessa's feelings for him.

"I'll not let him flirt with you in my presence," he'd said after he bought his GMC Denali truck. And he'd meant it when he left for his swim training without her yesterday.

Her stomach in knots, she slid on her go-to leggings and layered up with a blue top before putting on her running shoes, giddy to meet him. They'd start their day with devotions, stretch, then run before breakfast.

Taking the stairs two at a time, she strode through the quiet house to the front door. Mom had already left for work. Then Tessa jogged across the yard. The vibrant early morning light making its way to her heart, she hummed one of Leora's songs and rubbed her arms to chase away goose bumps the brisk air caused. Once she and Chad started running, she'd warm up.

She knocked and waited at the door. Wow, the potted geraniums at the door appeared more radiant. He'd taken good care of them.

She knocked again. Voices reverberated inside. Huh. Chad rarely watched TV.

After waiting and knocking one more time, she pushed open the door. Then her mouth dropped open. Chad lay in bed, focused on the TV. Two bags of chips—Doritos and barbecue Ruffles lay beside him. The barbecue ones had been ripped open and spilled on the comforter.

At least he was dressed, rather than exposing his hairy chest like the first morning. She left the door half open and moved closer.

He didn't flinch and kept his gaze at the TV.

Hmm, so strange.

The musty odor tempted her to open the window and fling the door wide.

"Hello." She moved to stand in front of him, blocking him from the TV. He gave her a cursory glance, his gaze distant as if he were far from the cabin.

Had he been too lazy to turn off the light last night? Made sense with him sleeping in the clothes he'd worn yesterday. Her fingers itched to brush away the white and yellow crumbs clinging to his stubble and shirt, and her heart constricted at the dark circles around his eyes.

"You okay?"

He shrugged. "What's up?"

She edged closer. Twinkies and candy bar wrappers, strewn all over the comforter, glistened in the bright light. She picked up a Twinkie wrapper and crinkled it up. "What are we celebrating?"

Although she sensed what was wrong with him, she wanted him to talk. Her chest tightened with the memory of Elias's despair.

"Where did you get all this?" She sat at the edge of his bed, and he scooted, moving his legs to the side and creating extra space.

"I have a vehicle. I know my way into town."

So not good! Just when she'd entertained the possibility of them together, this happened.

"You're late for our stretches. I'm assuming we're still running?"

"I know." Without looking up, he pointed to her printout on the board above his nightstand. "Your schedule is crystal clear."

She huffed. "Let's get going before it's hot."

"I'm not going anywhere."

Okay. She stared at the exercise mat at the foot of his bed. She could settle for stretches with him if he didn't want to leave the cabin.

"Next week, we're starting a progress report."

"Works for me." He'd refocused on the TV with cartoon dogs in training. What in the world? He must have the TV on for a distraction, not for entertainment.

"Looks like I'm not leaving this cabin today." She crossed her feet. Although uncomfortable on the bed, she sat taller. "We'll sit here all day and listen to lazy songs, but chips and sweets are not going to work."

She reached for the bags of chips by his legs, then walked to the counter, and set them on the microwave. She returned to clean his bed. Wrappers crushed in her hands as she moved to toss them in the trash can by the makeshift kitchen.

"I need to be alone today."

She should respect his privacy, but if Elias taught her anything, it was that she should never have given him the space he'd demanded while he drowned in sadness and food.

"Tomorrow is your recovery day. Today, we're training."

She slid her phone from her tights leg pocket. Then frowned at the screen, unsure how to make breakfast orders online. But if Chad was going to be impossible, then she'd make it two of them. "Let me order some chia seeds and yogur—"

"I'm not eating bird seed for breakfast!"

"If you're staying in bed all day, we're not loading on calories we can't burn."

He grumbled and glared at her. She stared back. The hard edge to his green eyes should make her cringe, but she didn't waver. She wanted to read his thoughts through those eyes.

Then his eyes softened, and a sizzle of attraction simmered between them. She almost blinked as she struggled to stare at him, then relaxed when the ghost of a smile curved the corners of his mouth.

"You're the most stubborn woman I've ever met."

"That so?" She lifted her phone to him. "Ready for breakfast?"

He pulled the remote from under his pillow and punched the power button, turning off the TV before tossing aside the blanket and leaping out of bed. "All right, drill sergeant." He huffed and ran a hand through his rumpled hair. "For your information, I like dogs."

Some sadness accompanied that simple statement. Was he just explaining why he'd been watching a kid dog show?

"You like dogs?"

Instead of answering, he rubbed the back of his neck, then winced as he raised his armpit. "Let me brush and clean up."

She scrunched her face to emphasize his point. "Cleaning up is a good idea."

"I feel sorry for your clients." His voice light, he walked past her to the bathroom.

"While you clean up, I'm taking your chips to the main house."

He threw his head back. "What choice do I have?"

He didn't appear bothered by her threat to steal his snacks. And he needed nutritious meals while doing such intensive training. She opened the window and back door to let in the morning breeze, then marched away with the chips and remaining two Twinkies. Chad would earn them as a reward, but he should eat them for enjoyment, not to forget his problems. Since he could go into town and buy more junk, she'd try to fight him whenever he wasn't cooperative.

She left his chips in the house. When she returned, he was standing on the back porch appearing ready for their workout. Today, they'd wait to do devotions while they ate their breakfast after the run.

"Let's do this." She swung through the open back door and stepped behind him.

Chad turned sideways, grinned with a yawn, but appeared more alive than he'd been minutes ago. He'd need a nap at some point if he let himself rest.

They crossed the small bridge over the stream and made their way toward the hammock. In the open space between the aspens, she'd start with relaxation exercises, given the circumstances.

She stood in front of him and blew out a breath. Usually, he followed her lead.

"With arms spread out"—she outstretched her hands, and he did the same—"breathe in, then out."

Chad breathed deep, then exhaled. It took almost thirty minutes to stretch, mostly with emphasis on his shoulder and hip to strengthen his muscles.

"Close your eyes and concentrate on your breathing." She closed her eyes, assuming he'd do the same. "Try to imagine something good—"

"Okay." He cleared his throat. "Right now, with my eyes closed, I see myself on some adventure with a beautiful trainer."

She opened her eyes, her heart racing at his sincerity.

With his eyes still closed, he appeared serious about his statement. "All I can see is... you."

Me too.

Then he opened his eyes, his green gaze finding hers, and her knees wobbled like jelly. She crossed her ankles to give her legs the needed support.

He raised a brow. "You didn't tell me what you see."

He didn't give her time to delve into her thoughts when he spoke his. "Your thoughts were supposed to be unspoken."

He threw his hands up. "Not fair. I told you mine, and you don't tell me yours?"

His charm was out of this world. How could she manage to keep things professional? Charming or not, he was too unstable, and if she ignored all the signs, she'd get burned. When she lifted her chin to him, he was waiting for a response, but as far as she knew, she was just his trainer and nothing more. Whether her heart got the memo or not.

"We're late for our run."

She started jogging, and he ran in step with her. She intended to keep their run steady being the first week of real practice.

The woodsy space from their yard opened up to a windy trail. Chipmunks scampered out of the way and vanished into the tall grass, and bees zipped past.

"Is this how you usually mistreat your clients, or is it just me?"

Tessa elbowed him in the ribs, and he groaned dramatically.

"Is that the mistreatment you mean?"

"Exactly." Laughter carried in his breathless tone. "And confiscating their snacks."

"Only those training for a triathlon."

"Unbelievable." His stride lengthened and ran ahead of her.

"That's impressive."

He turned, jogging backward and grinning. "I can be impressive."

Tessa loved long-distance running, but she was more motivated with Chad as her running companion this summer.

They jogged uphill, the run not too steep but good enough for strengthening during their training's early stages. Chad wasn't struggling on the run as she'd expected. Then, when they reached the lake where they did their therapy, they stopped to stretch. Dragonflies skimmed the lake's still surface, and a fish jumped in the shadowed waters.

She bent to the side, her hair trickling down her arm. "I mentioned Elias is one of the organizers of the 5K run for vets, right?"

With his legs spread apart, Chad moved one arm across his chest and held it in place with his other hand. "You're already confident enough in me to let me run this Saturday?"

Three and a half miles were nothing for him. The two days they'd run, he'd come close to nine miles even though she'd encouraged him to keep it slow. He liked to push himself by running an extra mile or two. "It will be good practice for the triathlon."

He moved his hand to wipe the perspiration from his forehead. The breeze swept through the trees around the lake and seeped into her damp top, refreshing her. "It's time I met your brother. I'm in."

Renewed energy surged through her at the thought of Chad meeting Elias. Talking to another soldier who'd been through trauma might remind Chad he wasn't the only one struggling. Either way, soldiers always had a special bond with each other. Tessa wasn't a soldier, but she sure seemed to be attracted to them. What a strange thing!

She brought her right knee to her chest and held it with both hands. "What do you think if we left on Friday and stayed the night at Elias's place?" Then Chad could meet more soldiers at Elias's workplace. "Instead of driving Saturday morning and diving right into the race."

Chad planted his arm on his hip. "Does he like soldiers?"

"'Course, he does." Tessa lowered her right leg and lifted her other knee toward her shoulder. "He's a veteran. He's organizing this run for vets."

She didn't blame Chad. Thanks to Mom's reaction, he now had doubts about their family. At least, Mom was coming around since she'd run out of questions to bombard him with.

Stretching done, they ran back home, looped around, and emerged on the side of the main house. A good ten-mile run. Not too bad for starters.

The white Chevy Spark in the driveway reminded Tessa of an appointment she'd spaced out. She stopped, bent over, and braced her hands on her thighs as she recovered.

"That's not your mom's car." Chad stopped beside her.

"I might have you make your own breakfast today."

"Who's that?" He tipped his head toward the car.

"A client."

"Doesn't seem like I have you to myself."

"You do. I'll explain later."

CHAD DIDN'T NEED AN explanation about Tessa's client, but he liked giving her a hard time. Teasing her came automatically, and most times, she understood his jokes. Except today, she didn't seem to get him when she explained she'd added a client to her schedule after her friend, Liberty, called her about a family in need. A patient in his twenties who had a procedure for a damaged disc to relieve pressure on the spinal cord.

After one look at the young man wincing in pain and his worried mom, Chad offered to help take them wherever Tessa needed them. He'd escorted them to Tessa's gym as he pushed the young man in the wheelchair. The guy wasn't permanently in the wheelchair, but walking across the yard would've been a stretch for him.

Tessa still needed more equipment in her gym-slash-therapy clinic. Chad couldn't remember everything she'd ticked off her fingers when she discussed it. But she sure had a heart of gold taking on clients without expecting them to pay. Good thing he'd insisted she get insured. Whether she treated people for free or for a fee, someone could file a complaint or a suit.

While he stood in her kitchen making toast, he stared at the bag of Doritos she'd captured from him, tempted to munch the contents. But he'd be betraying Tessa. That didn't mean he wouldn't resort to junk food the moment he felt downcast.

He reached for the bags. He'd seen her throw the trash under the sink cabinet after dinner last night, so he opened the cabinet and deposited the bags of chips. No temptation anymore. He didn't see the Twinkies. Maybe Tessa had already tossed them. Or maybe she'd sneaked a minute to eat one herself. He snickered, picturing his scrupulous trainer surreptitiously hunched over a sugary snack.

Other images followed that one. Memories of their morning. The passion and fire in her eyes had diffused his defiance and the unexpected anger that had been threatening to blow up.

The bread popped up from the toaster, and he swung open the refrigerator wondering what to add to the toast. What could he cook for Tessa, who didn't eat bread?

Ziploc bags contained collard greens, eggs, and—wait, bacon?

He pulled out the eggs and a vegetable bag.

His stomach rumbled, and he munched the toast while whipping up the eggs. Bettina had been amazing opening up her home, but he preferred not having her watch his every move. If she was home, he wouldn't be munching toast in her kitchen.

Bacon sizzled and popped on the stove top. With the eggs and bacon ready, he plated them and covered the food with paper towels. He'd wait for Tessa so they could eat together. Hmm, only ten fifty-two.

And she'd planned a long day of foam-rolling exercises, swimming, a 3K in the afternoon, and biking in the evening. He'd have earned a recovery day tomorrow, but who wanted a full day of doing nothing?

As he walked through the living room, his shoes thudded against the worn hardwood floor. Tessa had apologized about the dingy floors when he first came for dinner, saying she planned to hire an expert to polish the floors one of these days.

Could he do that tomorrow on his recovery day? He stopped in the living room to study the photos on the wall, photos he hadn't seen. With Bettina's watchful gaze on him, he usually escaped to his cabin as soon as he helped load the dishwasher.

His eyes caught a photo with Elias, Tessa, and Bettina seated by a Christmas tree. It had to be a recent photo since their dad wasn't in it.

Elias was in dress pants, but... He had a prosthetic leg. Odd Tessa never mentioned her brother had suffered an injury that cost him a leg. Apparently, Chad still didn't know a lot about her. He intended to find out soon.

CHAPTER 9

Chad didn't care what Bettina thought about him when he showed up at dawn with cans of wood stain. He rapped on the wooden door, then waited. He ducked when bugs under the porch light flew in his face.

Gaining Tessa's approval had meant compromising and allowing her to cut down his payments for the training. She'd agreed to let him buy the stain and varnish and get her one step closer to hiring a professional to restore the flooring.

He hadn't told her he was going to get the job done. Finding a pro for such a small task would be a waste of time and money. He had the money, but even with that, it wasn't worth hiring someone.

The door swung open, and Bettina's brows drew together. He'd known Tessa's mom would answer his knock since she woke up earlier than Tessa.

"Good morning, ma'am."

Bettina eyed the cans at his feet. "You, um—"

"I'm here to stain and varnish the floors." He pointed at the sander and two cans of stain by his feet. He'd left the varnish in the car with extra cans of stain if needed.

"I see you found the stain?"

Yesterday, at her hardware store, they didn't have the stain on the color chart Tessa provided him. Bettina had directed him to a paint shop in town.

"Come in." She ushered him in with a wave. "Does Tessa know about this project?"

"Yes and no." He followed Bettina to the kitchen where she had something steaming on the stove. "She would put up a fight if I told her I was going to do it."

She patted her short graying hair. "Can I get you some coffee?"

He didn't drink coffee with his sleep being a struggle. "No thank you."

"I need to go to work in an hour." She ticked her fingers with all the things that needed to be done before he could paint.

"I know. I'll clean everything." He didn't intend to move the piano, though. "Whenever I can get piano movers, I'll fix the floors under it."

"Sounds like a long-term plan." Bettina moved to the stove and mixed the white substance in the pot. "Have you decided to stay?"

He'd never said he was leaving, but she'd figured him out. "Maybe."

She kept her hand on the wooden spoon and gave him a warning look. "I see the way she looks at you and how you look at her."

"We're friends...." He rolled his eyes, realizing who he was up against. Bettina was a clever woman, and he shouldn't underestimate her. "Tessa is a very—"

"Don't you hurt my baby girl." She wagged the wooden spoon toward him, dribbling oatmeal on the floor, and he almost thought she was going to poke him with the gunky thing. "Tessa deserves someone who's fully committed to her. Someone who's figured out their future."

Without giving him time to respond, Bettina spun back to her task and turned off the stove. "Would you like some oatmeal?"

Even if he were hungry. "I'm good. Thanks."

Blood rushed through him as he walked back through the house. Maybe he should wait for Tessa to wake up. In the dining area, he stopped before a photo of Bettina's husband by the piano.

If the man were alive, would Bettina act differently? Chad could promise her he'd stay away from Tessa, but deep down, he wanted more with Tessa. More than he could offer, but he felt compelled to try. Tessa was different from his ex, Nelly. Selfless, hardworking, and self-reliant. She'd started caring for him before they met in person, before she'd known everything about him. Yet whenever he looked into her eyes, he saw affection, a reflection of the affection he felt for her.

He still hadn't asked about Elias's injury, but when he did, he wanted to know who broke her heart and wrecked Bettina's trust in soldiers.

"What do you need for your project?"

Bettina's words bounced off his back, and he turned, his chest rising and falling as he composed himself. "From you—a broom and a mop."

She left and returned with the cleaning items.

After emptying the bookshelf of board games and books, he stacked them on the kitchen table and moved the bookshelf to the kitchen. Intending to work in the dining room, then start in the living room later, he carted the dining chairs to the living room. Then he dismantled the table legs and stacked them and the heavy maple tabletop against the hall wall. By the time he finished moving things and cleaning the floors, Bettina had left.

Chad could finally breathe.

He drew the blinds aside, and natural light streamed through the room. He'd have to wait until Tessa got up before he ran the sander over the floors. Still, he returned to his truck for the paint roller and tray. When he returned to the house, Tessa stood in the dining room, yawning and frowning. Looking at her made him forget how to swallow, nearly forget how to breathe.

Not wanting to be caught staring, he cleared his throat. "Morning, sleeping beauty."

She jumped and then hugged her arms across her chest, obviously embarrassed to still be in her pajamas. The shorts emphasized her long legs, but he didn't let his gaze linger, afraid he'd be ogling.

"What are you doing?"

He set the roller and pan down next to the stain. "What does it look like I'm doing?"

"This is your recovery day—"

"That's why I'm not out swimming or biking." He pulled out his pocketknife from his shorts pocket, then flicked it to lift open the can lid, wincing at the stain's overbearing smell. He'd have to get it stirred before starting.

"I'm coming to help you."

"Nah. I'm good. Go rest some more—that is if you can stand the sound of the sander."

She left, but she didn't listen. Minutes later, she showed up, changed into shorts and a loose pink T-shirt sporting a petite female cartoon character carrying weights bigger than she was.

Yep, that was Tessa carrying him and his issues, should he pursue her.

"What can I do?"

"I only have one sander." Her scent was refreshing as opposed to the sharp stain that lingered even after he'd closed the lid. He plugged in the sander. The noise was almost too loud to talk over.

"Well," she shouted over the buzzing whir, "let me take a turn at least."

"How about you start by telling me about Elias's injury."

"Oh. Mom told you?"

He smoothed the sander across the floor, dust rising. Her mom was another conversation entirely. "The Christmas photo in the living room."

Tessa fell silent.

Chad moved the sander, careful not to go too deep or double up on his lines.

"His injury doesn't define who he is."

At the hurt turning her voice husky, he paused and switched off the sander to stare at her.

She stared back, her eyes glassy. "He's still my big brother, and I prefer not to mention his injury whenever I describe him."

Compassion tugged at him, and he moved the sander to his other hand, then touched her shoulder, giving it a gentle squeeze. "I understand. I shouldn't have asked."

She saw her brother for who he was, rather than the injuries that changed his physical appearance.

"When I finish this room, you're taking your turn in the living room." He smirked. But, realistically, he needed to take it easy with his shoulder. It didn't hurt him, but he'd rather save the constant movement for training purposes.

She crinkled up her nose. "We'll take notes on which room looks best."

"You're competitive."

"Competition in life is good for us." She sauntered away, returning with a shop vac to clean up the sanding debris.

As Chad continued to sand the floor, a sense of the family who had lived here swept through him, leaving him needing to know why Bettina had a love-hate thing going with soldiers.

"How was your experience with your ex?" He slowed his strokes, feigning only a slight interest. Although he'd never asked about Tessa's ex during their long-distance friendship, he'd learned she was single. "I presume you dated a soldier?"

"Yep." She edged the nozzle along, the noise scarcely allowing for an intimate conversation. "We dated for two years."

She shut off the vac, waiting for him to move on. "He was Elias's best friend, but like Elias, he struggled with PTSD and had unexpected anger outbursts. He used to come here all the time."

Chad gripped the sander too tight and accidentally jerked it to a sanded area, almost making a groove. He bit the inside of his cheek, willing himself to listen about the guy who used to hang out with Tessa every day but dumped her without telling her to her face.

She wiggled around to sit cross-legged facing him. "His sister told me he left and wasn't coming back to Pleasant View."

He'd better not come back. "His loss." Chad's gain.

If Chad had known Tessa then, he may have hunted her ex down and punched him for acting the way he did. Unless... "Is he still alive?"

"I called his mom, and he was going to rehab."

What if he came back for her? Did she miss him? "How long since you broke up?"

"Three years." Her arms slid around her middle, pain glowing in her eyes when he looked up. "He's now moved on with someone else."

The selfish thing to say was that he was glad she was still single so he could pursue her, but the practical thing to say was. "You deserve better."

Just like Bettina had said, Tessa deserved someone better than Chad too. But why was his heart thrumming so hard at the possibility of him being the man she so deserved?

MUCH LATER THAT EVENING, Chad stood in the kitchen with Tessa. The cutting board clicked as she cut the peppers and carrots while he pulled chopped arugula from a Ziploc bag and dumped it in the salad bowl. Although mindless work, he cherished it since

Tessa was close by. Moving to her side, he brought the half-filled bowl of greens to the counter by her cutting board. "What next?"

Her hand shook, and she lowered the knife to the board, turning and looking up at him. The pulse point on her neck was racing, and her moist lips parted as if she was about to say something. Then she pressed her lips closed.

He'd left space between them, but she was within reach. His mind spun, and his heart thudded as he fought to lift his hand to touch her. He'd better not. He fisted his hands to keep them at his sides. Why was it so hot? What was he telling her again?

Dinner. "Um, what time... should I grill?"

She bit her lower lip and shrugged, then spoke breathlessly. "Soon?"

He crossed to the fridge, needing some air to cool off but also needing to get dinner started. So he pulled out the covered container with the steaks he'd begun marinating last night.

The front door jerked and swung open. Bettina strode into the house. Good thing he wasn't making out with Tessa.

"Hey!" His voice came out raspy as he greeted Bettina before she noticed them in the kitchen.

She stopped by the living room, gasping. "They look like new." She gripped her black handbag to the side, then tiptoed closer. "This looks amazing."

"Hi, Mom." Tessa finally spoke, her chirpy voice high-pitched, and he knew why.

Without looking at Tessa, lest he gave himself away, he addressed Bettina. "Your daughter did most of the staining. The halls aren't done yet, but I wouldn't step on the living or dining room floors while the stain dries this evening. We'll do the varnishing on my next resting days—I'd like to do two or three layers so it lasts." Talking about that would transition them to normal. In the meantime, he needed real fresh air outside. He carried the meat container. "I'm gonna go get these on the grill."

Leaving should ease the tension for Tessa as she spoke to her mom. After all, Chad and Bettina didn't have much to talk about.

Crows gathered on the pines, cawing for scraps and attention, while smaller birds—sparrows and finches and chickadees—flocked around a feeder Bettina or Tessa maintained. The air smelled of propane and meat as smoke billowed while he grilled. He flipped the steaks when Bettina brought broccoli for him to add to the grill. He didn't grow up grilling, but he'd cooked at the bases. As for deployment, meals were always different.

When dinner was ready, they ate on the porch, shooing random flies and bugs away from the table time and again. Chad spoke with light humor when Bettina asked what he enjoyed most about his career. Talking about his boot-camp training was easiest. His brain hadn't been a jumble of explosives and nightmares back then.

"Everything the captain asked, the obvious response was 'Yes, yes, sir!'"

Bettina laughed and wiped tears from the side of her eyes when he told them the time he'd said "yes, sir!" when he should've said "no, sir!"

"That wrong response earned me a ton of push-ups as a consequence."

Tessa covered her mouth with her hand as she laughed, and he kicked her under the table since she was seated right across from him.

When he helped clean the dishes and was ready to leave, he stopped by the breakfast nook where Bettina was organizing the board games and books on the table. "Good night, Bettina."

She eyed him, then Tessa who escorted him as she'd done every night. Technically, they'd made it a game of her escorting him and him escorting her back to the yard.

"Why don't you stay and play a board game." Bettina's dark-brown eyes were softer tonight.

Although exhausted, he wouldn't fall asleep anyway. Sleep had become too elusive lately.

"Stay." Tessa's warm breath dusted his neck, and he shivered.

He tipped his head to one side. "What game do you have in mind?"

Bettina ushered him to the breakfast nook, then stepped around him. "I'll let you two decide, and I'll whip up some snacks."

"Mom!" Tessa rolled her eyes. "We just ate."

But Bettina was already rummaging in the pantry.

With the lights brightening the kitchen nook, Chad slid the first box from the stacked pile, a game about guessing movie stars. "I don't keep up with movies."

She moved aside a yellow box where a caption asked, "Do you *really* know your family?"

Nope. His family tree was too thin. "That's not for me."

He reached for the next box and grinned, remembering the last time he'd played the strategic board game of diplomacy, conflict, and conquest. "Risk."

Tessa rolled her eyes, her brows lifting in mischief. "Not a chance."

"Why not? It's fun."

She crossed her arms and tapped her foot on the tiled floor. "I can't play Risk with you because none of this"—she nodded between them—"bodes well for my survival on the battlefield."

"You'll survive. I'll make sure of it." Why did he feel like they weren't talking about the board game?

"I don't think I want to learn the hard way."

The microwave beeped, and the smell of popcorn permeated the air.

He set the board game back on the table and moved closer, leaving scant space between them so he could keep his voice low enough Bettina wouldn't hear him. "What if I said I'd play by your rules?"

Tessa drew out a slow breath. "In the real world, things don't operate like that."

"We could make it work." Blood pulsed through his ears when he lifted his hand and brushed loose strands of hair from her face. Her brown eyes searched his with a tenderness that quickened his blood through his veins. His gaze fell to her lips, and he cupped her chin in his hand, pressed to make her understand he wanted to take the risk and fall in love despite his issues looming in the shadows. "Do you think we can try?"

"Risk is dangerous."

"No pain, no gain."

Her chest rose and fell, her voice a whisper. "Let's try."

He almost forgot where he was when he leaned in to kiss her, but the shuffle of footsteps had them both tearing away from each other.

They glanced toward Bettina, who hummed as she carried a full popcorn bowl.

Chad grabbed the board game and waggled it. "We've agreed to play Risk."

Tessa eyed him, her soft smile a secret promise to whatever risks lay ahead in their venture into the unknown.

CHAPTER 10

Just before noon, Tessa led Chad toward a brick building. Care workers in scrubs, likely physical therapists, pushed individuals in wheelchairs and assisted others with their walking. Above the pathway, the brown words *Wounded Warrior Hope and Care Center* arched over a white sign. Tessa waved and greeted those they passed. Then the automatic front doors parted, and the scent of disinfectant bombarded them.

"T!" Elias shouted from behind a wide counter, lifting his hands in the air before leaning toward the brunette next to him. "She's my baby sister."

The woman waved, her smile warm.

Tessa's heart swelled as she sped to meet Elias where he rounded the counter. She wrapped her arms around him, savoring the familiar smell of soap and the warmth of his embrace. "It's so good to see you."

"Look at you." Elias moved out of the hug, stepped back, and assessed her. With a beard dusting his jaw, he looked so much like Dad. When his gaze lifted behind her, she remembered her companion. "You must be Chad."

Tessa scooted back. "Sorry. I forgot my manners."

"Hello, Elias." Chad grinned before shaking Elias's offered hand. Tenderness softened his all-too-familiar grin. "Thank you for your service, sir."

"Thank you as well." Elias cocked a hip against the counter, his prosthetic leg visible beneath his blue shorts. "Word has it that you're enrolled in the 5K tomorrow."

"I've been enrolled into a lot of things." Chad waved his hands, his wink at Tessa stirring butterflies in her stomach. "Not sure if I'll be running through thorns next."

"He's such a baby." She bit into her lower lip before switching her gaze to Elias. Staring at Chad would make her look like a lovesick fool.

"You guys came just in time for my lunch break." Elias ushered them toward a hallway on the left. Soft relaxation music played through the hallway speakers. "Let's go grab a bite."

"Now you're speaking my language." Chad fell in step.

Chad asked how many tours Elias had been on, how long he'd served, and what rank he'd held. The questions had the two men connecting with their love to serve their country.

After they ordered their meal at the counter, Chad insisted on paying and sent them to grab a table while he waited for their food.

Elias sank into a blue plastic chair across from Tessa. His gaze was serious as he studied her. "How's Mom?"

"You know Mom." Tessa rolled her eyes. "She still loves her garden, and she's taking on too many shifts at work. You should come up to Pleasant View soon. She doesn't say it, but she misses you. You must be lonely too."

He shrugged. "How can I be with Tag? That German shepherd has taken me on so many adventures since you gave him to me...."

His fond words slipped into the background of her thoughts as her gaze wandered to the big windows where Chad was waiting. Wow. He was staring at her. He winked, and her insides hummed a sweet melody.

Elias reached across the table to cuff her arm. "Seriously, Sis? The heat between you two could start the next fire."

She sat up straighter and swished her hair over her shoulders. She'd better act as if she'd stayed attentive the entire time. "You were telling me about work—"

"No, I wasn't." He guffawed and wagged a finger at her. "We were talking about Tag, and he's not work anymore since he's grown out of the puppy stage. You've got it bad, girl." His brown eyes searched hers, his smile falling away. "Are you two still just friends?"

Despite Chad's code language about Risk, nothing was a guarantee. "He has a lot on his plate."

"Lucky him. He has you to help him clear his plate."

Tessa almost understood what Elias said. But, as she was about to ask, Chad joined them with their food and slid into the chair next to hers.

While they ate, wounded veterans ate in the seats and wheelchairs around them. Some were being fed, no doubt paralyzed and unable to hold a spoon or lift it to their mouths.

Her chest tightened with compassion and an urge to do something. Maybe she shouldn't quit physical therapy while people could benefit from her gift.

Chad and Elias talked about baseball and triathlons, topics that normally kept her engaged, but she was half listening now as the people around them drew her focus.

When the guys finished eating, she finally moved her fork in the arugula chicken salad she'd barely touched.

Elias leaned back in his chair, arms crossed over his chest as he nodded to her plate. "If it wasn't salad, I'd eat it."

Chad squished his face. "If I eat more salad, I'll be growing roots."

Tessa covered a hand over her mouth, stifling a chuckle.

"She'll find a way of grinding those veggies into your smoothie."

"I'm never going to have those breakfast smoothies again."

Cute. She rolled her eyes at the guys, then gave Chad's side a gentle push. "The leftover salad will be your dinner, buddy. Never underestimate the importance of healthy eating and good rest if you want to become the next Ironman."

"You have a key to the house." Elias stood and balled the napkin in his hand before looping it into the basket. "I'll meet you guys at home."

Chad dabbed a napkin on his mouth, then set the napkin on his disposable plate. "Tessa said people could use company here?"

Elias beamed. A familiar glow sheened his eyes as he slapped Chad's shoulder. "Let's get you in the system first."

"Great. And Tessa promised me a tour of Colorado Springs this afternoon." Chad winked at her, and her body heated with affection and all sorts of emotions. But she looked away and to her brother who gave her a knowing look.

As far as Elias knew, she and Chad were friends. But their coded language two days ago had meant something. Had Chad been asking for a chance to date her? Besides their usual smoldering looks for each other, he hadn't bothered to explain what he'd meant or tried another attempt to kiss her.

With him being hot one day and cold the other, she needed clarity on whether their relationship stood a chance.

They spent the afternoon visiting veterans, playing board games, or listening to stories from the brave ones who spoke about the cause of their injuries. She couldn't tell how Chad absorbed the afternoon's events since his expression stayed unreadable. But, when they walked back to his truck, he stopped on the sidewalk, wrapped his arms around her, and squeezed her in a warm and protective embrace. "Thank you for bringing me here."

She squeezed him back before easing out of the hug and resuming their walk to the truck arm in arm. He kissed her cheek as he opened her door, leaving her with more questions.

HOURS LATER, CHAD SAT on the dark porch. He patted the soft fur of the German shepherd on the floor between his legs, his shallow breaths mingling with the crickets chirping and the cars passing on the highway. Elias's house was only a quarter mile from the busy road, but the nearby trees and tall apartments absorbed some of the noise.

If Chad struggled to sleep in the quiet cabin, no way could he sleep in a strange house with noisy cars. After tossing and turning, he walked out of his bedroom at eleven p.m., and the dog followed him. He'd turned off the porch light so the bugs didn't hover around his face.

Having spent an afternoon visiting with injured veterans, he understood why Elias appeared free and relaxed in his post-combat life. Who could dwell on their own problems after spending time around people who'd experienced such heart-wrenching war injuries?

Elias had found his stability at his work despite his PTSD and seemed happy living in his ranch house.

Chad could buy a home anywhere he wanted and find a job, but none of that appealed to him. What job would satisfy him besides detonating bombs? If he could go back to active duty and make things right with a successful mission, maybe then he'd feel free to settle down in a new career and a home with Tessa.

He was getting too attached to her—and that wasn't good.

Holding her hand or kissing her cheek felt too normal—and he couldn't do normal.

Not now. Maybe not ever.

Yet he liked driving her in his new truck. Her floral scent mixed with the new-car smell was a scent he'd never forget.

He jerked, startling when the back door opened and revealed a shadowy figure.

"Can't sleep?"

Tag stood and moved to his master. Here Chad had thought he had a loyal friend.

Chad huffed. He'd been careful not to wake anyone except the alert dog. "You should be sleeping."

Assuming he'd recovered from his PTSD.

"I heard someone walking in the house." Elias sat on the plastic chair to Chad's left. "Even after all these years, I still struggle to sleep."

That meant a shrink hadn't helped solve Elias's sleep problems. "Didn't you get help?"

"I got counseling if that's what you mean." The apartments' dim light radiated toward Elias's house, revealing his outline rubbing the tail Tag was wagging. "It helped, but it didn't take away the memories of what happened."

"What exactly happened?" He could ask Tessa later, but he owed Elias the respect of asking him directly.

Elias shifted, resting a hand on his chin.

The crickets and random cars on the highway absorbed the silent night until Elias cleared his throat. "I was the only survivor that day...."

His voice distant and sad, he relayed how an IED exploded with him in range. Four years ago, when Elias's life changed. As Elias spoke, Chad learned Tessa's brother was a year younger than Chad was. "I've never told Tessa or Mom how I lost my leg. I can tell you because you understand."

A sense of trust grew between them. Having Elias open up about his traumatic events almost felt freeing. Chad wasn't the only one struggling. Seeing the veterans who'd lost their eyes, legs, and hands, interacting with them, and hearing their stories had both troubled and comforted him. But their loss left him feeling "less than," knowing he had no room to fuss or complain.

"Tessa," Elias said suddenly.

What about Tessa? Chad crossed his ankles, bracing for another warning from a protective family member.

"I wouldn't be the person I am today without her."

Me too. And no wonder. Tessa was dedicated, but more than that, she took her love to a level that made those around her feel her care. Her almost-daily calls and emails while he'd been abroad had made the year fly by. "She speaks highly of you, Elias."

Silence passed before Elias spoke again. "She taught me never to be secluded while dealing with melancholy. To practice optimism and spend time with loved ones..." He continued talking about the need to seek professional help if his sister wasn't a great resource. Then he relayed what Chad already knew about Tessa. Compassionate, feisty, and dedicated to her clients and loved ones. Chad considered himself among Tessa's loved ones—or at least, she was his loved one since she was the first one to come to mind when he thought of loved ones.

And if Elias meant talking to a professional, Chad hadn't gotten comfortable with his new doctor, not enough to start blurting out his sleepless nights.

Elias slapped Chad's knee. "EOD tech, huh?"

"Yep."

"You must have plenty of stories to tell." Elias's statement should motivate Chad to open up, but he didn't feel up to unloading when they had a race to run tomorrow. They both needed to rest, even if sleep was out of the equation.

"Lots of good stories." Was all he could say.

As if he knew the battle raging inside Chad, Elias drummed his hands on his thighs and huffed out a breath. "Too bad you won't have Tessa to talk to."

"What do you mean?"

"Doesn't make it easier to share your darkest fears with your love interest."

Chad couldn't deny his feelings anymore. "I'm not the right guy for her."

"If she likes you and you like her, how complicated does it get?"

True. "Your mom—"

"Huh, I see." Elias chuckled. "She'd rather not deal with more soldiers to worry about. She's been through a lot. My dad, then me. I... I avoid visiting now. Mom literally cries whenever she sees me."

Talking to Elias was comforting as he assured Chad of God's goodness and their need to count daily blessings rather than hardships. If Elias and all the wounded veterans could get through each day, why couldn't Chad? He admired Elias's bravery and diligence to continue serving at the rehab center and clinic.

The next day, when Chad ran with Tessa and Elias among so many others to support the veterans, fulfillment ran alongside him as he accomplished the race with ease. They ran to raise money for the care facility so they could continue helping those who couldn't afford medical and rehabilitation care. So he gave a generous donation at the reception booth before he and Tessa left.

After they'd each showered and changed at Elias's house, he and Tessa went to an old arcade in Manitou Springs. They entered a room dedicated to horse games and breathed in air that smelled as if it had been locked up for ages. "It feels like this room hasn't changed since the last century."

"No kidding." Tessa stepped next to him and asked a man with a name badge to show them how to play the game.

"You'll need change."

The games required quarters to play, so Tessa traded her bills for coins. Neither of them had ever played the horse game, but after the man's instructions, the game seemed easy. With twelve horses at the start line, their goal was to move their horses by rolling a ball into the three different-color holes.

"There goes mine." Tessa jumped when her horse crossed his. Then she tugged at his arm, caught up in the fun.

"I'm not losing another race—not today." Chad rolled a ball in the holes. His horse sped up, and he rubbed his hands together waiting for it to pass hers. But she must have done something to her balls, something that caused her horse to move faster.

"Yes!" she shrieked, twirling in circles when her horse crossed the finish line.

Chad lost interest in following the trotting of his horse while Tessa was a far better sight. She'd tucked a navy top into yellow shorts. The sash emphasized her slender waist. How could someone look so beautiful in casual clothes, the way she always did?

She then turned to him, poking his chest. "Don't mess with me."

"Is that so?" Tempted to pull her in his arms and kiss that smirk off her face, he stepped further back. The man grinning at Tessa didn't need another show, so Chad rolled his eyes and linked his hand with hers. "Let's go and play something I'm good at. I saw a foosball table at the entrance."

"Your tickets." The man called after them as they approached the door. So they returned for a handful of tickets. Apparently, at the end of their game, they could claim a prize.

Unlike the horse room, people flowed through in the open arcade outside. Midmorning turned to afternoon while classic rock music rang in the background as they played foosball, Skee-Ball, pool, and more.

The beeping machines and pinging music reminded him of the fairs that came to Soda Creek, Virginia during his early teens. He and his cousins looked forward to those events. But what he loved now was Tessa's happy dance whenever she won. With it contagious, he did his own happy dance when he won at table hockey.

"That's what I'm talking about." Tessa high-fived him.

Then they walked to the main building where red horseshoes flanked the matching red words, *Arcade Derby*, above an old-fashioned red-and-white awning. When they presented their tickets, they'd earned enough to walk out with two caps sporting the Colorado state logo.

"We make a great team." Chad tugged at the brim of her cap, pulling it into her vision as they exited the building.

She gave him a sideways glance as she nudged her hat back up. Her beaming smile warmed him more than the afternoon sun could. "That we do."

"Let's go have some lunch."

Tessa touched her flat stomach. "I'm surprised you waited this long."

Having such fun, he hadn't even been hungry. When was the last time he had a good time and played mindless games?

Straightening her cap, she nodded to the diner next to the arcade. "Let's grab a bite in there."

How he loved her practicality! He scooted ahead of her to open the door, then followed her into a retro red-and-black painted diner his ex-wife wouldn't approve of. But with him hungry and bombarded by savory scents of fried food, grilled meat, and onions, surely even Nelly couldn't have begrudged him stopping to grab a quick bite to go.

Tessa ordered a hamburger with no bun, and Chad ordered a real hamburger, fries, and a vanilla milkshake. Then he handed his credit card to the man dressed in a soda-jerk paper cap and a white chef coat. "Make it two vanilla milkshakes."

"Two milkshakes?" Tessa slid off her cap and shook her hair loose. One brow rose over his dessert indulgence.

"One's yours." She wasn't allergic to dairy, but she still opened her mouth to protest. So he held up a hand. "We ran five miles, and we're still on this training streak."

"This one time." She smiled when the guy placed their milkshakes on the glass counter. "Could you get us two glasses of water to go with our food too, please?"

The guy promised to call Chad's name when their food was ready. So she carried their water, and Chad carried the shakes to one of the two empty booths.

While they sipped their milkshakes, he thanked her for bringing him to Colorado Springs. "I like talking to you." He had no other way of being honest without being straightforward. "I feel so alive around you—even before we spent time together in person. Talking to you on the phone was the highlight of my day."

She wrapped her hand around the frosted glass, and her eyes softened. "The feeling is mutual."

They looked at each other then, eyes locked, an awareness he'd never felt for anyone taking up all the air between them. His heart pounded against his ribs as if he were back running the 5K.

Even with her hair pulled back and wearing the simple outfits she favored, she stunned him, and he wouldn't ask her to change anything about herself.

"I meant what I said when we played Risk." He stacked his cap on hers to the side.

"You mean when I dominated the game?"

Bettina had opted out of playing Risk and slipped out to her garden while Chad and Tessa played. "I let you win on purpose. I had to play by your rules."

"Really?" She wiggled her brows, her teasing smile crinkling her nose and bunching up her cheeks.

"I had to make sure our code language made sense to you."

"Yes?" she whispered curiously, urging him to keep talking.

He set his half finished milkshake aside and did the same with her milkshake so he could hold her hands, which were so soft in his. "I'm officially not your client."

She frowned. "Too late. You already paid an advance."

"That contract ended the moment you helped me varnish the floors."

"The insurance you paid for." Her voice was low, so soft and laced with affection. Her words were too weak to be taken seriously. "I have to—"

"I'm not the right man for you, but I can't stop thinking about you." He rubbed his thumb across her palm, emboldened to take a stand and claim her. "Take a chance on me. Let's try to see if you'll like me or not."

"I like you. A lot." She beamed beneath the natural light radiating through the windows. "You might end up realizing you made a mistake in wanting me."

No way would she be a mistake. It was him. Only him who would mess this up. Ignoring the negative voice creeping into his mind, he lifted her hands to his lips and kissed her fingertips. "My perfect mistake. I can live with that."

CHAPTER 11

On the next day Sunday, Tessa stood in the line of guests to meet and greet the pastor. After the church service, some people scurried through the lobby and aimed for the exit. Others lingered to chat. Mom, in her traditional black cloche hat with its huge pink flower trim, was one of them, her laughter carrying through as they huddled in groups.

The stained glass windows, illuminated with afternoon light, shimmered color onto air scented with coffee and baked goods. Tessa had asked Chad if he wanted any of the treats reserved for first-time guests at the welcome table, but he'd scowled and muttered something about not wanting to interact with an entire church.

"You're sure you don't want to meet me at the car?" His warm breath tickled her ear, sending a rush of awareness and warmth to her whole body.

"It will be fast," she promised, still surprised her soldier would let a church group intimidate him. He appeared so carefree, even when he hung out with the veterans at Elias's workplace, but she was beginning to sense that attitude was his armor.

On Tuesday, he'll have been in Pleasant View for four weeks. Until today, he hadn't felt comfortable coming to church. When he'd said good night last night as she climbed out of his truck, he'd said he wanted to try her church. It would be strange if she didn't introduce him to their pastor.

Once they stepped up to greet Pastor Pedro, a Latino man in his midforties, he beamed. Streaks of gray highlighted his dark hair, and his smile crinkled up his dark eyes before he covered her hand with his and spoke her name in his thick accent.

"I want to introduce you to Chad, an army vet who's recently finished his tour."

Pastor's brightened eyes offered the only indication he remembered their conversation a month before Chad's arrival. Good thing she'd told her pastor, so she wouldn't have to explain how she'd met Chad in a line like this.

"I'm Pedro." He pulled Chad into an embrace as if they already knew each other. "Thank you for your service."

"Thank you for being the pastor. I liked your teaching." Chad stepped out of the embrace and scratched his jaw, no doubt ignoring the topic about service. He looked so handsome in his black jeans and the black button-down shirt he'd bought yesterday while clothes shopping after their arcade excursion.

While Pastor asked Chad how long he was in town, Tessa waved to the few people hovering in line behind them. Bummer that Liberty wasn't at church today. She'd gone camping with her family for the weekend before the Fourth of July, so they could be back in town for the Fourth.

If Chad was up for it, Tessa would invite him to the barbeque where he could meet her friends.

"Tessa?" Pastor's voice drew her from her thoughts. "I have good and bad news."

His expression didn't appear sad, but starting with a happy note was always best. She rubbed a sudden shiver from her arms. "What's the good news?"

Chad linked his strong fingers in hers, and they closed over her grip so warm and so right. She felt secure just like that.

"We have two truckloads of donations for your care packages ministry."

Wow! Her free hand flew to her mouth. "How...? Where did they come from?"

"Vran shared a photo from last year's packing. A stranger saw the social post and was so moved to donate that he got truckloads of stuff together."

Amazing that a random person would be so touched. From his generosity, more soldiers would get packages this Christmas. But she didn't have to ask the bad news. She already knew.

"And the bad news?" Chad asked, his thumb rubbing across the back of her hand.

Pastor cast a glance at Tessa. "Unless you've come up with a storage solution, I haven't agreed to the delivery."

She hadn't brainstormed ideas to rent space anywhere. A warehouse would be perfect, but real estate in Pleasant View was crazy. A warehouse could be a long-term goal, but she'd be okay if she could get any decent-sized space. She squeezed Chad's hand, even as a breakout of sweat slicked her palms. She needed his hand for support more than ever.

"Let's not turn down the donations yet."

Pastor Pedro gave her a curt nod. "Keep me posted."

"I will." She wished him a great day, and Chad added his goodbye with a promise to return next Sunday.

At Chad's truck, Mom wanted to sit in the back. The four-door Denali offered a spacious crew cab. Although Tessa hadn't sat in the back before, it should be as comfortable as the passenger seat she currently occupied.

While he drove, her mind whirled to the coming month. July was only two days away when she would kick off the package drive for soldiers. She'd begun by sending five or six packages to random soldiers in the Middle East—the last place Dad had served.

But then Liberty introduced her to some of her clients who were veterans. Then church members mentioned their family members who were serving. Soon, Tessa was turning care packages into a ministry and extending it to the church by asking for nonperishable food donations and money for shipping costs.

Vran recently returned home from a base in Germany. If a post he'd shared earned them truckloads of donations, he must be good with marketing.

"Bettina, if it's okay, I'm taking you ladies to lunch." Chad's voice pulled Tessa to the present.

Mom cleared her throat. "Lunch sounds nice after church."

"Do you both have a restaurant you prefer to go to?"

"There's a new restaurant at the end of Pleasant View." Mom scooted forward in her seat to touch Tessa's shoulder. "I heard it has the best smoked barbeque."

"Sounds good." Tessa nodded. "But my treat." Chad couldn't keep spending all his money on her and Mom.

He kept his gaze on the winding road as they passed middle-income homes. "If I remember the pastor's words, you have a warehouse to rent."

Uh? How did he know she was thinking of a warehouse?

"You found a place for your package ministry, honey?" Mom squealed.

"It's..." Tessa peered at the road, not needing to stress while she couldn't control certain things. "I will." With God's help, sooner rather than later.

After their lunch when the server brought the leather booklet with a receipt, Tessa reached for it, but Chad snatched it out of her hand. "What kind of man do you think I am? To bring ladies to lunch only to have them pay?"

"Mom, can you tell him we usually pay for our bills?"

Mom crossed her arms on the table, and the big pink bow on her black hat drooped to one side of her face. "Honey, if you're going to wrestle him for the billfold, be my guest."

"Thank you, Bettina." Although he was addressing Mom, Chad's gaze stayed on Tessa, his teeth too bright for his own good. "I'm up for the challenge."

"Of course, you are," Tessa mumbled under her breath as she rolled her eyes and surrendered.

That afternoon, Mom had plans to meet her friends for their Bible study, so Chad asked Tessa to join him for a walk to work off their lunch. After changing into shorts and a light floral top, she met him on the boardwalk beside the cabin.

Gone were his button-down shirt and jeans, replaced by a black T-shirt and dark shorts.

They strolled to the lake they normally ran to, enjoying a lazy walk with an afternoon breeze while she pointed out the local birds they encountered—chickadees, flickers, goldfinches, nuthatches, robins, sparrows, and wrens. Too bad they didn't sight an elusive bluebird. Then they sat on the grass by the lake. Seeming relaxed, Chad stretched out on his stomach, so she laid down next to him. She made a face when the wild grass poked her arms and legs. "We should've brought a blanket."

"You can sit on my shirt." He tugged at his shirt. The V-shape revealed the first letter—a script T—of the word inked on his chest.

"Keep your shirt on." She reached out to touch his hand where it hovered by the hem of his shirt. "I don't need you scaring the animals." Yeah, right. She was who he'd scare if she started to stare at his bare chest. Even if she was eager to ask about the tattoo, it could wait for another time.

He captured her hand, and she hadn't meant to be so close to him—okay, she liked his nearness. But the way he was looking at her made her want to lean in and kiss him, yet also run at the same time.

"I don't see any animals." His gaze fell to her mouth, and heat surged through her. Instead of leaning toward him, she tugged her hand free and glanced at the waterlilies across the lake.

"Why did you become a bomb technician?" She had no idea how she conjured up the sudden question, but she'd wanted to ask since they'd met.

Silence passed as swallows skimmed the lake, their song filling their surroundings. When it felt too long, she had to look at him to make sure she hadn't offended him. The last thing she needed was a repeat of that time he'd gotten angry.

"I was on my way to jail. My teen years... I fell in with the wrong friends and dragged my cousins along. We snuck into theaters to watch free R-rated movies—I got a thrill out of the pranks, the mischief, and we got into a lot of silly things unsupervised teens do."

Unease shivered up her spine when he talked about his abusive uncle and the consequences Chad brought upon his cousins for getting them into trouble.

"This one time, we got into some old sticks of dynamite and blew things up—including the shed in the backyard. Man, you should have seen that mess! It scared Aunt Abby's cat so much the thing ran away and never did come back." He chuckled. But a rueful twist flattened his lips, and his eyes didn't sparkle. "After high school, my uncle kept reminding me how I was going to spend the rest of my life in prison if I didn't get my act together. He talked me into joining the military to acquire some discipline."

He plucked some blades of grass, selected the widest, and fit it between his thumbs. Then cupped his palms as if holding a harmonica and blew on the grass, letting out a squawk like a duck. "I went to get him off my back, but I had no intention of joining the army. The recruiter that day was more interested in technicians as long as getting rich wasn't your type of thing. What seventeen-year-old doesn't like blowing things up?"

She flopped onto her side and braced on one elbow as his stories showed the level of maturity he'd acquired after boot camp. He'd trained for combat and risen in the ranks too. The afternoon shadows lengthened as he shared some different missions he'd gone on. She laughed with him over fun moments he had with his unit and gasped gripping the tall grass before her when he brushed off his near-death experiences, especially during his early years in the Iraq War.

But through it all, he hadn't mentioned Nelly. Tessa dipped her chin. "How old were you when you got married?"

"I was twenty-two." He swallowed hard, his shoulders hunching. "I had unrealistic expectations—you know, never having seen a real marriage work, but believing in it from movies and such. Just a naïve kid who thrust all these ideals on her, then took off on deployments without putting any real effort into building a relationship. I stayed tight with my buddies, but let the army draw me from my wife."

He fell silent, his green eyes turbulent. "We made it through three years of my service, but then a bit after I re-upped, my high school best friend gave her the attention I didn't offer. It didn't occur to me then, but now, I think maybe she wasn't expecting me to reenlist."

Tessa couldn't judge since she didn't know what it was like to be married to someone who was always gone, except for her observation in her family. Dad was always gone, and when he was home, he didn't seem to know how to interact with his wife and kids. Tessa had chosen to cling to him whenever he opted to go fishing, so she'd found a way to spend time with him. Because Mom endured and stayed faithful, Tessa assumed that, by marrying a soldier, one would know they were committed to serving their country—no matter the circumstances, you'd have to stick it out and honor your vows.

Her heart ached when he talked about the only dog he'd ever had and how his ex had taken it. Since she'd spent more time with it and he was always on the move, Chad hadn't demanded to have the pet he couldn't take care of. "Funny, I always wanted a dog since I was a child."

What had he said the day he'd had a dog cartoon on TV? *"For your information, I love dogs."*

"Guess I'm never meant to have one."

She could fix that if she could guarantee his plans after the triathlon. For now, he needed comfort. Reaching out, she clasped his hand, burying it in both of hers. "I'm so sorry."

"I have endless issues." He pressed his lips together, his jaw twitching. His gaze went distant as silence fell upon them.

"This last mission hit me the most." He winced, and she couldn't help moving her hand to touch his jaw to comfort him. He reached for her hand and sat up, staring at her with a tenderness that stole her breath.

He tucked a finger under the neckline of his shirt and tugged it down to reveal the ink on his chest. "I got this as soon as I landed in Virginia last month."

Curiosity moved her closer. Then her eyes widened. He had *her name* in black on his skin. "Oh." She blinked, gulping at the understanding of how much she meant to him. Her chest tightened, and her eyes moistened as she traced a finger over each line and curve of her name. "Why did—"

"You are the reason I made it through alive." Emotion roughened his voice as he let the shirt slide back into place over the ink and then traced his fingers on her cheek. "I don't know why I connect with you on a deep level. I just..."

There was probably more to the story behind the tattoo and his survival, and she wanted to ask. But now wasn't the time or place. She didn't have to know all the answers, not when she'd just learned she was important to him. All she could feel was the love shining in his eyes and her need to reach out and put her hand to the side of his face. She had no idea where her courage came from. But she leaned in and pressed her lips to the line of his jaw, light as a butterfly's landing, then the corner of his mouth, diffusing each kiss with her unyielding need to reveal her heart, to heal and make him forget all the unwelcome war memories.

Chad kissed her then, really kissed her with raw emotion, nestling her back against the grass as if it was their first kiss, a planned kiss that seemed so true and perfect. If she thought the airport kiss was raw, then she hadn't kissed anyone like him before. Tessa's heart thundered against his heart. She loved the heavy feel of him, the way she felt small and protected beneath him as if she'd found the place where she belonged. It felt like the world had stopped turning as she saw stars. While she moved her hands to the back of his neck, his fingers wove into her hair, and she savored his scent—forgetting summer's heat that would be turning to cool air soon and the sounds of nature as the rasp of their breathing drowned it out.

Chad kissed her neck and her ear, then propped on one elbow to look down at her. The longing and tenderness overwhelming her reflected from his eyes.

"You're too good to be true." His fingers caressed her face as his raspy words caressed her ears.

Somehow, she managed to respond. "Why's that?"

"I have a hard time believing you could like me."

"You have to believe it." With an ex who left him for his best friend and an abusive uncle who belittled him, no wonder he had doubts about relationships. She ran a hand through his soft hair. "I more than like you," she whispered, breathless. "How can I make you understand?"

"I don't know." He lowered his lips to hers and kissed her, and she kissed him back, slow and tender, with a reverence she hoped he could grasp, a promise of her love for him.

CHAPTER 12

In the days leading to July 4, Tessa continued to work with Chad, proud of his efforts to progress. Their five-mile runs turned to seven, then to fifteen, and yesterday to twenty. He could keep running, but she wanted to go in increments each passing day rather than do everything at once. The Ironman Triathlon was twenty-six miles, and she planned for him to reach that goal by the end of July. To run 26 miles, bike for 112 miles, and swim for 2.4 miles. Come September 6, Chad would be doing all three events in one day.

She should've signed up for the triathlon, too since she did everything with him except swimming, her least favorite task.

Thankfully, he'd taken his recovery days—Tuesdays, Fridays, and Sundays—more seriously since he was exhausted.

On his recovery days, she'd researched real estate as if she expected things to change overnight. But while he was resting from workouts, he was still interested in discussing the soldier ministry and how he could help.

Tuesday, he'd wanted them to look at rental warehouses and buildings in the area. She'd agreed to talk to a Realtor who showed them three buildings. The former boutique was perfect since it was in town, but it was the most expensive one. There was a warehouse and another building both outside Pleasant View.

"Let's get the one in Pleasant View." Chad had said on their drive home. He always spoke like a wealthy person whenever he jumped at big plans to purchase and pay for things, yet he didn't squander money on himself. He'd only spent money on himself when they'd shopped for his equipment and then when she'd taken him clothes shopping in Colorado Springs.

Even if he didn't show any symptoms of pain, she still insisted he do stretches and exercises for his hip and shoulder to strengthen his muscles.

On Friday—July 4—Chad helped Mom load vegetables in the back of his truck. Even though her market days were Wednesdays and Saturdays, a local restaurant needed vegetables delivered since they were cooking meals for the festivities.

Tessa and Chad dropped off the vegetables with Mom. While they ran the annual parade 10K, Mom joined the group cooking pancakes on Main Street. Pleasant View's community pancake breakfast was a tradition. After the run, Chad and Tessa were ready for the scrumptious pancakes.

It would be a big day as Chad met her friends. Once they returned home to shower and change, Mom was leaving with a couple of her friends to make jam and can vegetables.

An hour later, with the sun high in the sky, they met Liberty and her family at Eric Stone's house. One of Tessa's first clients, Eric had tested her patience with his surly mood—a result of traumatic events he'd been going through then.

Chad drove into a grand driveway, and although Tessa had been there for a barbeque twice, she never got tired of taking in the expansive property with its limestone mansion in the distance.

They followed Liberty and Bryce's SUV to the entrance where Tessa recognized the guard, dressed in black. He was grinning at Bryce as he waved them through the oversized metal gate. They pulled into a circular driveway and parked in the wide space on the side. Massive gardens separated the parking space from the house.

The moment they stepped out of the truck and Chad pressed a kiss to her lips, Liberty emerged from the SUV and shuffled toward them. She kept a hand on her protruding baby bump before spreading out her arms. Those deep dimples pinched through her flawless brown cheeks, and Tessa's wide smile stretched out her face.

"Oh my goodness, Chad!" Liberty squealed, then whispered to Tessa something she didn't hear before walking to Chad whose arm was over Tessa's shoulder.

Chad dropped his arm from Tessa when Liberty wrapped him in an embrace. "I've been dying to meet you."

"You can blame Tessa for our delayed meeting."

"He's to blame." Tessa eyed Chad playfully, tempted to rat him out for his hot-then-cold vibe.

When Liberty's husband plucked their two-year-old from her car seat to his hip, Tessa's heart pulled. Myra's gray eyes, the same color as Bryce's, brightened, and her pudgy hands clapped. She was so adorable in her navy dress with red and white stars. White ribbons tied up her curly hair in pigtails, the trailing satin already tangling with her glossy locks.

"Eta!" She flapped her arms at Tessa.

Tessa scooted closer to them, reached out, and scooped Myra in her arms. "Happy Fourth of July, my Starlight."

While Tessa squeezed her tight, Myra slobbered her with a wet kiss on the cheek. Then Tessa pecked the little one's amber cheek. With Bryce's light skin and Liberty's brown skin, Myra was blessed with an amazing skin tone.

Tessa had met Liberty when they worked together in a mutual client's home. Liberty had been pregnant with Myra then and starting her business while Tessa was also starting as a physical therapist.

With Myra's pigtails tickling her cheek, Tessa introduced Chad to the little doll who lit up their lives. The men shook hands and spoke before Chad stooped to Myra still nestled on Tessa's hip. He oohed and aahed about Myra.

"Do you remember when we FaceTimed?" Chad touched the red festive necklace around Myra's neck while speaking so tenderly to the toddler. If Tessa didn't know any better, she'd assume Chad was around kids often. "It's so nice to meet you."

The smell of fresh-cut grass, heady honeysuckle, and budding roses spiced the air while they crossed the lawn. Chad and Bryce walked ahead and talked sports. Tessa and Liberty followed while Liberty leaned in to whisper about Chad. "He's more handsome than in the photos."

That was the truth. Chad was strikingly attractive. Tessa shifted Myra on her hip, feeling the weight leaning into her. "He's one hot mess." She needed to see things from the bright side, but in case it didn't work out, she had to be forthcoming. She didn't intend to talk about his outbursts unless they got worse, but she needed her friends to pray for him.

"Underneath those green eyes, I see a lukewarm sweet mess." Liberty squeezed Tessa's shoulder.

Just the mention of lukewarm had her body heating up at the memory of his kiss—*kisses* if counting the airport.

"We kissed," she confessed.

And Liberty gasped, dramatically posing and clamping a hand over her mouth. "Wait until Iris hears *that*."

Iris, quite the romantic, might end up analyzing the kiss for a two-hour discussion. She was due to a FaceTime call sometime soon. "She's not here in person, so she won't know just yet."

Tessa resumed walking, then ducked, and shielded Myra with her hand when a bee zipped from the honeysuckle flowering along their path and buzzed over their heads.

Just as they rounded the path near the house, Eric emerged from behind the well-trimmed mountain laurel hedge near the front door. A handful of kids trailed him, their happy voices ringing through the gardens.

"Welcome!" His hazel eyes radiated with kindness as the early afternoon sun lit them up. He pulled Bryce into an embrace before shaking Chad's hand. "Chad, right? I'm so glad you could join us today."

Eric Stone was a living miracle, a testimony to what God did every day. He was also one of the kindest people Tessa had ever met.

When Liberty and Tessa joined them, Eric arched a brow at Liberty, then Tessa. "Is this *the* Chad?"

"The one and only." Liberty elbowed Tessa.

Eric slapped Chad's back and man-hugged him as if they'd known each other for years. "Thank you so much for your service."

"Thanks for having us in your lovely home." Chad eased away from the brief hug, his voice emerging a bit rough.

Myra wiggled out of Tessa's hold, and as soon as Tessa set her down, Myra broke out into the cutest waddle to join Eric's kids, who were now running around the shrubs.

His biological triplets were about Myra's age and played with her whenever Liberty's family hung out with Eric's family.

Eric's wife, Joy, who'd become a good friend, soon joined them. With her skin, brown like Tessa's and Liberty's, damp in the afternoon warmth and her curly hair frazzled, she must've been running after the kids.

Eric glowed as he moved to his wife and leaned in to kiss her cheek.

"I can't believe our friends are here." Joy smoothed a hand over her rumpled patriotic dress. Blue and red with a white decoration on her shoulder. The sparkly red hair band was as vibrant as her sunny outlook on life. She beamed, moving to Tessa and squeezing her then Liberty in tight embraces. "So good to see you guys."

Tessa introduced her to Chad. "Joy painted the abstracts in the cabin."

He'd raved about the peacefulness of the paintings and how relaxing he found them. "Aha, *the* Joy." Chad winked at Eric, tossing his words back at him, before facing Joy. "You're a great artist."

She dismissed his compliment with a wave. "You'll be surprised what you can draw. But if you're interested in art, you should make

Tessa bring you to the opening night gallery in September for new artists."

"I'm not an artist." Chad raised his hands to protest.

But Eric slid an arm around his wife's waist, his gaze roaming to Liberty, Bryce, Tessa, then back to Chad. "My wife believes everyone has a hidden masterpiece they need to release."

Pointing at Joy, Bryce nodded. "We've all been to her studio and painted something under this lady's guidance."

Tessa's phone rang from her shorts pockets, but she only brought it out because she knew who was calling. Iris had known when they'd be at Eric's house and had wanted to greet Chad. So Tessa lifted the phone to Liberty and then Joy, displaying Iris's photo on the screen. "We'd better answer."

When Liberty nodded, Tessa pressed the camera icon, and Iris's brown hair danced over her shoulders.

"Is Chad there?" Iris asked rather than starting with a greeting. So Tessa lifted the phone screen, moving it around to show everyone standing around, and Iris's eyes brightened. "Hey, big brother."

"I'm still mad at you for not being here in person." Eric wagged a finger at her, a teasing smile revealing his soft spot for his sister.

"Your offer to send a jet was enticing, but I'll be home at the end of the month for the reunion."

"Don't forget Gavin's wedding."

"How can I miss a wedding? I'll plan to stay an extra week until the wedding."

With a promise to see her brother later that month, Iris waved and asked to talk to Bryce. As soon as she'd greeted Bryce, she said, "Put the phone in front of Chad."

Hoping Chad was okay with all the attention, Tessa handed him the phone. She and her friends had talked about and prayed for Chad so many times, so it didn't seem odd that Iris spoke like they were friends.

His face pinked as Iris's questions bombarded him, and he gripped the back of his head with his other hand. "I've heard great things about you from Tessa."

Iris squealed. "I can't believe you're in Pleasant View! Will you come to the wedding in August? When is your triathlon again?"

Iris rarely left time for him to answer and had him chuckling by the time he said goodbye and returned Tessa's phone. Since Iris still wanted to chat with the girls, Joy told them she needed to tend to the kids while the men caught up.

Iris had been Liberty's best friend, but when Tessa and Liberty became friends, the three of them had become like the three musketeers. Now Joy joined their trio, although they rarely hung out due to her obligations with the eight kids. Joy never wanted to spend more than two hours away from her little ones.

Tessa and Liberty moved to the newly built gazebo further down the property and sat on the outdoor sofa set. The waterfall's distant whisper and the kids' nearer squeals offered a cheerful background noise.

"Oh my word, he's so handsome," Iris gushed. "After he went MIA on you, I didn't think you two would pull it off."

"How come you didn't tell me about your doubts?" Tessa tucked her legs up beside her, knowing her friends had comforted her after his stretched silence.

"They'll pull it off." Liberty's hair brushed against Tessa's cheek as she drew closer to the screen.

"I'm not so sure." Tessa had to be honest with her friends. The three prayed for each other, and her relationship still needed prayers.

Iris frowned. "The man is in your town, staying in your home. What more proof do you need?"

"Chad has no interfering mother." Liberty bumped Tessa's shoulder, no doubt speaking from her experience. "If Bryce and I did it, so can you."

Not all mothers were like Bryce's mom, but each relationship has its ups and downs. Tessa still shook her head, afraid to come to any conclusions about Chad. "Remember Elias's condition?"

"PTSD and depression?" Iris raised a brow, and Tessa nodded, almost convinced Chad had war-related trauma.

"Elias never left the cabin." Liberty slid an arm around Tessa's waist and squeezed. "Chad's here at the picnic. Your career has prepared you for such a moment."

"Chad was smiling!" Iris bounced in her seat, and something like clapping sounded through the speakers. "Have you forgotten how my brother never spoke to anyone?"

Who could remember how grouchy Eric Stone had been until he met and married Joy a few years ago? He'd changed so much once Joy came into his life.

"God was probably using my brother to prepare you for Chad."

"Iris is right." Liberty nodded.

Could Iris be right? Had Tessa's career experiences been preparing her for a spouse who needed her help continually? She wasn't a psychologist to help him with his emotional battles. But Chad had retained his sense of humor and the sparkle in his eyes, so he wasn't as deep in darkness as Elias or Eric had been.

"We have to do something to make this a happy ending for you." Iris sighed dreamily, being the romantic she always was.

But Tessa was ready to switch the topic. "It's odd to have a party at your brother's house without you here."

"You guys are family." Iris waved her manicured fingers at them. "Makes it even easier that my brothers are best friends with Bryce."

Liberty scooted in closer to the phone again. "We need to plan a getaway when you come for the reunion—maybe a trip to the cabin. Only this time, you girls *actually* show up."

Tessa laughed with her friends over their antics to get Liberty and Bryce back together by luring her to a girls' weekend at the cabin while Bryce's friends lured him there to a guys' weekend. Then they'd left the estranged couple alone together. "Hey, our ploy worked, didn't it?"

Liberty beamed, her dimples flashing. "Best Christmas gift—*ever*!"

"But seriously"—Iris waved—"let's plan something together. I have an entire week before the wedding. We'll catch up and go to a spa for a massage and get our nails done. We need to start scheduling hair appointments for Saturday morning."

Iris seemed more energized just talking about the wedding, but as much as Tessa enjoyed her time with her friends, she'd committed herself to Chad.

"I'm not so sure I can hang out for more than two days." Although Chad claimed he wasn't her client anymore, the triathlon was just over two months away.

"Bring Chad to the reunion. You girls *have to* plan on staying the night at my parents' place. You can't say no—just think of that mansion. Plenty of room."

"Myra will love it if Eric's kids are staying."

Despite what she said, with Iris's family coming into town, there wouldn't be enough space to accommodate the extra friends.

"Seriously, girls, plenty of room. Some of our siblings will be staying at Eric's house."

"July twenty-seventh." Liberty tapped Tessa's shoulder. "You'd better start preparing Chad for all the upcoming parties."

"We'll have a virtual call next week to do online shopping for wedding dresses," Iris added.

A thrill ran through Tessa. Iris's enthusiasm could excite anyone. She didn't even know the bride and groom, except that the groom, who'd been the Realtor to show her places around town, was Bryce and Iris's family friend. Iris and Liberty were the your-friends-are-my-friends types.

How was Tessa going to convince Chad to go as her date to a stranger's wedding? She wiggled in her seat, jittery. "I don't even know the couple."

Iris wagged her finger. "When I come to Pleasant View, I want to spend every minute with you girls. I don't even care that I'll be the only one without a date at the wedding."

Her voice rasped with the last line, betraying her. She dipped her head and spoke with her face down. "I guess you know how to pray for me, ladies."

"This is going to be your year." Liberty raised her hand as a silent plea to God. Tessa agreed.

Beautiful and cheerful, Iris never lacked suitors, but she was set on finding the one person meant for her. Sparks and chemistry topped her requirements list—all the things Tessa felt with Chad.

"I'm still single until I'm married, you know." Tessa wasn't sure enough to consider herself someone's girlfriend. August's wedding was a long time away. Anything could happen between her and Chad in the meantime. He was as unstable as they came, and as much as Tessa wanted to jump every time he asked her to, could she trust him with her heart and survive the outcome?

CHAPTER 13

Kids' squeals reverberated in the air, creating a soothing kind of noise Chad drank in thirstily. Tessa and her friends chased the kids in the open grass. The little ones had unending energy even after Chad, Bryce, and Eric had tried to wear them out in the backyard's shallow fenced-in pool. Chad's gaze shifted to the glittering adult pool yards beyond the small one. Maybe he could come back and swim in it sometime.

For lunch, Eric's chef had served grilled chicken and, for dinner, filet mignon. Both meals had a variety of sides to choose from. Too full, Chad had declined dessert after dinner. He still felt full even now as he shifted in the soft padded chair before the rectangular unlit fire pit.

The sun was rolling out of the horizon, casting touches of golden rays on the steaming mountain while Chad relaxed with Bryce and Eric in the gazebo. Strung lights flickered on the arches and crossbeams, glittering now in the gathering dusk.

He'd earned the break after helping the guys entertain nine kids under the age of ten. Despite the two nannies helping with Eric's kids, the little ones preferred wandering to their dads. Eric and Bryce had stopped whatever they were doing each time to tickle, chase, or throw a ball. And Chad had watched, mesmerized by how dads interacted since he hadn't grown up around a dad who played with his kids.

Bryce and Eric, both successful investors, hadn't talked about their careers until Chad asked. Now, after five hours in their company, he knew their passion for God, their love for family, and their commitment to the town.

Bryce showed no regrets over moving from New York where his business had been so he and his wife could raise their children in Pleasant View.

Chad only learned about Eric's financial company when he'd been looking for the bathroom and stumbled into an office with trophies and awards in a glass display case. Stone Financial Services earned its place as the most admired broker company and held three others trophies he hadn't had time to read.

"We meant it." Eric's voice pulled Chad out of his thoughts. "We golf, play chess, bike, or whatever hobby you want to introduce every Thursday evening."

"We talk about spiritual struggles and victories." Bryce set his water on the marble part of the fire pit.

If Chad stayed in town, he wouldn't mind making new friends. He stretched his legs out and crossed them at the ankles, relaxing back in his seat. "How did you guys come to discover this place?"

"My parents live above that hill." Eric pointed to an extensive expanse of woodlands, but with the thick forest elevated above them, Chad couldn't see any structures.

"My folks had homes in the Hamptons and Pleasant View." Bryce spread his arms out on the couch he occupied. "Their place here was just supposed to be a vacation home, but they spent more time in Pleasant View as time went on. Mom even ran for and served as mayor once. So yeah, we kinda stuck here. Then Liberty and I—"

One of the kids fussed, and the guys turned to where the ladies were. Each one had a child, and Tessa looked as if she was one of the moms with Myra's head nestled on her shoulder.

The older kids must have left for the house with a nanny since they weren't in sight.

"You have a good one there." Bryce tipped his chin to Tessa as she secured one arm around the child while lowering herself to reach for a stuffed toy from the grass.

"Yeah. I'm lucky." Chad kept his gaze on Tessa, her full focus on the toddler. What would it be like to start a family with her? Would he be a good parent, and what kind of dad would he be, having never had a father or a decent father figure?

He could be a good dad if Tessa could be the mother of his children. She'd teach him what a father was like, based on her experience with her dad.

"Did Tessa tell you I was one of her first clients?"

Eric's voice had Chad tearing his gaze from Tessa to Eric, who was setting his sparkling water beside the fire pit.

"She said something about you being her client."

Eric chuckled. "Did she also tell you I was the worst?"

"No." She never pinpointed her clients, badmouthed them, or revealed their personal details. Whenever she spoke about them during their FaceTimes, she'd talk about the ups and downs of her job. "All I can say is after training me she'll have lots of stories to tell."

"Romantic stories are the best." Bryce crossed his legs and clasped both hands to the back of his neck.

"I'm sure Tessa is a good trainer, but she has a lot to offer as a therapist." Eric closed his eyes as if reflecting on the darkest days of his life while he spoke of Tessa's patience and kindness whenever he'd barked at her. When he reopened them, a twinkle flashed in their depths. "I bet I'm the reason she's switching careers."

"I don't think so." Chad rubbed his hands on his thighs. Tessa had such passion for her clients, but Chad hadn't made her job as a trainer any easier. "If that were the case, then she'd rethink it."

The ladies joined them in the gazebo. Joy sank onto the seat next to Eric, curling up beside him in a way that made Chad ache for Tessa to do the same. She let out a low sigh. "I've got to get our littlest ones to bed." But with her head on Eric's shoulder, she made no move to leave.

Myra was now on Liberty's hip, clinging to her mom, a thumb in her mouth. Bryce tucked an arm over his wife's shoulder.

"Would you like to stay and watch the fireworks here with us?" Eric looked at Bryce, and Bryce eyed his wife, who nodded.

While everyone else tended to their kids, Chad studied Tessa to figure out what she wanted to do. Then he lifted his hands in question since he had no idea what plans she had for the early part of the night.

"I don't see friends often, and when I called Mom earlier, she was having fun with her church friends." Tessa leaned her head to the side, a secret plea to stay.

He reached for her hand, entwining her fingers in his, and relished the softness and warmth it radiated.

She squeezed him back. "As long as you're with me, I'll go wherever you go."

Chad stared at her, her face aglow beneath the soft strings of lights. "I, too, will go wherever you go."

She gave a gentle shrug. The red top she'd worn over blue jean shorts encased her soft curves. With her hair cascading down her shoulders, his fingers itched to touch it, but Joy declared they were taking kids to bed, reminding him they weren't alone. Then Liberty and Bryce took Myra, following Eric's family toward the house.

Alone with Tessa for the first time all day, Chad pulled her onto his lap, and she wrapped her arms around him. He slid his arms around her waist, pressing his nose into her hair. Her familiar shampoo and her wildflower scent drew him in, and a warm feeling of comfort ran through him.

"You were so good with Myra. You'll make a great mom someday."

"You think so?" Her warm breath whispered against his neck, and his heart beat faster.

"I just know." He shifted so he could look at her face under the lights and tucked a piece of her hair behind her ear. His heartbeat stuttered. Oh, man!

Overcome by desire, he leaned in and kissed her ear. She shivered, and an outbreak of goosebumps puckered her arms. So he wasn't the only one feeling things. She then shifted on his lap to face him. Her fingers trailed along his jaw, and he sucked in a breath. The longing he felt reflected in the glow in her eyes.

"You were so good with the little ones too," she whispered.

"I was left with no choice, being around them all day." Hide and seek was starting to grow on him. "Would you like to have kids someday?"

The words rolled off his tongue without permission from his brain. It felt right since they were talking about kids.

She leaned in and softly kissed his lips. "With my future husband, yes."

Unwelcome questions crept into his mind. Did she see him as a potential husband? A dad to her kids someday? He couldn't ask her, and she interfered with his thoughts when she spoke.

"What about you?"

If she agreed to marry him, he'd try anything. Tessa inspired him to believe in himself. Her presence made him forget his restless nights.

"As long as the child is as beautiful as their mom." Of course, God was in control of the future. Tessa could decide to leave him tomorrow or next week like Nelly had. His blood chilled, and he moved his hand away from her shoulder.

She curled her hand around his neck. "What's going on in that busy mind of yours?"

No way could he voice his doubts and fears while she was looking at him with such tender affection—the same love he felt for her but wasn't sure how to express.

So he groped for a safer topic. "Eric thinks he's the reason you're switching careers."

"Really?" Her forehead puckered.

"He thinks he was your worst client but says you have a lot to offer as a physical therapist."

Tessa put her hands on his racing chest. A brief silence passed before she added, "When we visited Elias's hospital, it crossed my mind not to give up on being a physical therapist just yet."

"Maybe you shouldn't. Pray about it." That's what she would suggest to him. She'd told him to pray about his decision to run the triathlon this summer or to wait. Chad had prayed, but God responded by making Chad's last mission unsuccessful.

"I'll pray and think." Her face glowed in the twinkling lights, which seemed brighter now as the day lost its light.

He wagged a finger at her. "I'm not sure I want you to train a bunch of snob guys who might end up swooning over you."

She playfully punched his chest. "Nobody is swooning over me."

"Like Kinkaid, for starters." Chad hadn't bothered asking how she'd met his swim coach, and he wasn't ranking himself to know any of those details.

"Is that why you stopped me from coming to your swim sessions?"

He couldn't deny it, and he had no better explanation for why he felt protective and jealous whenever she had admirers. "I'm a very insecure man. At least, until I'm sure that you are mine."

His heart was racing when she took his hand and pressed it to her pounding heart. "I'm yours. Because of this."

Low and raw, her voice sliced into him, tearing down his defenses with her vulnerability. He moved his hand from her chest to cup her face. Her skin was so soft and so perfect. "I'm yours too," he whispered, and his lips found hers.

Everything else vanished, save for the pounding of his heart and the feel of his fingers in her hair. He kissed her soundly, not caring if he should or shouldn't. She kissed him back. Her hands rose to clutch the sides of his T-shirt and pull him closer, filling his heart to overflowing.

BY ALMOST NINE THIRTY, the sky was dark. Chad had his arm around Tessa, her body warm as she leaned against him on the blankets sprawled over the grass on the hills above Eric's home. Liberty and Bryce sat in a similar position. The triplet boys, not much older than ten, sat a ways behind them with Eric and Joy, glow sticks on wrists and worn as necklaces while they stared at the dark sky shooting sprinklers of fireworks.

From their angle, they overlooked the entire town with its glittering lights. According to Tessa, Eric Stone usually paid for a fireworks show over the lake in the park he'd built for the town. The recreation center where Chad trained for his swimming was also Eric's doing to provide affordable activities and places for the locals without breaking their wallets.

A booming rocket, louder than the last, soared into the air. Chad jumped, and his heart started racing. It shouldn't startle him, but it'd been a long time since he'd gone to a fireworks show. He tried to keep his attention on the sparkling red, white, and blue, then gold and silver in the sky, willing himself to calm down by taking focused breaths. He didn't mean to tighten his arms around Tessa's waist, but he felt it through his stiffened muscles.

In need of a distraction, he moved his head to the side and peered at her. The fireworks' shimmering rays illuminated her beautiful face, and her mouth spread into a grin as the display captured her full attention. He could get through this show. For her.

He held his breath while rockets fired into the air. As the volley after volley had people gasping and oohing and Eric's kids chattered their excitement, the bang after bang had Chad's palms sweating and his mind working on an escape plan. He couldn't interfere with anyone's fun, though.

Memories of his last mission stirred. The boom of the explosion, the cloud of the dust that had remained of his friends. His heart thrummed against his ribs, and he struggled to breathe.

Tessa must have felt his heart pounding against her back because she nestled closer, then whispered, "You're okay, love?"

He might have responded with a groan, but it could've been his rapid breathing. "I'll be back."

He eased out of her arms, stood, and walked off into the open space in the darkness. One heavy step in front of the other, his ears echoing from the blasts and his vision blurring from the smoke of dust from several months ago.

He was breathless, and his legs buckled. He sank down and raked his hands through his hair, tugging at it as if it would block every unwelcome flashback.

Why had he followed the wires of possible IEDs instead of leaving as his crew had suggested? He'd already deactivated the three bombs they'd come for while his men stayed back, covering for him should there be an unexpected attack.

But like the hero he assumed he'd been at the time, he'd ignored his friends when they radioed him.

"There's a few eyes on us, sergeant...."
"We've been here so long...."
"We'd better let the engineers handle the rest...."
"There's vehicles driving past...."
"What's the update on the possible IED?"

All the voices he'd told to give him a few more minutes. Yeah, just another minute. Just one more IED. Always another IED needed his skill. Just because he'd disarmed several in his career, he'd let his adrenaline surge take control, not the teams' safety.

A warm hand draped on his shoulder. "I'm here, sweetheart." Kindness laced the voice of the woman he'd come to love. "Are you okay?"

He was hot and cold. An outbreak of sweat dampened his shirt.

"Oh, my sweet, sweet Chad..."

Unlike his last nervous breakdown, when she'd asked questions, this time she didn't. She sat in silence and ran a comforting hand on his shoulder, moving it around his back. After moments of the gentle caresses, the tight knots in his shoulder loosened, and so did his heart.

"I was the only survivor."

At her slow exhale, her hand stopped moving on his back and rested between his shoulder blades.

"I just... It was a call on the roadside... in the desert." With each word a struggle, he could hardly form flowing statements. But he needed to explain.

One minute, a soldier was speaking on the radio. The next, a booming explosion cut off his voice.

With his elbows on his knees, Chad ignored the tall grass that poked his legs and through his shorts. Ignored the pounding in his head and the guilt chilling his heart. Told Tessa how he'd survived the deadly shrapnel effects like those that left Elias's leg needing amputation.

Seeming to ignore the discomfort, she moved in front of him. The stars didn't provide light for him to see her face, which made telling her the rest of the story easier while she couldn't see his agonized expression.

"I was suited up...." His throat was thick as if lodged with shrapnel. He'd only ended up with the cuts because, horrified and confused by the explosion, he'd tried to run toward his men. He'd taken off the helmet and attempted to ease out of the heavy suit so he could run faster as if he'd bring his friends back to life. Then debris tossed him backward, and he'd forgotten what he was supposed to do.

He'd been found unconscious, probably twenty-four hours later. He couldn't remember what they'd told him.

"It's all my fault."

"Chad." With her voice tender, she touched his wounded shoulder and squeezed it. "How many bombs have you disarmed?"

He'd been asked that a lot, but he wasn't keeping track. "Six hundred or so?"

"Is this the first time anyone died under your supervision?"

They'd died before if they were ambushed and shot at. This was different. "This time, I lost everyone because of my foolishness."

"You don't have the power to end someone's life unless God decides. And you're not responsible for all the evil in people who choose to carry it in their hearts." Her voice cracked, and her grip tightened. "It's not your fault." She repeated it as if she could say it enough for his mind to register her words.

She added practical reasons of God's power and His having everyone's days numbered—no matter what Chad could or couldn't do or did or didn't do. A slight assurance settled over him for the first time. Maybe, just maybe, he wasn't 100 percent responsible for the deaths that day.

But that what-if lingered. What if they'd left two minutes earlier?

"People die all the time. If not in battle, someone is on their deathbed as we speak. Someone just died two seconds ago somewhere around the world...."

She was good. Was she a counselor too?

Crickets chirped. The fireworks faded in the background and so did the memories in the desert, diffused as if she were the EOD tech deactivating the bombs in his mind.

She leaned in, wrapped her arms around him, and squeezed him in a comforting embrace. Her body shook against his, clearly affected by his dark story. Either way, she gave the most genuine hug he'd ever had or felt in all the long years since his mom.

"Can you do me a favor?" She moved from the embrace and kissed him tenderly on the lips.

"Anything."

"Call your cousin."

What an odd request. "Why?"

"Surrounding yourself with family is one of the best medicines when carrying such a burden."

"You're my family." He hoped she knew that.

"Yes, I am." She kissed him on the cheek. "The more family the merrier. Plus, I'd like to meet one of your family members."

"Lucky for you, I don't have a string of them for you to meet."

"That's all right." She touched his jaw. "We have plenty of friends and room in our hearts to make new friends."

As her friends' voices drifted on the breeze, they must have finished the fireworks. He hadn't heard any bangs going off anymore. The bombs in his mind seemed disabled as well, the flashbacks having fired their last shot for the night. He pressed his jaw against her soft palm, grateful to have her tenderness diffusing the angst in his life.

And maybe, just maybe, she was right. Maybe he couldn't have saved the lives of those under his command. Maybe he could leave the matters of life and death to God.

CHAPTER 14

July flew by. In one week, it would be August. Tessa didn't have to remind Chad about his training routine anymore. He did his therapeutic stretches daily and went through his other activities. Then, later in the day, when warmed up, he met Kinkaid to swim in the open water, a reservoir rather than a pool. Tessa had also taken him to Boulder to run on the triathlon's trail. Knowing what they still needed to work on helped improve Chad's approach to the terrain.

Enthusiastic, he woke earlier than she did and let himself into the main house to cook her and Mom breakfast.

At the end of the day after dinner, Mom suggested they pray together before Tessa escorted him to his cabin—kissed him good night only to kiss again when he walked her back to the main house's porch. Tessa often found him and Mom laughing in the kitchen, especially on Wednesday and Saturday mornings when he helped pack the vegetables before he took them to Mom's customers in town.

Mom seemed to enjoy having him around for morning companionship—but so did Tessa. His opening up to her at Eric's house deepened their bond and took their relationship to another level.

With his intentions clearer, she had hope for their future. They did things as a couple, and she looked forward to his spontaneity on outings lately. Like when he'd surprised her by getting tickets to a boat festival and taking her there. Also, he'd asked to go back and visit the veterans at Elias's hospital, and they'd gone twice.

Last time, he'd taken her on a date to a romantic restaurant that played live music, and they danced. But her favorite date was when he'd driven her to an open space and packed a picnic. After eating, they watched one of her favorite rom coms that he'd downloaded on his phone.

Two days later, she'd taken him to a summer outdoor concert. After the concert, they lay side by side with their backs on the blanket, talking as they gazed at the stars long after everyone cleared out of the park.

All those moments gave her heart extra reason to race whenever she heard his voice. Waking up this Friday morning was no different when Chad's deep laughter drifted downstairs. A sweet scent wafted from the massive bouquet on her nightstand—a delivery Chad ordered from a floral shop. He'd had two bouquets delivered that day, and the pink roses had Mom's name on the card.

Today was his recovery day, and lately, he'd turned those days into adventures with her.

Her heartbeat quickened as she showered and dressed in a cream-colored top, tucked it into olive-green shorts, then wrapped the sash into a bow. Not only were the shorts comfortable but also she liked how the sash kept her waist snug.

Of course, none of this had to do with Chad.

Yeah right.

She rolled her eyes as she stood in front of the full-length mirror. She patted her hair and gathered it into a ponytail before deciding against it. She'd free her hair today.

Again, she hadn't kept her hair free for Chad. Lately, she barely tied her hair in a ponytail unless she was biking and running with Chad. But that change of habit wasn't because of him, of course.

He was a part of her life now, part of her family.

Anticipation tightened her stomach as she climbed the stairs one at a time, her knees weakening with each step forward. Mom asked Chad a question, and he responded in a lighter tone.

As if he'd heard her footsteps, he stopped talking, and when she reached the threshold, his eyes were focused on the stairs. She swallowed, her legs almost buckling, and stood there crossing her arms.

Chad walked toward her with a wildflower bouquet. Dressed in faded jeans, a white T-shirt, and a red-checkered shirt unbuttoned, he looked so handsome and appeared so at home.

She swallowed hard, breathless.

"Happy morning." He leaned in and kissed her on the cheek, and oh, how she loved his spicy scent! Then he straightened and handed her the Colorado blue columbines, silvery lupines, and pinky aspen pea flowers. "Picked these this morning."

"Thank you." Her heart warmed. Evidently, he thought of her as often as she thought of him. Except, she was still wondering how she could do something special for him too. She touched the petals, dew wetting her fingers. "These are so beautiful."

"Not as beautiful as you." He tugged at the sash at her waist. "You look lovely."

She struggled to look at his face, but when she managed, the smoldering look in his green eyes mirrored hers for sure. "You look nice too." Always.

Spoons clanked in the kitchen as Mom tried to mind her business. No doubt she was listening, though. The morning after July 4, Tessa had told Mom that she and Chad decided to date.

"I hope you know what you're getting into," Mom had said. "But I like him."

Lucky for Tessa, she liked him a lot.

"I have big plans for us today." He placed his hand on her lower back, urging her toward the kitchen.

"I like plans." Plans that didn't involve running and biking but relaxing with him.

"Hey, baby." Mom wiped her hands with the kitchen towel, her knowing grin suggesting she knew what he was up to. After reaching for her purse next to her pink roses on the counter, she slung it on her shoulder. "Looks like you two lovebirds want me out of here."

"You can stay as long as you want." He brought out a glass vase from the cupboard, filled it with water, and lifted it toward Tessa. She nestled the bouquet in it before carrying it to the living room table and following Mom and Chad back to the kitchen.

After Mom said goodbye and left, Chad leaned into Tessa and kissed her lips. "Go get your handbag. Meet me at the car."

The stove clock showed seven ten. "This early?"

"We need to utilize every minute of daylight."

Anticipation danced in her stomach, little fires of excitement sparked by the mischievous grin lightning his green eyes. So she ran back downstairs for her handbag.

Despite needing to know what he was up to, she liked the surprise when he drove her to a nearby town for breakfast. From there, they listened to her favorite Leora Crisp's songs as he drove somewhere she'd never been.

A bracket of mountains surrounded them when he parked by a clear lake. Gentleman that he was, he stepped out and ran to open her door for her.

"I hope you remember your fishing skills." He took her hand to help her down, then led her to the back of the truck where he pulled out a fishing tackle box and two fishing poles.

She grabbed the black box and yanked off the tag dangling from it, then shoved the paper into her shorts pockets. "You didn't tell me you fish."

He set the rods on the grassy area, snagged the kit from her, and opened it. "I've never fished before." He retrieved a booklet and flipped it open. "But I've watched enough YouTube videos for dummies in the last two days."

Her heart swelled, gratitude causing her to move to him. The booklet fell when she wrapped her arms around him. "You did this for me?"

"For us." He kissed the top of her head and winked. "But don't forget you might be teaching me to fish if YouTube didn't get the job done."

She locked her hands behind his waist and leaned back to see his face. "It would be more comfortable if we had chairs."

He flicked the hair away from her shoulders. "They're in the truck."

He'd planned this through. Her chest swelled, her heart beyond full.

They returned to the truck to fetch the chairs, her skipping two steps to his one long stride. "You shouldn't have bought chairs without just asking me for some. I have camp chairs, you know."

"And how would it have been a surprise if I asked you for the chairs?"

Being the only ones at the lake allowed them to choose the best grassy spot along the edge where they set their fishing supplies and chairs.

He handed her one of the rods. Wow. Even if she wasn't an expert at fishing, she knew a good rod when she saw one and told him so.

He blushed. "I did my research."

Speechless, she watched him add bait to the hook.

"Apparently, fishing will test my patience."

"That it will." Feeling light, she arranged her bait. Memories of fishing with Dad danced in her mind the way sunlight danced on the water—light and carefree. She'd dreaded days when Dad would take her and Elias fishing at dawn, yet she'd never forget those special memories of her dad.

Dad and Chad would get along fine. Perhaps they'd talk about war stories and whatnot.

Chad stood next to the chair and cast his line into the water, and she walked to join him. The lake wafted a subtle smell of fish and damp grass. The morning sun cast their shadows behind them, mist rose from the lake, and the breeze tousled their hair. Not cold, just right.

Tessa flicked her hook into the water. "I haven't gone fishing since Dad died."

"I had that feeling."

He already read her in mind-boggling ways.

"Why do you think your dad liked fishing?"

She'd always found fishing to be boring. She elbowed Chad. "Already bored?"

"Not when you're here."

Warmed by his firm statement, she ducked her head and breathed in deeply, absorbing the perfect moment. "Unexpected results," she whispered, not just thinking of what her dad used to say when she asked him. "The unexpected results with fishing was why he loved it."

Chad's brows furrowed. "What does that mean?"

"He liked the fact that it was mindless. He could still enjoy the sport, even if he didn't catch anything." She smirked. "Dad said it was the one place he'd have us kids with him, and we'd be quiet since he told us not to scare the fish. Lucky for him, we obeyed."

"I hope you don't plan on being quiet." He recast his line. "Your voice is soothing."

Her hands shook, the certainty in his compliment overwhelming her. "I like... hearing you too."

A silence passed as they stood there, recasting their lines and gazing into the lake as if in their own thoughts. Then he broke the silence. "What do you miss most about your dad?"

"Having deep spiritual conversations."

Chad peered at her. "It all makes sense now."

"What's that?"

He looked back to the glittering lake. "Talking to God like you would to your dad."

When he'd asked how to talk to God who wasn't visible, Tessa had told him to envision God as a father, but that was the wrong analogy for him. "He's there, and He's listening. You just have to believe it—you know, like our fishing here today. Believing He's there and cares is like believing there are fish in this lake, even though we can't see them."

He shrugged. "It's hard for me to connect the dots."

With the rod in her right hand, she closed the space between them and slid her left arm to the back of his waist. "I understand it may not make sense to you. God knows you don't have to connect all the dots. Even a tiny dot matters to Him." She squeezed him. "Think of the mustard seed. Even faith as small as that is all that God wants from us."

He kissed the top of her head. "If God is okay with my doubts from time to time, then I can live with that."

She scooted away and recast her line, and Chad laughed as he copied her.

"Too bad Jesus can't talk to us right now. He'd tell us where to cast our lines to catch these silly fish."

She snickered. "Be patient. It's not like we need to haul in full nets. He's already given us more than we need to take care of ourselves today and tomorrow."

Chad filled his lungs with a deep breath. "That's faith, huh? Trusting Him for what matters."

An hour later, Chad reeled his line in and packed up the tackle box. "Let's get out of here."

Letting her line still drift with the current, she eyed the water striders scooting over the surface. The little bugs probably offered better temptation than her bait. "We can't leave yet. We haven't caught anything."

"It's not like I don't have faith there are fish out there," he teased, nudging her with his shoulder before reaching to grab her pole. "I haven't given up on fishing or on God, but we have other things to do besides stare at the lake all day. C'mon." He reeled in her line, then folded up their chairs and tucked them under one arm while grabbing the poles with his other hand. She scooped up the tackle box and followed as he lugged their items back to the truck.

When they sat and he started the truck, the dashboard clock displayed the time at only 11:52. They still had an entire day, but if he was so eager to get going... She buckled up. "What kind of things do you have in mind?"

His lips quirked and his eyes twinkled. "Things you'll soon find out."

He took her to an all-smoothies café, and they talked while sipping fruity drinks before he drove her to another lake where two canoes bobbed in the water beside a wooden dock.

"Leave your purse in the car." He held his hand out for her when she stepped out of the truck. The same place she'd left it while fishing.

Then he guided them to a shed, let himself in, and ushered her forward.

She stopped in the worn wooden doorway. With the lone window closed, she could barely make out the contents, but he was busy shuffling through things from the wall.

"What are we doing?" Knowing his teenage adventures, she didn't want to join him on a trip down memory lane.

"I'm not trespassing, if that's what you're worried about." He held a handful of life jackets and gestured her outside, then followed, and handed her a small orange vest before setting the rest down. "Huh, apparently, all these are the same size. We better get suited up."

"Why are we the only ones here?" She lifted onto her tiptoes, craning her neck. The silence stretched, save for the crickets chirping and the aspens rustling.

"You'll find out soon." He buckled his jacket on.

Saving her curiosity for later, she slid one arm into the vest, then the other arm. "At this point, I have no choice but to trust you."

"That's a wise choice." He winked, crouched to reach for the two other vests, walked back to the shed, and tossed them in before closing the door.

The sun was still high and warm against her back. How nice to have the weather cooperate with the adventure Chad had in mind. She hadn't ridden a canoe in years, and she still had no idea where their destination was, except for trusting the man leading her toward the dock.

Chad untied the canoe and steadied it while she slipped into the front seat, but sat backward, facing his seat. He handed her an oar, and the craft rocked when he slid into the back with his own. He pushed them off, and the canoe glided across the surface, light and quick like the water striders bugs. In the shadows, the water lurked as green and enticing as his gaze. Just like most of the unique scenic views in Colorado, this place stole her breath. How did he find such a place?

A peaceful silence descended as they crossed a canopy of overhanging boughs. A flock of birds fled from the shrubs and darted into the sky.

With his strokes long and steady, she set her oar between her legs and let her fingers make little wakes in the water. She winced, surprised by how frigid the water was on such a sunny day.

"I've never been here before."

He tipped his chin to the scenery ahead, a big white barn coming into view, and he chuckled. "I'd have plenty of questions for you if you'd been here before."

The protectiveness in his voice warmed her. "Is that so?"

In less than ten minutes, he glided the canoe ashore, but she was already sweating from the minor strokes she'd managed. She discarded her life jacket, and he did the same.

The barn nestled beneath a stunning mountain peak left her jaw hanging. Three stories high, flanked by lean-tos with rows of colonial windows and veiled with a white-tiled roof, it gleamed like a puffy wedding dress in the midday sun. So romantic, designed for couples. She now understood his comment about having questions if she'd been to such a place before. "This is beautiful."

"You're more beautiful." He leaned in to kiss her cheek, then stepped out in ankle-deep water, and helped her from the front.

The canoe tipped from side to side when she stood, and she lost her balance, falling forward against his chest. He caught her with one arm around her waist, and they stood there in the shallows, looking into each other's eyes. She didn't care that her toes were wet as water seeped through her tennis shoes.

"Thank you—for being you." Chad's hoarse voice caught on the words, his deep-as-the-lake green eyes reflecting his sincerity.

Her lips parted to respond, but her mind went blank. The water rippled in gentle laps against the shore, but she was more aware of the sound of their breathing as it drowned out everything else.

"Let's go have some lunch." Chad clasped her hand and started to lead her toward the bank, but she tugged him back.

"The boat's drifting."

"Oops!" He let go and sprinted back into the water, then pulled it ashore. His chest muscles flexed as he tied it to the shady willow overhanging the lake.

They strolled a flagstone path with LED lights shooting from the ground to the expansive barn nestled in waving grass. When a woman dressed in a white blouse and black trousers met them, Tessa asked, "Is this a wedding venue?"

The woman glanced at the trees along the manicured lawn framing a dramatic horizon for an open-air ceremony. "Yes, it is." In her midtwenties, she had a kind smile as she beckoned them. "Your table is ready."

"Um..." Chad pointed at Tessa's feet, then his. "Do you have any flip-flops?"

"Of course!" She ushered them inside and to one of the back rooms where they stored spontaneous items for emergencies.

The words had already vanished from Tessa's mouth earlier, and they weren't about to return now as their hostess led them to a lone table in the center of the rustic-modern barn. Soft instrumental music played, the sound vanishing somewhere in the lofty ceiling. This sprawling barn with sparkling lights glinting like stars overhead, swaths of silk floating like lazy clouds, and thick-planked floors beckoning dancers to swirl into the dream world could easily host a hundred and fifty people. A stone fireplace climbed the far wall, and a magnificent white rose and orchid bouquet graced their table. But the mountains and wildflowers enticed her eye to the windows. What a picturesque backdrop!

Her neck would tire from turning around, so she faced Chad and laughed. "You really had a plan."

He beamed, his eyes aglow as his smile crinkled up their edges. "There aren't too many romantic things in a mountain town."

A delectable aroma of gourmet food drifted through the massive space, and a warm feeling of comfort ran through her. Soon, servers wheeled buffet-style food trolleys to their table, and she blinked several times, opened and closed her mouth, wanting to ask if more people were joining them.

But just the two of them were feasting and celebrating—what she had no idea. After filling their plates with different salads and fancy meats, then praying, she asked, "How much did you pay for all this?"

He was a soldier, almost a volunteer since her internet search had revealed how little bomb technicians earned. She should have insisted on training him for free.

A grin stretched out his lips while he retrieved silverware from the white damask napkin. As their gazes lingered, heat rose up her neck.

"Just relax, okay?"

She was relaxed since she was here with the man she loved. She reached for her napkin, but was nervous to think he was going into debt on her behalf.

"I've never been on such a date before."

He must've meant a luxurious date. Clearly, he'd taken his ex-wife on dates. "It's a first for me too."

With Kanon, they'd had picnics, and she'd initiated them, not the other way around.

Forks clanked as they ate, her mind awhirl with worries that Chad would have to work for the rest of his life to pay off their date.

The server, a man this time, appeared with two fluted glasses and then poured champagne.

"To a new beginning." Chad lifted his glass, and Tessa clinked hers to his.

"To forever." She whispered her hope—forever with him.

After their meal and a lazy stroll on the grass, they sat side by side on chairs and utilized the offered blanket in the gardens. Chad had stripped off his checkered shirt and given it to her, and she'd snuggled into it, savoring his scent.

With the lake below them and rolling mountains towering above, they talked about all sorts of things. She fretted about getting back to the lake to get to his truck before it grew dark, but he assured her the facility owners would drive them back.

"We could've driven here, but I wanted to make it romantic by taking a boat."

A sigh slipped free. "This was more than romantic."

He clasped her fingers in his, resting their joined hands on his lap. "I wanted to do something special for you."

"And you have." Way more than she'd ever thought.

"I know you wanted to know why I went AWOL on you earlier this year."

She now knew he'd been injured then. "I think I know."

He cleared his throat and brought their hands to his mouth, kissing hers, then settling them back on his lap. "When I thought I was going to die... I had your photo that I kept in my wallet. Somehow, I managed to take it out. I kept staring at it, hearing your voice in my mind, knowing I would do anything to survive just to hear and see you again."

Tears blurred her vision and clogged her throat. Unable to speak, she rested her head on his shoulder. She couldn't imagine losing him. Just the thought of it lifted the hairs on her nape.

He must have sensed the tension in her hand because he draped his other arm over her shoulders. "That's why I didn't want to call you when I was in bad shape. I knew you'd panic."

She cleared her throat to rid the lump clogging it. She *had* panicked. "I thought something happened to you." Or worse. "I also thought maybe you didn't want us to be friends anymore."

"Trust me—I wanted to leave you alone. Save you from me." He drew out a breath. "I even called you so I could hear your voice, but I didn't say anything."

"You did?" She elbowed him. "Why didn't you say something?"

"I was conflicted." He squeezed her shoulder. "I wanted to be more than your friend."

And so did she. "If you didn't kiss me at the airport, I might have kissed you by now."

"And go against your client code?"

"We didn't sign any contracts, after all."

"You're so bad." He nibbled at her ear, and she shivered. He smelled as fresh as the mountain air. "You're worse than I am."

A stirring noise boomed across the lake. Two rockets soared into the air and exploded with a deafening bang.

"Oh, Chad." She jumped and grabbed onto him. "There's fireworks. We need to leave."

But when she pulled to stand, he tugged her back to her chair. "It's okay, baby."

He was too relaxed. That was too odd. "But last time—"

"I messed up your fireworks show. We're having a redo." He stretched the blanket up to her legs and drew her closer to him.

Okay. He was okay, and that was good. But was it even legal to have fireworks on any given day?

As if reading her mind, he rubbed her back and placed a kiss on her cheek. "Don't overthink. Let's enjoy the show."

Another rocket shot through the sky, lighting it all in a dazzling canopy of sparkling gold and white that reflected in a glittering shower over calm water. Her jaw dropped as more rockets fired into the air and exploded in a kaleidoscope of color.

Her heart was racing as rocket after rocket ignited and bang after bang resounded. She'd never seen such a stunning fireworks display.

She glanced at Chad, the light illuminating his chiseled jaw. "It's not bothering you?"

"I watched a lot of them on YouTube to prepare for this day."

Her heart melted, and her muscles liquefied. "Oh, Chad." She slid her hand to touch his perfect jaw, so full of gratitude. He'd gone so far out of his way to give her this romantic date. "This is the best thing anyone ever did for me."

"You're the best thing that ever happened to me."

She was so in love with him. How could he ever understand the extent? And he was overcoming his fear, perhaps getting past the PTSD one step at a time. Her hand moved, trailing his cheek.

As more silver fountain rockets shot into the sky, she leaned in and whispered against his lips. "I love you so much."

He moved his hand to the back of her neck and raked it up her scalp as it climbed into her hair. "I know. I know you love me." His voice emerged gruff, almost pained, as he captured her mouth with his. The fireworks faded in the background as the beating of their hearts dominated the night.

CHAPTER 15

Tessa's love for Chad deepened with each passing day. She savored the moments with him, the sight of his smile, the sound of his throaty laugh, the fun of his humor. Happier than she'd been in a long time, she'd been praying and hoping to do something for him—something to make him smile the way he made her smile.

God answered her prayer on Wednesday evening when Liberty called her.

"One of my clients has a foster collie." As Liberty talked about the border collie that needed more attention than the older man could offer, Tessa's heart skittered, and her mind moved to Chad.

"He's only four and energetic. Elias loves his German shepherd, but—"

"He already has a dog."

"You just interrupted me, lady." Liberty laughed playfully.

Restless, Tessa shifted her feet, opened and closed her mouth, and clamped down on her tongue before she could shout out that she would take the dog. She bit her lower lip to keep from interrupting her friend.

"Getting a dog cheered up your brother, so Chad might love a companion too."

"*I* should be Chad's companion," Tessa said, despite her need to get to the topic.

"Yes, but until he marries you, he might need a furry friend."

Tessa hadn't told any of her friends how Chad enjoyed hanging out with Elias's dog or how he'd always wanted to have a dog in his childhood.

"Even if Chad doesn't want him—"

"He will love him." A thrill pitched her voice higher. "You'll make his day."

"Um, this will be *you* making his day. Do not mention my name."

Either way, she couldn't wait to do something for Chad. She hadn't owned a dog after she'd lost hers two years ago. "How soon can I see the dog?"

"I'm sure any time tomorrow would be fine."

"Is seven too early?"

"My client wakes up at three. He has apnea. I'll talk to him as soon as we hang up, and I'll let you know what's the best time."

Things moved faster than Tessa had expected, and Liberty called back almost an hour later with an address to pick up Dusty the next day any time after six. So Tessa could leave the house at five thirty before Chad showed up at the main house.

Before she went to bed, she told Mom her plan, and Mom hugged her. "Funny you say that. He was talking about buying a dog sometime soon."

That only kicked up Tessa's urgency, so she woke up earlier than she'd intended. With no traffic in the silent morning and just a peek of mountain sunshine, Tessa made it to the older gentleman's house in less than twenty minutes. She listened to gospel music while waiting in the driveway.

Light illuminated the ranch house curtains, leaking out onto the white siding. The front door opened, and the man shuffled out. A dog followed at his heel before he closed the door and squatted before the dog. Morning light and the porch light radiated on the dog's black and white coat and revealed the man's taut features. The poor guy was clearly struggling as he spoke to his dog and rubbed behind his ears. The dog wagged its tail.

Tessa should've brought a treat or something. Excitement to get a dog had overtaken her thinking brain.

"I didn't mean to come so early."

He stood, and the dog moved to her, sniffing her shoes and jeans.

She squatted to pat him. "Hello, Dusty." The dog licked her hand, and she laughed. "You must be a morning person."

"He gets antsy. Good thing I'm a morning person."

And so was Chad.

The man held out a hand, then gripped hers in a callused clasp. "I'm Tom."

"Tessa."

"Dusty likes you. I hope he likes the soldier just as much."

Liberty must have told him about Chad already.

"I'm sure the soldier will spoil him rotten." Chad's desire for a dog couldn't be any different from hers and Elias's when they'd wanted a dog and their parents got them their first puppy one Christmas. She'd been ten, and they'd spoiled the rottweiler.

"You and that soldier came with a high recommendation from Liberty." The man shared the dog's short history and regimen from what he'd learned about the dog over the three months he'd had him.

"He's my eleventh dog since I left combat." Tom squatted to rub behind Dusty's ears. "I got a therapy dog when I returned and fell in love with dogs. I've had one ever since. So, when Liberty told me Dusty is going to a soldier's home, I had no doubt he'd be in the right hands—and by *he*, I mean both my Dusty and your soldier."

Your soldier. That sounded nice. "Thank you for your service." Tessa laid her hand on the man's shoulder. "My dad and brother both served. I guess I'm the finicky one who didn't serve my country."

Having secured her promise to bring Chad and Dusty to visit, the old man walked her and Dusty to the car, and her chest squeezed as the man kissed his dog goodbye. Only three months, and he'd bonded with the dog so much.

"Are you thinking of getting another?"

He nodded. "Only if it's an oldie like me."

The ache stayed as the dog whimpered during Tessa's drive home. Maybe she'd made a mistake assuming Chad would love the dog as much as Tom did.

At almost seven fifteen, she walked into the house. Chad and Mom were sitting at the dining table while Mom had her breakfast before heading to work. They turned at her footsteps and the dog's clicky nails on the polished floors.

Mom arched a brow, a soft smile lighting her face.

"Good morning." Tessa smiled at Chad, who was frowning at Dusty.

"Who's this?" Chad walked toward them, knelt in front of the dog, and stroked his furry back, then rubbed behind his ear. The dog wagged his tail and moved to Chad, sliding his tongue on Chad's jaw.

"Hey." His voice was so tender, his grin so wide.

"This is Dusty."

"He seems to like you, Chad." Mom walked over, crouching to pet the dog, then patting Chad's shoulder. With a wink, she kissed Tessa's cheek and scooted away.

Chad probably hadn't noticed her leave as he crooned to the collie. "Dusty, you don't look like Dusty."

Dusty leaned into Chad's hand, and Tessa's heart squeezed at the way the dog was nestling into him as if they knew each other.

"You seem like a fine dog."

She could barely contain a squeal. "He's more than just a fine dog—he's *your* dog."

Chad's brows drew together as he looked at her, then Dusty.

Bouncing as her excitement burst loose, Tessa clapped. "I got him for you!"

"You did?" He sucked in a gasp. His head jerked up, and his eyes focused on hers. "How?"

She moved to kneel on Dusty's other side. "You've always wanted a dog. Don't you think it's high time you had one?"

His expression softened, and a tender glow lit his green eyes as they studied her. "This..." He swallowed. His low voice sounded thick as the whisper caught in his throat. "This is the best present anyone has ever given me."

And she'd been blessed to be the one to give him his first special present. She winked then as Chad's attention returned to the dog and she lifted her head thanking God for Chad. And for the dog he would cherish.

CHAPTER 16

Just after four p.m. on August 5, Tessa met with her volunteers in the church lobby to discuss their gifts-for-troops strategy. The smell of cookies permeated the lobby as she greeted her helpers and answered their questions regarding the gift-packing day—questions she would be covering in the meeting, but some people were always ahead of schedule. She almost doubled her group of volunteers compared to the nine she'd had last year.

Nearby, Dusty sat still on the carpet at Chad's feet. With the attention Chad had given him since he'd become part of their home, the dog had bonded with his new master. Chad handed out flyers to people who went through the line for cookies and lemonade on their way to their seats. Some of them picked up the volunteer forms to fill in and commit to specific tasks in planning for the packing day. Chad had not only helped bake the cookies but also suggested printing out the flyers rather than emailing information.

"Some people don't check their emails." He'd shrugged. "I haven't been active at checking my email since I came to Pleasant View."

When everyone settled in the folding chairs, chatter died down, and Tessa addressed the group. She smiled at all the kind faces staring at her—faces including Chad's who had joined the group and claimed the lone chair in the back row. "I wouldn't entertain the idea of expanding this ministry without your support."

As she continued to share her vision of the ministry, she sensed Chad's gaze on her, and without permission from her brain, her gaze wandered to the back seat. His soft smile sent warm tingles through her body.

"As I was saying..." What was she saying? She rubbed at her forehead as if her brain would do her any justice. "The packing day." Right, she needed to talk about packing. She knew the date by heart, but now her brain was fuzzy, thanks to Chad. "I'll get back to you about the exact date."

"It's the tenth!" someone shouted as they lifted Chad's printout.

Right. Tessa usually relied on Quinn, the pastor's brother-in-law, to help her deliver the packages to the post office. There'd be too many boxes for her to carry by herself.

"Until then, these are things you can tell people when they ask how they can help...." She explained their need for space in reference to the shipment they'd deliver to the church on September 10, on their packing day, three days after Chad's race. She pointed out the need for donations to ship the packages, the cost of each package, and their opportunity to pray for the men and women who daily put their lives in harm's way. "So... does anyone have any questions?"

A silence passed as people looked at each other before clapping erupted from the back.

Chad. Dusty barked. Tessa's neck heated as the group clapped for her.

Several minutes later, everyone helped fold the chairs and return them to the closet.

Dusty got lots of attention from the crowd admiring his blue eyes, but he seemed to shy away from unsolicited touches as strangers tried to pet him. Interesting that he'd not shied from Tessa the day she'd picked him up. He'd also let Chad pet him when they'd met. Could it be that, with Chad's unyielding attention, Dusty didn't need anyone else? The border collie moved between Chad's legs, clearly not interested in making new friends.

Colleen, their music director, cornered Tessa. "I wanted to thank you for this service—um, you probably remember my granddaughter served a term overseas?" Colleen patted her white hair, ruffling up its feathery pink tips. "This is going to be a great event, and you've surely got together an enthusiastic crowd. But we should plan food for the packing party just so the day has a real festive atmosphere and people come back next year."

They didn't need to turn the day into a food fest. Tessa needed to tone down Colleen's enthusiasm. "We'll have a lot of packages coming in, so we won't have much space or time for planning. So it's better that—"

"We can just do a potluck."

Chad lifted his hand and winked at the woman. "I'm sure a restaurant could cater and bring food here."

Did he think Tessa kept a stash of cash for this occasion? They'd need every penny donated to go toward shipping the many packages this year. The church members brought nonfood items throughout the year, and now they had that large shipment from a generous donor.

Between Bryce and Eric, Tessa could have a building by now. Bryce had money, and Eric owned most of the buildings in town or at least supported the owners to stay in business. However, he had a ton of organizations to support.

Chad said goodbye to his and Dusty's new fans, and Tessa waved and embraced some women who walked over to say goodbye. "You and Dusty are quite popular."

His smile was sweet and warm. "Dusty and I weren't the one giving speeches while everyone was listening to us."

"Sorry, I'm late." The male voice caused them to turn and Dusty to bark.

"Quinn, you are really late." Tessa hadn't expected the pastor's brother-in-law to show since he'd not marked on the shared spreadsheet that he'd be at the meeting.

He leaned in to kiss her cheek, his golden hair tickling her forehead. "Your hair looks different. It's nice."

"Oh." She touched the hair she'd left free and draped over her blouse as opposed to her usual ponytail.

Quinn stuck his hand out to Chad. "I don't think we've met before. I'm Quinn."

"I forgot everyone knows everyone here." Chad stood military stiff as he took Quinn's offered hand. "I'm Chad."

"I usually help Tessa to take the packages...." While Quinn spoke with more enthusiasm than usual, he almost made it sound like he'd talked her into starting the packages-for-soldiers ministry.

Chad lowered himself to pet Dusty, clearly bored when he straightened and eyed the door as if indicating he was ready to leave.

"Tessa and I go way back to junior high when we played trumpet in the band."

"You played the trumpet?" Chad cocked his head and arched a quizzical brow.

"Not good enough to talk about it." That was the one time she'd quit before finishing what she started.

"Anyway, Tessa is a very wonderful person."

"I know." Chad's jaw twitched, but Quinn didn't seem to notice.

"So what did I miss?"

"Chad was handing out some flyers. I'm not sure we have any left."

"We're out of flyers." With his tone flat, Chad addressed Quinn. "Just show up on time at the packing party. It's on the tenth."

Quinn brushed Chad off with a wave and leaned into Tessa so close she had to take a step backward. "You can always text or email me."

Quinn moved in front of her, almost blocking Chad from her, but with Chad taller than he was, Tessa could still see his grim face.

"I heard about the package, the big shipment?"

Oh dear. What was Quinn up to now? Sure, he was a friend, or at least, they'd stayed friends since he'd asked her out six months ago and she turned him down. He was handsome and kind, a genuinely good man, but she'd had feelings for Chad even before she'd met him in person.

"Have you figured out what you're going to do with all that? Do you have any updates on a building for it?"

Pastor must have shared Tessa's vision with Quinn. As she decided to ignore his questions, Quinn continued to be an encouragement, touched her shoulder, and said he'd keep praying for God's provision.

"This year, I want to do more than deliver the wrapped packages." Quinn's hands moved as he suggested his ideas to make this year's packing experience the best for the volunteers. "Next year, you'll have no idea what to do with all the volunteers and donations!"

Catching his enthusiasm, Tessa crossed her arms over her thudding heart. Was he right? Could they lease space in the next town where rent would be cheaper than Pleasant View?

Tessa looked above Quinn's golden hair to glance at Chad, but he wasn't there. Her gaze darted toward the door where he was making an exit. She cupped her hand to her mouth and called. "Chad!"

Either he didn't hear her or he ignored her on purpose.

"Anyway—"

"I'm sorry, but I need to leave." She cut off Quinn. "Chad is my date... I mean, we're dating, and I don't want him waiting in the car."

"Sorry to keep you." The light dimmed in Quinn's eyes. "You should go."

"We have to pick up his cousin at the airport." She added that detail so Quinn wouldn't think she was blowing him off. "See you on Sunday."

"Yeah." As Quinn lifted his hand to wave, the whole situation left her uneasy. She'd made two men sad today.

When she met Chad at his truck, the engine was running, and Dusty was in the back, his head peering over the console.

Tessa rubbed at the black spot on his forehead before she faced a fuming Chad, the muscles in his shoulders stiff.

"You're okay?"

He grunted and started driving.

She may have to stay home with Dusty when Chad dropped the dog off. Either that or she and Dusty could call Iris so they could get together. Chad's cousin had chosen the perfect weekend to visit since Iris was in town. She'd been in town since last week for the Stone family reunion Tessa and Chad had attended. Having Bryce and Eric there had helped Chad feel comfortable, and he'd chatted with them most of the time. While Chad visited with his cousin tomorrow, Tessa would spend time with the girls.

"I assume I'm still going with you to the airport to get your cousin?"

"Did you think I forgot our plans?"

If he intended to stay glum, he'd ruin their dinner.

She huffed and crossed her arms over her chest. "We need to talk before we get Liam."

When she met his closest family member for the first time, they didn't need this... awkwardness.

"There's nothing to talk about."

The silence stretched as he drove them home and walked Dusty to his ball and Frisbee sessions, despite the long run and bike ride they'd taken the dog on earlier that day. With the kind of attention Dusty needed, Tessa understood why the old man couldn't keep him, but he sure was an intelligent and loyal dog.

Regardless of the training Chad had instilled in Dusty, leaving him at home was better than taking him to the restaurant after the airport.

Chad was still brooding as he navigated the freeway toward the airport.

"Ready to talk to me now?"

"What do you want me to say?"

Usually cheerful, he wasn't good at hiding his tension. Although she didn't mean it, she wanted to get him to say something, anything, even though she knew why he was upset.

"If you won't talk to me, you need to pull over and let me call an Uber to get me home."

His chest rose and fell before he let out a breath, his focus steady on the road. "Who was that man?"

She doubted he even paid attention as he shook the man's hand. "You mean Quinn?"

"I don't need to know his name."

She bit her tongue against the urge to remind him to stop talking in codes. Although she felt like chuckling, she had to remember why he was jealous. His ex had cheated on him, so his overreaction made sense.

"He's the pastor's wife's brother."

"You've heard me play the harmonica several times, and you didn't think that was a good time to reveal your bass skills?"

"What Quinn failed to mention is that I quit the band after three weeks. I was terrible at it."

"Is he married?"

"His wife died."

Chad twisted his grip on the steering wheel, his forearms flexing with the tension in his body. "He probably wants to make you his next wife." Telling Chad that Quinn had asked her out before and she'd turned him down would be pointless. His jaw clenched, and he spoke through his teeth. "First Kinkaid and now Quinn."

Having an ex who cheated would be jarring, but she didn't want that looming over their relationship.

"If we're going to date..." She sighed. They *were* dating, weren't they? "You're gonna have to trust me."

"I tried that once, and where did that leave me?"

So it had to do with his ex now? "I interact with all kinds of people all the time. I'm a trainer and a physical therapist. I must interact with people. But you're the first client I've been attracted to." Mainly because their relationship didn't start out professionally. "I was attracted to you before you showed up to be my client."

"I'm not your client. Never was." He mumbled under his breath, but despite his growling, his shoulders relaxed as his chest rose and fell.

"You were never my client, huh?" she felt warm, glad that he'd felt drawn to her, just as much as she'd felt about him.

Every so often, a car drove past them, but traffic stayed light.

"I could've hired a trainer somewhere else, but I wanted to spend time with you as... more than a friend."

"I'm not your ex." Nelly had married him knowing he was a soldier who'd be traveling for work. "I'd never leave you for someone else—unless you make it clear you don't want me."

She doubted she could handle another relationship should things not work out between them.

He frowned, remaining silent and hopefully processing her words. They needed this conversation now rather than later.

"You're not the only one whose heart has been broken by someone they loved. You're not the only one with doubts."

They stayed silent the rest of the drive to the airport, so she punched his phone on the console and played one of his mom's songs from his playlist.

CHAPTER 17

Chad ground his teeth. If only he could go back in time to when Tessa addressed her volunteers and stole glances at him, then got all flustered and lost her train of thought. Everything had been going well until that guy showed up, hugged Tessa, and kissed her cheek.

Chad didn't need to be a psychologist to see that the guy's feelings ran deeper than he was letting on. The guy probably had some good insights for Tessa's packages and whatnot, but he'd been trying to impress her more than he'd been interested in the cause.

And she'd given Quinn her full attention.

But Tessa wasn't Nelly, and Chad better get his mind straight. Tessa was independent, confident, and loved him. Could be because he was older now, but this time, he could tell Tessa had everything he needed in a friend, lover, and lifetime partner.

She didn't deserve to have him panicked because of lingering insecurities. If only he could rewind the clock! When Quinn introduced himself, Chad could've said he was Tessa's boyfriend and put an end to the guy's agenda. But timing was never Chad's thing, and he lived for regrets. Regrets for a failed marriage. Regrets for treating Tessa like Nelly. Regrets and guilt for losing his men on a routine mission.

Ugh. How was he going to endure dinner with Liam, Bettina, and Tessa while he was all jumbled up?

Especially now that Liam was getting chatty on their drive from the airport.

Tessa had volunteered to sit in the back, leaving the front seat for Liam, but Chad's cousin must have picked up on Chad's pensiveness because he twisted in his seat to jabber with her.

In the year since Chad had seen Liam, a lot had changed for his cousin, who was Tessa's age. He'd had a girlfriend, but if that relationship had ended, he could be using this opportunity to secure a date with Tessa.

Chad's jaw stiffened. Daylight was vanishing, his headlights now illuminating the road, and wildlife becoming more of a hazard. So he tried to concentrate on driving as Tessa boasted about all the fun things Pleasant View had to offer.

"I have one weekend to squeeze in all that fun." Liam tinkered with the collar of his white polo. A polo and jeans was casual at its best for him. As a detective, he wore dress suits and kept his dark hair parted neatly to the side. He would've made a good bodyguard or any career that called for dressing up.

"I don't see a ring on your finger."

Whoa. Liam's words had Chad swerving and slamming on his brakes to avoid rear-ending the car ahead.

"Wow, you want me to drive?"

"I got it." He didn't intend to be curt. Not that Liam paid any attention. He was already back to facing Tessa.

If his cousin wanted to tick Chad off, it was working. Chad white-knuckled his grip on the leather steering wheel. No doubt by the time they met Bettina at the steak house, Liam's neck would be ready to fall off from his constant craning to speak to Tessa.

"Besides entertaining my boring cousin this summer"—humor tinted Liam's tone—"what else have you been up to?"

"Training. Not entertaining." Great. With his voice so gruff, Chad sounded like a protective boyfriend, and he'd acted like a child who needed all the attention. Who could blame him? He never got the attention a child should get from both parents, and now Tessa was paying for it.

Apparently, their heart-to-heart on their way to the airport hadn't registered.

Tessa was selfless and cared for him. But how was he supposed to move past those roiling emotions, all that doubt, insecurity, and fear?

He tried to keep it under control when they met Bettina at the steak house on Main Street. He'd wanted to take Tessa here last night, but she didn't want him wasting money at either of the two high-end restaurants in town. Since she didn't want to go there just the two of them, tonight was as good as any while his cousin visited.

The hostess showed their party to a middle table, the tables around them occupied, and the room abuzz with soft chatter and soothing background music.

"Liam." Bettina closed her menu and set it down. Great, unlike her first reaction to Chad, she was warm toward his cousin. "I see a resemblance between you and Chad. Those eyes."

Liam laughed and batted his eyelashes. "Seems the eyes are what people notice first whenever we're together. We got our greens from our moms."

Their server arrived with their drinks and took their orders. All of them ordered steak with different sides, except Tessa. Seated next to Bettina and across from Chad, Tessa ordered grilled chicken. He shuffled his feet, tempted to step on her foot just to interact with her secretly, but they weren't at that point of playfulness now.

Despite conversations around them, their table seemed the loudest, ringing with Bettina's and Tessa's laughter. Since when did Liam become the fun guy?

The ladies asked about their childhood, and Liam obliged by sharing the mischief the three of them had gotten into. "Mud racing with tractors…"

Chad tried to fake smiles for everyone's sake mostly when Tessa glanced at him and covered her mouth, pausing from her laughter. A soft glow tinted her face beneath the ambient lighting, and an electric current crackled between them before she looked away when she reached for her water. He needed to apologize for his tantrum if he got a moment with her any time soon.

Just before nine, they returned home, and despite Chad's earlier plans for sleeping arrangements, Tessa and Bettina pleaded with Chad to stay in the main house.

"I already set my bed in the gym." The air mattress he'd bought two days ago.

He and Liam said good night to Tessa and Bettina when they climbed from Chad's truck and the ladies stepped out of Bettina's black Forte.

Tessa looked stunning beneath the porch lights that illuminated her summer dress, and he willed his tongue to speak to her and summon her for a private chat. But that wasn't going to happen, not when Liam was visiting and Bettina was standing right there, questions narrowing her graying brows.

Chad lifted his hand to Tessa, who so happened to be gripping the straps of her handbag, probably nervous.

"'Night." Her word was a whisper. Her gaze drifted to Liam who was retrieving his bag from the truck. "Good night, Liam."

Liam responded, and Bettina wished both of them a good night with a promise of a hearty breakfast in honor of Liam's visit.

With the moon lighting their path, Liam rolled his bag as Chad walked with him to the cabin. The lights illuminated the cabin blinds. Chad had kept the room lit so Dusty didn't get scared.

The moment they opened the door, Dusty barked, and Chad moved to the kennel he'd put in the place. He unlatched the kennel, and Dusty bounded to Chad's lap. "Did you miss me?"

He rubbed the back of his ears, and Dusty smeared his cheek with a wet tongue. Chad's heart melted.

What a loyal friend and a joy to have around! Thanks to Tessa, Liberty, and a stranger willing to part with him. But his gratitude remained with Tessa who'd thought of him.

"Who's this?" Liam let go of his bag and lowered himself to pet Dusty. Not one for belly rubs, Dusty walked away from Chad's lap.

"I got him last week." Chad's muscles loosened as he shared how Tessa gifted him with the border collie.

"You finally have a dog back." Liam stood. "Not a German shepherd, but hey!"

"It's good to have a different breed. I'm not trying to replace my first dog." After several days with Dusty, Chad wouldn't ask for a better dog.

"Tessa is something else, eh?"

Chad stiffened at Liam's fond tone. Grinding his teeth again, he stood. Dusty needed a walk after all, now that he was scratching the back door.

"I'll let you change. Dusty and I will meet you on the porch in a few."

Chad retrieved some dog treats from the makeshift kitchen, and the dog all but leaped for his hand.

"Let's go and eat outside." He pointed toward the door, and the dog darted toward the back door. Chad's research about the border collies had paid off. With their extreme intelligence, they needed boundaries and were easy to train as long as they had attention. Chad had taught Dusty to flip and turn. Jump and twist. He'd had a lot to teach the dog, rooted from years of wanting a dog he couldn't have.

After feeding Dusty his treats, Chad took the dog to relieve himself. He then picked up the potty and tossed it in the bear-proof trash can in the clearing he'd designated for the dog.

Fresh air whispered through the trees, crickets chirped, and the moon offered silvery light. Chad reached for one of the rubber balls with flashing strobe lights from the toy bin.

Dusty panted as he fetched the ball Chad tossed for him. After several back and forth, Chad put an end to the fun. "All right, bud. It's late for this game."

He returned inside to wash his hands. Liam had already changed into shorts and a white undershirt. So they headed to the porch to catch up. They sat on the wicker chairs, and Dusty stretched out at Chad's feet, the creek rippling under them.

"Man, I'm so relieved you finished your term without getting blown up." Liam's voice held the concern that came with his birth order as the bigger brother. He'd always had a protective nature, even though Chad was older.

"It's unfortunate that others got blown up." Chad rubbed his damp palms together and concentrated on Dusty's breaths panting at his feet. "It's not fair."

"I see unfairness every day." Liam blew out a long low breath and drummed his fingers against his thighs. "Unresolved cases of missing or dead people whose murderers are still on the loose somewhere... Talk about unfair..."

Then Liam scrubbed a hand over his face as if rubbing away grim thoughts. "Why don't we talk about why you never called me while you were overseas?"

Chad hadn't thought of staying in touch. "You have enough to deal with." Tessa had dominated his free time that last year in deployment. "You didn't call me either."

Liam leaned back in the chair, the moon silhouetting his frame. "I always assumed you might be off somewhere blowing up something."

That brought to mind the years they'd blown up all sorts of things. "Remember that time we blew up the shed?"

"The one time I listened to you and Dylan." Liam's lips twisted with his mirthless laugh. "You brought excitement to our family."

Chad grimaced at the whips that they'd earned for the act. "Not when you paid the consequences."

"Blowing up that shed was the best thing we did."

Their dad would take them to the shed and whip them for any little mistake. One day, Chad conjured up the idea of burning the structure. Dylan's eyes had lit up, and he'd known where to find the dynamite. The neighbors had called the firefighters when the trees caught fire.

"I'm surprised none of us became firefighters." Chad ran a hand through his hair.

"Apparently, we had to take after the old man. Except for Dylan, who decided to take the wrong end of things."

Their dad had been a former military man, turned to crooked dealings, then carried that with him as a police officer.

"We all took a portion of him. Me taking on the old man's military background, you joining the police force, and Dylan delving into the shady dealings or whatever he's doing now. Have you heard from him lately?"

"He's somewhere in the Caribbean. As soon as I nail his location, I'll take a two-month leave and bring him home."

Liam would execute his plan to talk his brother out of his life of crime, and Chad admired him for not giving up. "If I can be of any help, just let me know."

"If we need to blow up anything, I know just the man."

They talked about life in general before Liam asked how Chad felt about Tessa. Not wanting his cousin to go after Tessa, Chad had to be forthcoming. "I like her, but you know my history with marriage."

"So Nelly cheated and left you, doesn't mean your fate is sealed." Liam clamped a hand on Chad's shoulder. "I can tell Tessa likes you."

Said the guy who'd spent the entire evening impressing Chad's girl. "And how would you know that?"

"You weren't good at hiding your reaction on the drive from the airport. With the lasers you were shooting at me, I was a few seconds from being shoved through the window! I had a blast testing your patience by conjuring up conversation with Tessa."

Chad laughed, remembering the drive. "I was already mad before we picked you up." He told Liam about his tantrum after meeting Quinn.

"I don't remember you being angry at me when I laughed with Nelly. You're totally in love with this girl."

That was just the problem. Chad's feelings for Tessa went deeper. Maybe because he was older and wiser than he'd been when he married Nelly. Maybe because he'd gotten to know Tessa in ways he'd never known his ex. Now he could tell good from bad. But he wasn't ready to venture into the unknown. Time to bug out of this conversation. "What about you and your girlfriend?"

"We're on and off, but... I don't know."

Chad couldn't blame Liam for his doubts. Not after the home his cousin was raised in.

The sky grew darker, and the moon rose higher. The crickets chirping, the tree toads croaking, and Dusty snoring masked the silence while Chad and Liam lost themselves in their thoughts.

Tessa's words rang in his mind. *"I'm not your ex."*

Meaning he'd have to trust her.

"You're not the only one whose heart has been broken by someone they loved. You're not the only one with doubts."

Was she having doubts about him? What kind of doubts and why? They'd had a good time at the lake as they ended their day watching fireworks. The most romantic date he'd ever planned, and he'd felt so safe and secure in her presence. With just the two of them basking in the wedding venue's picturesque scenery, he'd imagined them exchanging vows there someday.

He'd felt terrible for his breakdown during the fireworks. After telling Tessa about the loss of his men, it had been easier to talk to Elias. Elias encouraged him to try to stay active, doing fun things. Spending time with Tessa was the main fun thing Chad had going, and planning things for the two of them was even more fun.

He'd never gone out of his way to plan a romantic outing, but when he'd looked up romantic places within fifty miles, the wedding venue showed in the results. They didn't do private parties. Still, he'd spoken to the owner about the possibility of marrying there someday. Then Chad presented a request for a one-day tour and food service. He'd added an amount the woman couldn't refuse.

It wasn't fair of him to assume Tessa would fall for anyone who swooned over her. *"You're the first client I've been attracted to.... I was attracted to you before you showed up to be my client."*

After saying good night to Liam at midnight, Chad started down the path with Dusty on his heels. The dog barked at the sound and movement swishing through the tall grass.

Whatever was moving in the grass stopped. The grass wasn't tall enough to hide a bear, mountain lion, or any fierce creature that would hurt Dusty in Chad's presence, but he still stayed alert, in case something wound up attacking the dog.

Instead of walking to the gym where he was supposed to sleep, Chad walked toward the main house. "I guess we need this pit stop, buddy."

He needed to make things right with Tessa and put his mind at ease.

Walking around the house, he went to the back and crouched to knock on the glass of Tessa's bedroom window. He'd been in the basement getting his laundry done, so he knew where her room was, although he'd never gone into it. It was probably for the best because he got unclean thoughts whenever he imagined what her bedroom looked like.

Beyond the blinds, the light turned on, so he knocked softly again, this time speaking in a hushed voice. "It's me."

The blinds moved, and the window slid open. Tessa rubbed at her eyes, her rumpled hair enticing him to run a hand through it. "You scared me."

"I'm sorry. Can we talk?"

"I'll meet you on the back porch." Her sleepy voice made him wonder if she was even upset with him. How could she be upset and sleep?

The back door slid open, and she emerged with a blanket hugged to her chest. Then she stood there, moths kissing the porch light that made her face glow.

Dusty walked toward her, already forgetting Chad was his master. He sniffed at Tessa, and she oohed over him. "You should be in bed, big boy." Unlike Dusty's rejection of Liam's pats, he stayed still as Tessa rubbed his back.

Chad shifted, almost jealous of the affection the dog was getting. But again, he didn't deserve any affection after how he'd reacted.

They sat on the deck, the cool breeze seeping through his jeans.

"I'm sorry for acting out earlier."

She spread the blanket on her legs, extended it toward him, and covered his legs too. "I know you are."

"How do you know?"

"You had a battle raging in your mind during dinner."

Man, she was good at reading his mind. Dusty settled on Tessa's other side, and Chad took her warm hand in his. "I'm scared to fall in love, but I'm afraid it's too late." His heart for her was beyond his head, and it terrified him.

"Why is it too late?"

Her breath feathered soft warmth on his face. And despite the full moon and porch light behind them, it wasn't too bright to terrify him to speak his mind. "I've fallen in love with you."

He'd fallen in love months before they met in person, probably since the first letter she'd written to him. She'd appeared in his dreams often over the months of their FaceTime. In fact, he'd kissed her way before they shared their first kiss. "I fear you might leave me for someone better."

She lifted their entwined hands and put Chad's on her heart. Something she'd done before. Her heart thrummed against his palm. "Can you feel that?"

His heart was no different. "Yes."

"It only beats for you. Whenever I think of you and when I'm around you."

"Me too." He pressed her hand to his heart.

"I'm not leaving you. I love you."

"You love me?" Just a rhetorical question, really. He knew she loved him, and she'd confessed as much more than once.

"I'm no saint, but why do you think I canceled my clients this summer just so I can focus on you alone?"

She still took on spontaneous clients like the boy with back pain. He couldn't remember why she'd left to go and help an older woman who'd called her.

"Because you love me." He kissed the back of her fingers one at a time before setting their hands on his lap.

"Dinner was good by the way," she said out of the blue. "Thank you."

"Any time."

"I just... I feel you've been blowing a lot of money." She hesitated, quietly letting out a breath. "I know you love me, but it's not like you're rich or anything. I don't want you going into debt for me."

Her concern compelled him to tell her he wasn't in debt and didn't intend to get into debt. "I'm not filthy rich, but my mom left me an inheritance. I have her music royalties. Her merch, investments in the cosmetic and film production company she inherited from her last spouse—who also included me in his will. I also get income from some beach rental properties. I've got a good accountant and people in place, managers I don't need to talk to since everything's still organized and run by corporations." He tugged at his hair. "I vaguely remember him, except for his warm brown eyes. I met him three times when he came while Mom was home from her tours. She was half his age, but he loved her enough to put her name and mine in his will."

By the time Chad was approached by a lawyer about his inheritance, he'd matured and was already dedicated to serving his country, rather than blowing up money. It had been held in trust for him until he turned twenty-one.

"When I got married, I didn't reveal everything to my wife, but I needed to build trust in my bride." His chest tightened. Maybe he'd had trust issues all along if he'd gone into marriage without trusting Nelly. Sure, she'd betrayed him later, but he'd betrayed her by expecting it all along. "Two of my buddies had been divorced, and their ex-wives emptied their bank accounts when they walked away."

Tessa looked up to the sky where stars shimmered. "So your ex didn't know you were rich?"

"No."

"But you just told me."

He was older now, and he trusted her. Snuggling her closer to him, he savored the warmth that seeped through her pajama shirt. "That should tell you something."

"Yes," she whispered, turning to look up into his eyes. Man, she was beautiful, so beautiful he ached. He'd fallen in love, and there was no turning back. He lowered his chin until his lips brushed hers tenderly as feelings spiraled inside of him.

She kissed him back, a soft kiss, and spoke over his lips. "That being said, will you be my date next week to a stranger's wedding?"

He chuckled since they'd already had this conversation and met Gavin, the groom, at the Stone reunion last weekend as well as when he'd showed them around some properties for her warehouse. The Stone reunion was for family, but they seemed to have friends who'd become part of the family like Eric had said when Chad asked.

Chad had told Eric and Bryce he'd show up at the wedding when they discussed another opportunity for Chad to meet the rest of their friends and family.

"I'm the one supposed to ask you for a date, but I'd be honored to be yours."

"That's solved."

"Does that mean I have to dress up?" He knew and didn't intend to go overboard, but...

"You can show up in your exercise shorts. I think that should be okay."

Her humor offered the assurance he needed to conquer the day's stress.

He sensed it when he fell asleep on the air mattress and woke up next to Dusty with the bright morning sun streaming through the gym windows.

CHAPTER 18

The crisp smell after rain wafted through the massive tent canopy where Tessa and the others retreated for Gavin's wedding. Long tables with pink sateen runners were set along the flowing fabric "walls." Muted whispers about the rain intruding on the couple's big day, accompanied the chairs clattering while immaculately dressed guests found their seats at the tables under the shelter. Some ladies unrolled the damask napkins to dry their faces, their dates hovering and offering advice. The mothers of the bride and groom pinned back an entryway, and the fathers edged tables aside, creating an aisle for the bride's grand entrance while the groomsmen carried the now-drippy rose-covered arbor beneath the tent's central crystal chandelier. Its golden light gleamed on the sparkling white dance floor as the minister joined them.

A soft breeze swayed the billowing silk drapes, their backdrop shielding all from the now-gentle drizzle pattering against the canvas in rhythm when the soft background music started playing.

Tessa touched her wet bare shoulders, rubbing them up and down. Even with Chad's hand offering extra warmth on her lower back, the coolness in the open-air tent seeped through her damp cream-colored dress.

The rain couldn't have had worse timing. The clouds had been dark when the procession began with the mothers of the bride and groom taking their seats in the front row. Then the groom, groomsmen and bridesmaids, and best man and matron of honor had made their way to the altar under the floral-covered arbor.

While the guests waited for the bride's grand entrance, the first drops fell and became a torrential rain. After the unexpected downpour had everyone retreating for the tent, Tessa vowed she'd use a tent if she were to have an outdoor wedding. She'd had fantasies of her wedding ever since Chad took her to the scenic venue on their date.

Despite his revelation of his wealth, she'd want to keep things simple, as opposed to Gavin's luxury wedding. Billowing drapes, cascading floral installations, chandeliers, and classic centerpieces adorned a tent fit for royalty.

"Will it be offensive if I stay in my undershirt?" Chad's breath whispered warmth into her ear. His crisp white buttoned shirt made his green eyes pop.

She rolled her eyes. "You'll do no such a thing."

Amusement teased his handsome face as he moved his hand from her back. Tingles shot through her body when he ran his warm hand up and down her arm. "You're cold, and I don't have a jacket to give you."

"I'll be fine." Just looking at him warmed her. A smile lifted her cheeks. How good God was! How deeply He'd blessed her by bringing Chad into her life! Tessa had always been happy, but she found herself smiling even more lately.

"Have I already told you you're the most beautiful woman in the world?"

"More than once. Yes." Her cheeks stretched as her heart warmed. He told her every so often. "And you're the most handsome man in the world too." In her eyes. Well, she'd never spent as much time with any man as she'd spent with Chad. Plus, he was the first man who'd taken her on thoughtfully romantic dates.

A hand tapped her lap under the table, and seated to Tessa's left, Iris mouthed, "Wow." Her silver earrings danced on her cheek when she shook her head, smiling and keeping her gaze on the classic centerpiece before them.

Tessa slapped Iris's hand beneath the table. To Iris's left sat her two sisters while the rest of their family occupied the next table.

The bridesmaids now joined the bridal party once again at the arbor and lined up by the cascading floral installations. Bryce stood with the three men standing next to Gavin, their tailored navy suits offsetting the bridesmaids' pink gowns, the same blushing rosebud color as the table linens and their delicate bouquets. As the effect created a picturesque scene almost prettier than the planned wedding ceremony, Tessa imagined Gavin and Lucky forever looking back on this day with fond memories.

Silence settled when the background music stopped, and everyone took their seats waiting for the grand entrance. Then the wedding music started, and heads turned to the entrance. Kids' voices sounded, mostly kids Tessa knew. Liberty and Joy had taken the back seats closest to the exit, so they could whisk the kids away if they got squirmy.

Strings of Mendelssohn's "Wedding March" continued, but no one walked into the entrance. Had the rain somehow interfered with the flow of the ceremony?

Tessa had been to three weddings including Liberty's, but this was the longest time the bride had taken to emerge. The song ended and played again.

"Where's the bride?" Chad lowered himself to whisper in her ear.

Tessa squeezed his arm in response. Women needed longer to get ready than men did, so that might explain the delay. And after the rain, she'd probably needed to touch-up something.

When Tessa glanced at the bridal party, Gavin was adjusting his tie, worried crinkles evident beside his blue eyes as he narrowed his gaze at the entrance.

The man next to him—the groom's brother according to Chad who'd spent time with the guys at the bachelor party—whispered something to Gavin.

Chatter and whispers erupted as people craned from peering at the arbor to the entrance and the music faded.

Gavin's brother strode toward the side of the tent, edged aside the drape, and made his exit. Bryce was now talking to Gavin. The minister's frown deepened as his gaze switched between the groomsmen and the bridesmaids.

Soon Gavin's brother returned and whispered something. Gavin's frazzled face reddened. Then he loosened his tie and slipped through the drape with Bryce and his groomsmen.

"Oh no!" Iris's voice expressed more concern than Tessa dared admit.

"The rain must've spoiled her dress or something," Tessa said, rooting for the groom. They'd fix the delay any moment now.

After interacting with Gavin when he showed them the buildings for lease, then at the Stone reunion, she knew he was a wonderful man who deserved every happiness God could offer.

"Do you think she stood him up?" Chad's moist palm slid against hers when he entwined their fingers.

Tessa's heart ached. But surely, that wasn't the case. Chad's hold tightened around their clasped hands, and she lifted them to kiss the back of his. The last thing he needed was to witness another woman dumping a man. She shivered with selfish thoughts of how that would intensify his doubts about their relationship.

An elegantly dressed woman marched out through the back door. The minister seemed to be talking to the groom's father, a heated discussion ensuing.

Then Gavin returned, looking disheveled. He cleared his throat and announced in a crackly hoarse voice, "The wedding is off."

Then he left.

Tessa almost jumped. A sharp pain jarred in her chest.

"That's awful." Iris spoke the words Tessa felt, but Tessa could only shake her head as shocked as everyone looked.

"That stinks." Chad huffed, pulling his hand out of hers.

Everyone just sat there motionless, unsure of what to say.

Tessa slumped in her chair, deflated. She'd never had the misfortune of witnessing such an embarrassing moment.

"I can't imagine what Gavin is going through." Iris's shoulders sagged beneath the stylish straps of her one-shoulder navy-blue dress. As Tessa's most stylish friend, Iris always looked stunning.

Iris had been so excited about the wedding and helping Tessa, Joy, and Liberty choose the right outfits for the occasion. She'd even managed to talk Joy into joining them at the spa and getting their nails done last Saturday while Liam was still in town. Then Iris insisted on paying for the day's luxurious outing.

Besides her excitement, Iris believed in happily ever after, so she seemed almost as wounded as the groom. When Tessa wrapped her arms around her friend, Iris sighed. Then, as their hug ended, she wiped the moisture from her face, the eyeliner smudging her fingers.

Needing more than words to calm the doubts expressed in Chad's narrowed brows, Tessa leaned into him, pressed her cheek on his chest, and slid her arm to his back and around his waist. He draped his arm over her shoulder in return. Although tension radiated from his taut muscles, he dropped a kiss on her head.

Surely, he understood she'd never do something like that to him.

The elegant woman returned and announced the reception would go on as planned. They didn't want the food to go to waste.

Life wasn't fair sometimes, and Gavin didn't deserve to be stood up. Regardless of the unknown in her relationship, Tessa assumed that, by becoming engaged, both parties knew where their relationship stood before they invited friends and families to a wedding.

When they left that evening, Chad was pensive, and once they got home, he gave her a brief peck before wishing her good night. Tessa caught his hand as he turned to go. It was only seven, after all. "Why don't you join Mom and me for our nightly prayers?"

"That's okay." He freed his hand, edging away from her already. "Don't bother escorting me to the cabin. I just feel tired."

Slightly bothered, Tessa tried to understand what his change of attitude stemmed from. When she returned to her room, she knelt and prayed for strength for Gavin, his ex-bride, and whatever issues they had to resolve. She also prayed for Chad, for God to give him a different perspective, and for him not to determine his future by the failures around him.

With his triathlon approaching, he'd need to be mentally stable and physically fit.

AS THE TRIATHLON NEARED, Chad's adrenaline kicked up. In the two days since the gut-wrenching wedding fiasco, the whole thing had messed with his mind. But Tessa hadn't left him alone like he'd preferred when he retreated to the cabin. She'd shown up on Sunday morning as if unaware of his mood the night before. She'd brought a tray of food, set it and a note on the kitchen table, and left.

He closed his eyes, seeing the note again:

> Hi, sweetie,
> I thank God for you and pray for you every day.
> You're the best thing that's happened to me in a long time.
> I love you.
> Tessa.

Her dear handwriting brought back the earlier letters they'd written during his deployment. He'd then showered and changed into jeans and a polo, his church attire for the day. With Dusty in tow, he'd carried his tray to the main house and joined Tessa and Bettina for breakfast.

Chad had only hung out with Gavin a few times. When he showed Chad and Tessa the buildings for rent, twice at the reunion, and then during the bachelor party Bryce threw.

Chad had declined that invitation. But, determined to involve Chad in their lives and friendships, Eric and Bryce didn't let him off the hook.

Twice Chad had met them for golf, technically praying as they golfed. When was that a thing? Didn't you have to pray while kneeling and closing your eyes? The guys seemed to think you could bike, golf, or run while praying. And somehow, that drew God closer into Chad's thoughts and life—as if he were sharing his sports and everyday experiences with God as he prayed.

Eric shared his fear of his wife's cancer returning, and Bryce talked about his fear of his marriage failing like his parents' marriage had. Their transparency about their struggles and the urgency to pray reminded Chad that everyone had a problem in one form or another and he wasn't alone with fears and regrets.

Because of the two men—or at least, Chad assumed they were the reason—he was up early praying for Gavin this Monday morning while stretching and doing the muscle strengthening exercises Tessa insisted he did every day.

Still, the pain and shock in Gavin's eyes haunted Chad. At least, Chad had been married by the justice of the peace. Not that Nelly would've left him at the altar, but if she had, having her do it at a simple justice-of-the-peace ceremony would've been less humiliating than in front of an audience.

The morning air smelled fresh, and Dusty sat surprisingly still, watching without barking at the buck in the distance. The intelligent dog had learned Chad's expectations in such a short time. As long as Dusty was fed and got attention, he seemed as content as could be.

Just before six thirty, Chad walked back to the cabin. His phone chimed a text seconds later as Tessa checked in to see if he was ready for the quinoa breakfast. His lips quirked, and his fingers twitched to text that he'd *never* be ready for quinoa and birdseed wasn't his favorite meal. But he needed something light, protein-packed, and nutritious. So he huffed and texted the response his trainer deserved.

Chad: Good thing you know a way to cook odd foods and make them tasty. Always grateful for light meals before running!

So true. Especially since this morning they were driving to a more challenging trail for their twenty-six-mile run. He would run that distance in the Ironman in less than three weeks.

Shortly later, he climbed the terrain with Tessa on one side and Dusty on his other. Morning sun radiated through the tall trees, shimmering as it burned away last night's dew. The peaceful trail was perfect for their run.

Halfway into the run, his body was starting to drag, his mind telling him he was done. But he was far from done and had to finish if he intended to succeed through the big day.

"Run in such a way as to get the prize..." The words he read often from the Bible rang in his mind. The verses Tessa had read to him the first time she'd shared her devotions with him. With all his training this summer, he couldn't imagine better verses to cling to than 1Corinthians 9:24–27.

His chest burned, and he steadied his breathing. Why had Tessa chosen this strenuous trail? It didn't make sense. The hills and obstacles here were far harder than on the trail they'd run for the race.

"I do not run like someone running aimlessly." He forced his feet to go faster.

"If we can finish this trail without any problems, the trail on the Ironman should be a piece of cake." Tessa spoke breathlessly as she jumped over a jutted root, and Chad did the same. She continued talking him through the things he needed to improve, based on her observations while they'd run the trail in Boulder a few weeks ago—the same trail for the race, which was probably closed off now in preparation for the triathlon.

"See that hill?" She nodded up ahead of them.

Chad glanced at the hill, bigger than the one on the Ironman trail he'd struggled to run. Three-quarters through that trail, his legs had hurt badly, and his body gave up the fight.

"What about that hill?" He blew out air, eager to know how to approach the looming giant.

"Don't slow down. Take gravity and find your pace. Even if your legs start to hurt, don't slow down until we attack that hill."

"Good thing I still have my pace." So did Dusty, who'd proven himself to be a work dog who rarely got burned out.

After attacking the hill while maintaining their pace, Tessa kept running and put the valve in her mouth, which dangled from her hydration pack. She reminded Chad to take a drink from the hydration pack on his back.

"I'm going to run ahead of you, and when you get ready to pass me," she said as they approached another hill, "kick up the speed slightly and try to pace yourself."

Her stride lengthened, and she ran faster. Chad kept his pace, trying not to get distracted by Tessa's swaying hips as she attacked the hill like she was having fun.

He lengthened his stride and tried to remember her words when they'd run last time—*"Running is a mental competition."*

In no time, he passed Tessa with Dusty right at his heels.

"Good job, honey!" she shouted.

Seriously, she was better at this than he was. So he called over his shoulder, "Why aren't you doing the race with me?"

"I'm not a good swimmer, remember?"

Whatever minutes she lost at swimming, she could catch up with running and biking. "I'm sure you could pull it off."

"Someone has to cheer for you!"

As they continued attacking one hill after another, Chad had to ask if she wanted him to get hurt. "This trail is three times worse than the other."

"It doesn't hurt to be over prepared. Makes the real race easier." Her voice was closer, indicating she was about to catch up. "I want you to win, but it's more important that you know why you're doing this race in the first place."

Chad pushed his legs. He must be dragging. His chest burned, and his lungs were exhausted.

"Don't let me pass you." Tessa spoke from behind. "Keep your eyes on the finish line. We're almost there...."

The finish line sounded good.

"And when you remember why you're doing the Ironman, that'll enable you to finish or give up."

Why was he doing the triathlon? He had a different response to that question now. It had all been for him and spending time with Tessa. But, as he marveled through the lives lost, it became clear that doing something challenging, enduring, and painful was possible when doing it in remembrance. And just the memory of the lost lives had him ignore the pain in his legs as he ran further and faster... not caring that his legs and lungs were worn out or his mind was spinning. With a surge of energy, he pushed himself all the way to the finish line.

Panting, Chad wiped sweat from his face. He could feel Dusty's breathing and crouched to pat him.

Tessa beamed when she caught up, her face glistened, and he swiped at his sweat again.

"You did it!"

All sorts of emotion rolled through him. Caught between exhilaration and exhaustion, heat and energy, he felt his chest swell and his throat close up in admiration of this beautiful and supportive woman he didn't deserve. He moved to her, pulled her into his arms, and wrapped her in an embrace. He wanted to yank the hydration pack blocking his arms from roaming on her back.

With his heart so full, it surged in its beats against her. No doubt God loved and cared for him since He'd brought this selfless woman into his life.

Chad still wasn't sure he could pull off the big day. All he'd done today was run, but come the triathlon, he had to swim and bike and then run the twenty-six miles. Winning wasn't even on his radar, but for now, he'd cherish this moment with the woman who'd come to be the love of his life.

CHAPTER 19

Chad sipped vitamin water as he sat across from Elias in the food court. Two other guys occupied some of the many empty chairs and tables around them. Tessa's brother squinted, straining to read the screenshot message on Chad's phone—an email that required counsel and guidance from Tessa's big brother.

After two missed calls from an unknown number, Chad received an email from the captain of the ordinance group he'd been a part of. The captain requested Chad access his military account by using a one-time password to read the message they'd sent.

They needed him to fill in for the IED (Improvised Explosive Device) division training. The planned instructor had had an emergency surgery and wouldn't be up and ready to train students in the division that was starting in three weeks.

Not only had Chad trained students in the division before, but IED also held a soft spot for him. That, and he still needed closure somehow. Still, he didn't feel capable of making the right decision at the moment.

Today being his recovery day, he'd called Elias to discuss more than the email.

"What are you gonna do?" Elias slid the phone back to Chad and then reached for his cup of soda.

"My only hesitation is leaving Tessa for six weeks. Otherwise, the class is easy since the students have been through several classes and are eager for the IED specialist division class." He shrugged, then grabbed the back of his neck, the taut muscles hurting with the stress. "It's not like I've figured out a job to do yet."

He wanted to stay in Pleasant View and help Tessa run her soldier ministry while she pursued her training and therapy career. Once her ministry was up and running, he'd look for a job, perhaps at the fire station or somewhere that could use his engineering and electrical skills.

"We spent the last hour shopping for a ring for my sister." Elias pulled Chad out of his thoughts.

Chad kneaded his neck harder. Although they'd discovered an outstanding ring... "I'm still not sure I'll get the right size." He'd studied and held her fingers and assumed he could tell her size. That was still a gamble. Just like he'd be gambling trying to propose while considering leaving for six weeks.

"You're also leasing two buildings in town for her businesses." Elias continued ticking off all the things Tessa would need to have her business up and running. Employees, supplies, and start-up costs.

"You've already talked to a couple of suppliers." Both in Denver with outstanding reviews. "You said they'd contact her to choose the equipment she needs. Then they will deliver and set up the gym whenever Tessa's ready, right?"

"Right."

Last week during his two recovery days, Chad had told Tessa he had things to do, and since he'd previously gone to meet with Eric and Bryce, then to visit Elias and the vets at Wounded Warrior, Tessa had wished him a good time assuming he was doing something with one of them. When he'd spoken to Gavin, Chad had learned he was a property investor but also managed various properties in town.

Since Tessa had favored the vacant boutique due to its location, Gavin, who owned the building, was willing to have it remodeled to suit her needs to be used as a packaging center. Thankfully, another vacant space had opened up on the same street and offered two sections she could use as a gym-slash-therapy center if she decided to pursue that profession.

Chad would send extra money to her Venmo and PayPal accounts as soon as the triathlon was over. He'd underpaid her for training him since she kept arguing against him paying at all.

"Back to the email." He tipped his chin to his phone on the table, partially regretting having left his forwarding address and phone contact when he'd finished service.

"You and I know that, at the end of the day, deep down you have the answer." Elias's gaze drifted to the pink banner stringing photos of ice cream cones across the food court. "Just pray for clarity."

Chad huffed. "Clarity is one thing, but what will Tessa think?"

"It's only six weeks." Elias crossed his arms over his chest. "Mom is the one you should worry about. Dad's deployment strained my parents' marriage, and she's so worried about Tessa going through what she endured."

"Bettina…" Chad grabbed his neck again. "Winning her over hasn't been easy—I wouldn't even say I've managed it yet, but I would say we've settled into a truce. I'd sure hate to wreck that. She's something else, you know? I've missed having a mom, but being around her now… Well, it almost feels like I have a mom again."

Elias nodded and sipped his soda. "Just don't go dying on them now." He wagged a finger, seemingly trying hard for a teasing tone even as his dark eyes dulled and his thin lips tightened. "That will crush my little sister."

A tightness constricted Chad's chest when Elias talked about Tessa's worry in the weeks he'd gone AWOL on her.

"She thought you'd been blown up."

Chad ran a hand over his face, his stomach churning. The food court smelled like every fast food stuck together. Smoky, complex, herbal, and fruity, just like his emotions.

Reaching for his phone on the table, he trailed his thumb over the screen, ready to log in and respond with no. Yes would mean him leaving right after Tessa's packing party. But training candidates would mean him getting the closure he needed to move on.

"Don't type anything when you're emotional or conflicted."

Elias's voice pulled Chad's gaze off the phone screen. His friend smiled in understanding. "When do you want me to share the news about the house?"

Chad scratched his jaw, a grin stretching it out. Good thing Elias had his name on the property title along with Bettina and Tessa. Otherwise, they couldn't have pulled it off.

"Before the date of their monthly mortgage payment." Which was usually the sixth of the month, according to Elias.

"I'll back you up. Whatever you decide to do." Elias grinned back. "I know you love my sister."

"Thanks." It meant a lot coming from a fellow veteran. One of the times he'd gone to the veterans' hospital, Chad had told Elias about his struggle with the loss of the men on his last tour.

Elias responded the same way Tessa had, saying Chad wasn't responsible for who died in battle or anywhere else. It was God's job to determine who died and when.

Chad was coming to terms with the belief that his life and everyone's lives were in God's hands.

Following Elias's suggestion to think and pray about the looming decision, Chad responded to the captain and told him to give him less than a week to think. The captain responded by saying he had backups in case it didn't work out for Chad. In other words, they were not pushing him to commit.

The rest of the week, Chad trained and prayed, and one evening, he called and spoke to Bryce, asking him to let Eric know to pray for Chad's decision. He also asked them to keep it confidential. The last thing he needed was their wives mentioning it to Tessa.

Chad didn't want to blurt anything to Tessa yet. Still, as the deadline for his response neared, he felt more inclined to say yes.

It seemed easy to tell Tessa, but he struggled to form the words. One week before the triathlon, he texted her on his recovery day to meet him on his porch. Then he paced the small deck as he waited.

She showed up with two bags full of items, beaming. She set the bags down and pulled out a full-body wetsuit with the word *Army* on the chest. "I got you something. And"—she unfolded a gray cycling jersey with Army stamped across it and held it across herself—"I got myself a cheering shirt."

Sinking to her knees and letting the shirt drop to her lap, she rummaged in another bag and waved a treat for Dusty. "Something for you, big boy. Hope you didn't think I'd leave you out of the fun."

Dusty wagged his tail as he leaped for the treat, and her radiant smile lit Chad's heart. His chest about to explode, he scooped her up into his arms and kissed her cheek, neck, and forehead.

"Thank you for thinking about me." Not that he needed another suit since he'd bought one, but Tessa's was better. Just for him.

Not wanting to ruin her joy, he held off on telling her until he tried again two days later when they stayed in the movie theater after everyone vacated. Tessa sat tinkering with the popcorn and telling him to open his mouth while she tossed one kennel at a time for him to catch, and he gave up on the idea.

Then he tried telling her one evening after dinner with one of the veterans who used to be her dad's friend. The man had poured out his struggles to adjust to civilian life, overcoming drugs and hardship to keep a job ever since his homecoming. Chad's heart went out to the man, and Bettina and Tessa's eyes shone with tears. It wasn't a good time to dampen anyone's spirits further.

Now, the triathlon day was upon him, Saturday morning dawning with sixty degrees. Perfect for biking and running, but not so much for swimming.

The energy was high, and excitement buzzing where men and women, young and old, gathered at the reservoir. Spectators stood aside, shouting as Chad marched with a parade of fit athletes toward the lake. He didn't have to see Tessa to know that she, Dusty, Bettina, and Elias were in the crowd rooting for him.

Cameras on tripods along their path filmed their procession to the start line, and a man carrying a camera followed an interviewer who was asking athletes their inspiration to race.

Someone shoved a microphone toward Chad's face. "Sir, we're seeing the word *Army* on your wetsuit. Can you tell us about that?"

His throat closed, but he gave a curt nod. "I'm running in memory of friends I lost in battle."

"Wow." The interviewer turned to her cameraman and spoke to her audience. "That will give anyone the drive they need to complete such a grueling race. Remember that, folks, so we can cheer this guy on."

But Chad was already moving to his position for the start.

Minutes later, they were given the go to dive into the lake. Cool water sluiced over him, chilling his face, feet, and hands and leaving him grateful for the stretchy material keeping the rest of him warm as he swam. His arms cut through the lake, and his legs churned behind him, his body moving in smooth rhythm with the practiced strokes as he completed the 2.4-mile circuit in the crystal clear reservoir.

Then he emerged, following four others, as panic threatened to take over. He'd convinced himself it wasn't about winning, but finishing like a winner wouldn't hurt.

He was still one of the top five. That wasn't bad as long as he maintained his pace.

Cameramen followed him and the athletes as they ran toward the bike course. While the crowd chanted out cheers, Chad tried to focus. Ignoring his racing heart, he unzipped and started easing out of his wetsuit. Yanking off a wetsuit while running wasn't easy, but it had kept his cycling jersey and shorts dry underneath. By the time he reached the bikes lined up at the start of the cycling course, he had his wetsuit off and tossed it on the ground.

He had his pedals already facing the right direction and his shoes too, a step he'd taken to prepare before the race, which now saved him time as he slid on his shoes, strapped on his helmet, and climbed on his bike.

For the rolling 112-mile bike ride, he pedaled a pleasant course past cows grazing in pastures, the meadow grass waving on undulating hills while the Rocky Mountains offered their breathtaking backdrop. Cycling wasn't hard today. The trail wasn't as uphill as the ones Tessa had taken him to bike, but the high altitude still made it a struggle to gasp for air.

He'd undergone intense training to handle pressure, but it had been a long time since he'd been in boot camp and busted himself to pass the EOD training. So the cloudy sky was a blessing, as were the volunteers standing along the trail handing water to the athletes. Chad stopped for a fast drink before pushing himself to finish the bike race.

His chest was heaving. Hot and panting, he started the twenty-six-mile run. Man, his body was already telling him he was done before he even started!

Remembering Tessa's words during the last weeks of training, he kept a steady pace, and when he approached to pass the woman in front of him, he lengthened his stride. He'd been leaping over harder terrain during his preparation for the race. Now, the hills that had challenged him when he'd tried this course seemed to smooth out beneath his feet.

When he felt like his body had hit a wall, he reminded himself why he was running.

Compelled to lengthen his stride, he found a steady pace before passing the woman. He then passed two more people. Then three.

"Keep your eyes on the finish line." The words echoed in his mind.

"*Think like a winner.*"

"*Attack every hill in your way and don't think of your pain. Focus.*"

The word *Finish* fluttered on a red banner. What? He nearly stumbled. Was he in the lead? It couldn't be.

But the crowd squealed and shouted. Their faces beaming, they jumped and chanted his number with victorious fists while others put out their hands to high-five him, motivating him to push forward and burst through the banner with unexpected force.

Emotions exploded like a grenade in his chest. Hot and shivering, exhausted and elated, sore and exhilarated, he'd crossed the finish line. He palmed sweat from his forehead. Then, ignoring his sore legs, he craned to peer over the hundreds of heads for Tessa.

"You're the winner!" The woman with the microphone moved to him. "You broke the record time for previous races—finishing with eight hours, fifty-two minutes, and sixteen seconds. How does that feel?"

The army discipline and Tessa's rigorous training had made all the difference. The more he'd trained, the stronger and better he got.

"How do you feel?" The woman spoke into the microphone and then scooted it toward him.

"I..." He was squinting at the loud crowd. Where was Tessa?

"I feel blessed." Tears blinded him when the men he'd lost came to mind. Friends who didn't have the chance to come back to civilian life. He said a silent prayer for their loved ones he'd never met.

Someone slid a heavy medal round his neck. Ironman stamped the red lanyard with bold white letters while FINISHER engraved the medal.

"What are you going to do with the thirty thousand dollars?" The interviewer pressed the microphone his way again.

Hmm? There was money involved? Chad only wanted to finish strong, and winning wasn't the driving force.

But with the interviewer awaiting his response, the words slid smoothly from his mouth, and the idea settled as right in his heart. "I'm donating it to a veteran's hospital, Wounded Warrior Hope and Care Center." Where Elias worked.

His gaze drifted back to the crowd when the interviewer asked him something he didn't quite grasp. He wanted to see Tessa and used the opportunity the microphone offered.

"Tessa Richardson!" With so many people holding up so many signs for their loved ones, he'd be lucky to see Tessa. "You're my rock."

She emerged from the sidelines, a white banner in hand displaying bold letters in black.

YOU MADE IT, MY SOLDIER!

He moved away from the microphone and strode to her. She tossed the banner to the grass when he conquered the space between them.

In her presence, he could always block out everything around him, and at that moment, it was just him and the woman he so loved as he lifted her off the ground, swinging her and kissing her with an explosion of pent-up emotion.

Tessa pulled back, her eyes aglow. "You did it, Chad! I'm so proud of you!"

But he was shaking his head. He cupped her face between his hands. "*We* did it. I'm so grateful for *you*."

The excitement faded in her eyes, replaced by a glow lasting and tender. And his burning throat closed over as the emotions blasting through him settled and calmed with a feeling of coming home, a wholesome, secure, forever feeling. Closing his eyes, he pressed his forehead to hers and breathed her in, absorbing the true prize God had given him. "I love you, baby."

Later, when they presented the giant check, the forty-something woman who came in third and took first place in the women's division donated her share to the veterans' hospital too. She'd been training with her dad for the triathlon four years ago when he died in combat.

Chad hugged her, thanking her for her support, amazed by how he kept encountering wounded warriors or people related to an injured veteran and, now, someone else who'd lost a loved one, another soldier.

God was, indeed, in control. He put people in their lives for a reason. The men and women at Elias's workplace had taught Chad to be grateful and made him quit focusing on himself and his problems. The woman today taught him he could invest in veterans and those on active duty like Tessa did, instead of dwelling on the past. He didn't need to return to the army for closure. He didn't need to run a successful mission to atone for the one that went wrong. He could find a purpose—a fulfillment so much more than closure—right here, serving the men and women who served their country.

CHAPTER 20

Packing day couldn't have gone any better, and Tessa wanted to have a party as big, if not bigger next year. She beamed as she followed Quinn and another couple out of the post office and through the door Chad held for them.

"Thanks, honey." She slid her arm through his, then nodded toward where Quinn and the couple stood on the sidewalk by the parking lot. "Do you want to come with me to thank them?"

"I'm all good. Take your time." Chad closed the glass door and leaned in to kiss her cheek. "I'll be waiting in the truck."

The sun was high in the sky, not a bad day for a hike, but Tessa wouldn't want to go without Chad. She doubted he'd want to be anywhere near a trail, pool, or bike path for another week. Not after his long race three days ago.

Something had shifted in his attitude during the final two weeks leading to the triathlon. She'd thought he was anxious about the race, and she'd attempted to distract him with various activities. But now that the race was over and he'd won, shouldn't he be his normal lighthearted self?

He could be struggling because his win brought back memories of his colleagues. Or maybe not, since he hadn't dwelt much on that regret lately.

She shook off her curiosity, crossed to the trio of volunteers, patted Canita's arm, and shook her husband, Hezekiah's hand before turning to Quinn. "I can't thank you guys enough. You've gone above and beyond to make this packaging day a success. I still can't believe we stuffed and sent almost a thousand boxes!"

She jittered from foot to foot and checked the postal receipt again—957 boxes, to be exact. Words couldn't express her gratitude for all the volunteers and donors.

"You did all the hard work." Quinn lifted his shoulder.

Canita nodded. Her brother had returned from deployment recently, and she'd offered to help with packing and then driving the boxes to the post office. It had taken Chad's, Quinn's, and the couple's trucks to transport so many packages.

"Chad and I would like to take you out to dinner sometime." Nothing fancy, but she wanted to express her gratitude.

"You guys already fed us a gourmet lunch." Hezekiah put his hand on his wife's lower back.

But Tessa held up both hands, shaking her head. "If we're going to do this again—which I sure hope we are—then it will be great to spend an evening getting to know each other better."

The couple beamed at each other, then nodded their approval.

"I'd have to check my schedule." Quinn nudged the toe of his loafer along a crack in the pavement, chasing a beetle as he drawled the words out. He probably didn't feel comfortable around Chad yet, but Tessa had seen them chatting while they carried boxes to the truck.

With a promise to touch base with them about their dinner date, Tessa hugged each of her volunteers and said goodbye.

God had provided for the ministry this year, and no doubt, He would provide next year. Now she was dreaming about sending packages twice rather than once a year. She usually sent Christmas packages in September so they could get abroad and into the soldiers' hands in time. Bryce had paid for shipping and the boxes, and Chad had hired a company to cater brunch for the packing party while he'd done way more in preparation for the packing day.

This year, they'd sent packages to different bases—Germany, Japan, and South Korea. It was bittersweet not to send to the base she'd always sent to in the Middle East, the place where her dad was injured. They airlifted him to Germany, but he'd died en route.

The Middle East motivated Tessa to start the ministry. Now that American troops were pulled out of that location, she'd needed to find another base, but the place Dad last served would always hold a special place in her heart. Now if God could open her eyes to see what she needed to do with her career next? She rubbed her arms as she crossed the parking lot. The boutique space she'd been eyeing—and couldn't afford—wasn't listed anymore. Even with that obvious sign suggesting she'd better stop dreaming of something beyond her reach, knowing someone could afford to lease it and she was left daydreaming, stung.

A part of her wanted to remain a physical therapist. She'd found joy and fulfillment being part of someone's recovery. But she'd had to give that up or agree to contract through a company that could afford the insurance rates. So she'd been forced out of her field and grown passionate about starting her training business while catering to her soldier ministry. Now she had insurance again.

When she met Chad in the truck, his gaze was distant, his arms crossed as he stared at the white building ahead. To be exact, he was staring at the blue post office sign. He barely acknowledged her as she slid into the passenger seat and closed the door. He looked so pensive!

She touched his arm. "You okay?"

He shrugged and started the truck. It felt like déjà vu of the last time he'd been upset with her while in the truck after the packing meeting.

"I hope none of this has anything to do with Quinn." Now, why had she even said Quinn's name? Chad had been troubled before today. But Quinn might have caused his mood to get worse.

"Quinn's the least of my problems," he mumbled as he backed out of the parking lot.

Whatever it was, it sounded like a conversation that required them to sit down. She'd better wait until they got home, but a fifteen-minute drive was a long wait. She squirmed in her seat. "Can you park so you can tell me what's been eating at you?"

"I don't want to leave you."

Excuse me? She blinked at his fast response and tried to study him to grasp understanding. But he kept his gaze on the unpaved road from the post office. At times, he reminded her of a body that was always steady but a sudden twist left it with a strain or a torn ligament.

Seriously, was he considering breaking up with her? If so, why would he if he didn't want to? She shivered. Needing to hold on to something, she reached for her handbag on the floor mat between her legs and hugged it to the sudden hollow in her chest. "Then don't leave."

Maybe he needed assurance on her end. They hadn't discussed his future plans in Pleasant View. He'd been busy and focused on the race. He had money, but he didn't need to use it here while she and Mom had no intention of asking for rent from him.

If they needed more money, Tessa could take on the clients Liberty would pass on to her. Liberty, being a caregiver, often encountered patients in need of therapy. Thanks to Chad, Tessa had liability insurance and coverage for both physical therapy and training.

With the silence stretching, she'd better clarify what he had meant, rather than let herself go crazy guessing. Twisting her handbag straps around her fingers, she braced herself and asked again. "Why... Why did you mention leaving?"

"They want me to instruct a division."

That didn't make sense when he was already out of service. "But you're retired."

"I left them a forwarding contact."

Why did she get the feeling he wanted to reenlist? "You're not considering—"

"I already said yes."

She inhaled and glanced through the window at the cars they drove past before he turned to the country road leading home.

"Did you pray about it?"

"Affirmative."

"When did they ask you?"

"Several weeks ago."

"When do you leave?"

"Three days."

"What?!"

The truck jerked. No doubt her screech startled Chad as much as it startled her. "You've known for weeks, and you're just telling me now?"

Appearing void of any emotion, he kept his focus on the road. "I'm sorry. Telling you wasn't easy for me. I talked and prayed about it with Bryce and Eric, and..."

But she wasn't listening anymore. He'd talked about it with the guys, but not with her. Her shoulders sagged, and a weight pressed on her chest. Feeling unsettled, disheartened even, she hugged her purse tighter to her chest, the betrayal cutting deep.

Her throat constricted as heat burned in her eyes. "You didn't... think it was good to give me a heads-up or maybe even *include* me?"

"Tess." His chest rose, then fell. He reached his hand to touch hers, but she dropped the purse and snatched her hand away, having no desire to hold him now.

What could she say? Weren't couples supposed to be each other's best friend? Telling each other everything?

She'd assumed he'd retired. His sudden change of plans should've been a topic they'd discussed. Dad had died, and Elias had been injured, probably come close to death. What if Chad didn't make it this time?

Dread shivered over her spine, its icy fingers clawing at her throat. How could she mentally prepare for his departure with such short notice?

"I'm sorry. I should've told you."

He should have. She clenched her fingers into fists. "You're going to go diffuse bombs again." She struggled to speak through the cold grip on her throat, having no idea what instructing entailed or where he was supposed to go, but bombs were dangerous in any form. "I'm supposed to be okay that you're leaving in three days."

"Please, Tess..." His voice was hoarse. "I have to do this."

Her chest tightened, and when he parked, she didn't leave him time to get out of his seat like she usually did. She snagged her handbag, swung open the door, and hopped out. Ignoring his voice as he called her, she walked past the house and stormed through the tall grass until she stumbled onto the trail where she'd taken Chad during his assessment.

Critters darted out of her way as she tramped between pines and aspens. Perhaps she couldn't see clearly, but it seemed some leaves were hinting at a golden color.

Blinded by—what? Betrayal, confusion, fear, and panic all stormed through her. She stopped short of rampaging straight into a tree.

Chad was a soldier, but *they* were a couple. Shouldn't he be eager to start a life with *her*, instead of marching off on another assignment?

How long was he going and to what country? There wasn't a war zone at the moment, but any deployment could be dangerous.

But... She slowed her crazy pace. With everything catching her off guard, how was she supposed to be a supportive girlfriend? Was she capable of being the woman Chad needed her to be?

Panting, she arrived at the overlook where they'd stopped to eat on that first hike. She slumped onto a boulder and stared at the towering waterfall.

Memories of Chad rushed through her like those waters tumbling over the edge, whisking her along in a current she could no more control than something caught in the falls. His daring grin and urge to swing the ropes when he learned she'd done it before, his hand helping her over the rocks, his enthusiasm to share everything she enjoyed...

He'd ignored pain while she'd led him on the technical trail. Then he'd swung on the rope? Maybe he wasn't good at communicating after all.

But what about her? Had she expected him to fit into her life without her trying to accept his? He'd been so supportive of her dreams and goals, but had she considered his plans? What if he wanted to reenlist? Would she be strong enough to love him and respect his goals then?

"Oh, Lord." She breathed the fresh mountain air and set her handbag on the pine-needle carpet. "Why am I drawn to another soldier?"

As turbulent as that waterfall, a mix of emotions cascaded through her with memories of their adventures together. Hiking and running, fishing and boating, going to outdoor movies and watching fireworks at the wedding venue for the most romantic date of her life. She shuddered, her chest hollowing as new tears seared her eyes.

Chad wasn't just *any* soldier—he was the love of her life. It could've been worse. He might have taken off like her ex, Kanon, had.

Maybe she had to support Chad, even if his goals and dreams took him back to the army. Hadn't she thought as much about his first wife, thinking Nelly should have known that, in marrying a soldier, she'd have to stand aside as he committed to serving his country? Would Tessa now have to face the same challenge to her commitment? Did she love him enough to do that, to find her place in his life and future, and not try to change him?

Or was she not as strong as she thought she was? Parts of her still felt like the little girl she'd been, begging her daddy not to leave.

"So, God, am I overreacting? Am I asking too much to hope he'd want to stay with me?" Tired of sitting, she was tempted to follow the trail and swing on the ropes to dive into the lake, but she was too unstable to perform a daring task.

Instead, she strolled to different trails, savoring the solitude and grateful for the snowcapped mountains and vibrant wildflowers. Afternoon turned to evening, and evening to almost dusk with cool air brushing her shoulders. Her tank top had worked fine in the earlier warmth, but not anymore. So she returned home with a slight sense of peace and understanding about Chad's decision and his inability to tell her earlier.

When she got closer, she stared at Chad's cabin in the distance. Light peeked through the blinds. Was he inside or on his porch with Dusty?

Her feet started on the path to his cabin, but she thought better of it and turned toward the house.

Mom had returned from work, and the kitchen light was bright on her face as she mixed something on the stove. A fruity aroma sweetened the air. At Tessa's footsteps, Mom glanced her way and set the mixing spoon on the plate next to the stove. Her brows narrowed with genuine concern.

"Baby..." She wiped her hands on her brown apron as she crossed to Tessa with open arms.

Perhaps it was Mom's concern that caused tears to well in Tessa's eyes again.

"Oh, honey." Mom pulled her into an embrace, and Tessa threw her arms around Mom, holding back tears as she breathed in Mom's scent of fruit and lotion. "Chad told me about his assignment."

Tessa sniffed, nodding in Mom's neck. She felt young again, remembering all the years she'd cried in Mom's arms when Dad left. It must have been so hard for Mom when her husband took off for years. It sure had been hard on Tessa. Blowing out a breath, Tessa wiped tears from her face as she stepped out of the warm hug. "I thought he was done."

"Sweetheart." Mom grasped Tessa's shoulders, and the maternal glow in her kind eyes seeped their love into Tessa's. "If there's one thing you should know before falling in love with a soldier—"

"Too late. I'm already in love with one."

"—it's in their blood. Something that burns in their hearts urges them to serve their country. It's an unquenchable longing driving them."

Dad had never turned down a deployment. That much Tessa knew. Perhaps it would have helped if Chad gave her a heads-up.

As if Mom could read Tessa's mind, she continued. "At least he told you he was leaving."

Tessa winced at Mom's reference to Kanon, who'd left without saying anything and never bothered to call. Chad was a better man, and Tessa wouldn't have had it any other way. Loving him had to be worth whatever came next... even if she had to watch another man leave her life for the army like she'd watched her father.

She leaned in and pressed her lips to Mom's cheek. "Thank you. I think I'll call it a day."

Mom pointed to the stove clock displaying seven fifty-two. "I'm making some jam, but we could microwave the leftover meatloaf."

"Thanks, but I'm not hungry."

Mom looked at her sadly. "Unfortunately, Chad isn't joining us for dinner either."

"It's for the best." Yet deep down, Tessa wanted to see him so they could talk and spend every last minute together.

After a long shower, she felt better and understood why Chad might want to go back. He needed closure.

The first day while they ate, he'd said if they called him back he would be happy to serve. He'd ended his last mission by losing his friends. Perhaps he needed a do-over.

Tessa prayed again that night, then feeling renewed hope and understanding, slid into her bed. She tossed and turned as she fought the urge to leave the house and go to Chad's cabin. She needed to apologize and tell him she would support him, then hear all the details about his deployment or whatever kind of instruction he was going to take on.

By the time she got out of bed, she felt as if more than a night had passed—as if she'd grown up and put aside the last fragments of the little girl she had been, so as to become the strong woman her mother was. The woman she'd been raised and trained to be. A woman worthy of her soldier.

When she woke up the next day, as soon as she brushed her teeth, Tessa headed outside, intending to cook a hearty breakfast after mending things with Chad.

But something was off as she crossed the yard and didn't see his truck. Clouds tinted pink and orange lit up the sky as she all but ran along the path to the cabin.

The porch light was off, which was unusual too. Most days he forgot to turn it off until later. She scooted up the front steps and stopped between the still-vibrant geraniums, then lifted her hand. Her knuckles rasped on the door.

Dusty wasn't barking. Maybe they'd gone into town.

She edged open the door to a vacant room with askew dresser drawers, no clothes in the laundry basket, and no dog toys on the rug, and her heart sank.

On weak legs, she wobbled toward the dresser he'd started using. She pulled out one empty drawer, then another. The triathlon swimsuits and bike shirt and shorts were in one of the drawers, and the bottom drawer had a phone charger and the paper fans she'd sent him while he was abroad.

She moved to the bed which was nicely laid and tucked in, the way he always did. Had he left without saying goodbye? The bed creaked when she sank onto it, and her gaze wandered to the pillow and the letter folded there, Mom's special stationery with her company's vegetable-basket logo. He must have thought this through and even asked Mom for paper.

Her hands shook as she reached for and unfolded the paper.

My dearest Tess,

I decided to leave early before I cause you any more pain.

Leaving you even for a day is the hardest thing I'm doing. I hated saying goodbye to you, but there's no need for goodbyes. I'll be seeing you in six weeks.

Her shoulders felt lighter as tension evaporated. He would only be gone for six weeks?

I didn't get a chance to tell you the details of my assignment, but I'll be at the Explosive Ordnance School at the base in Florida.

I needed closure. Otherwise, I wouldn't choose to leave you. For some reason, I think this will be good for both of us if I end my time in the army on a good note.

I don't intend to die, but like you told me once, God is responsible for who dies and who stays alive.

Tell Bettina I said goodbye.

I love you so much.

Chad

"I love you too," she whispered, fighting tears as she set the letter on the bed.

Her chest tightened. What was wrong with her? Why had she lost it on him?

Of course, he'd made friends with Bryce and Eric. She'd been glad they'd included him, and she should've been glad he'd asked them to pray. Didn't she go to her friends the same way and have them pray with and for her?

She pressed her hands to her head and slumped against the bed, weighed down. What if the last conversation they ever had was of her ignoring his touch so she could walk off and throw a fit on a trail?

Although the training base was stateside, the dangers with bombs were inevitable.

She needed to call him. Maybe he wasn't too far, and they could hang out while he was still in town.

When she returned to the basement and sat on her bed to call him, his voicemail picked up. "This is Chad. Leave a message."

So precise yet deep and romantic. She called again just to listen to his voice as if that would make him magically appear.

Then the notifications on her phone forced her to tend to her messages.

A "you've got money" message from PayPal caught her attention, and she tapped the bubble. The crazy amount of money had her thumb shaking on the screen.

Yet another "you've got money" from Venmo flashed. Both from Chad.

She tucked her feet up beside her, the whole thing seeming surreal as she wrestled with her emotions. Wondering how she was going to use the money, she just sat there, frozen as if she were having a dream. She couldn't accept all that money. They'd made a deal when he paid her in advance for her liability insurance and stained the floors in the house too. She tried calling him again, but the call went straight to voicemail.

Great.

FRIDAY, TWO DAYS AFTER Chad left, getting ahold of him was still harder than getting back to her routine before she'd started training him.

She'd called two of her past therapy clients, but they didn't need a physical therapist anymore. Liberty had called with a potential client. The daughter of one of Liberty's clients would be in Pleasant View for the winter and needed a personal trainer and life coach to help her reach certain health and life goals that weren't yet clear to Tessa.

Either way, Tessa had something to look forward to, besides Elias's visit tonight that had Mom taking off work early so she could make his favorite dinner since she rarely saw him.

Come to think of it, it was probably Mom's favorite meal too.

After the roasted chicken and vegetables that reminded Tessa of Chad's first day with them, they sat around the table for angel food cake. Elias's favorite.

"I still can't believe the floors look this good." Elias pointed his fork at the hardwood floors gleaming under the fluorescent light.

"At first, I didn't like having another soldier in our lives." Mom extended the Cool Whip bottle toward Elias's plate and squeezed fluffy white foam on his half-eaten piece of cake. "But God is determined to bring them into our family."

Elias winked, grinning at Tessa, so she pointed her spoon at him. "What's so funny?"

"Mom's talking about your soldier, in case you were wondering."

If only she would hear from Chad, she'd have peace about his absence. If only she hadn't chased him away so early. "I can't get a hold of him."

"I was the last person he called before his phone died."

Right. Chad forgot his charger. But couldn't he borrow one somewhere? She'd mail him his if she knew where he was.

"Too bad he didn't call me first." She tried to keep the hurt out of her voice.

"Before you get all pouty"—Elias slid his cake plate aside and tipped his chin to the brown envelope next to Dad's portrait on the piano—"Chad wanted me to bring you that."

"What's that?" she asked.

Mom frowned.

"We have the title for the house."

Mom's eyes widened, and Tessa felt hers do the same as Mom walked to the piano and reached for the manila envelope.

Tessa's mind was spinning as Elias talked about Chad paying off the remaining four years of their mortgage. The land was in Tessa's, Elias's, and Mom's names, so Chad had gone through Elias to pay for the house. No way would Tessa have let him pay.

"It's not just the house by the way." Elias slapped the table, his dark eyes dancing under the light. "He leased a building for your business."

Tessa could barely register the rest of Elias's words as her head whirled with happy confusion. She didn't know whether to smile or cry, too overwhelmed to fathom what Chad had done. Chad was going to be broke because he'd poured his money in pursuit of her dreams.

"You'll need to meet with the Realtor—Gavin Kress, I believe Chad said—to sign a lease not just for the boutique you guys can turn into a storage and donation center for the packages-for-soldiers ministry but also for another nearby building. Chad leased that one for you to run a physical therapy and training gym." Elias reached across the table and rested his hand over hers. "As if that wasn't enough, Chad contracted with a supplier for you to pick out the equipment you need for your business."

"Oh, honey!" Mom sprang from her chair, leaned over Tessa's back, and hugged her neck. "I knew there was a reason I always liked that boy!"

Elias snorted. Perhaps guessing Mom's originally cool reception, or perhaps Chad had told him. He pulled his dessert plate closer and forked an oversized bite, then spoke with his mouth full. "He's planning to be your first employee at the soldier packaging storage center."

Mom dropped back into her seat and planted her chin in both hands, her eyes glowy. "A little birdie told me Chad might get a job at the Pleasant View Fire Station too."

Elias nodded and wiped a dollop of creamy substance from the side of his mouth. "If you still have doubts about your soldier"—he patted Tessa's back—"then I have no way of convincing you he loves you."

Hot and cold with a spinning mind, Tessa felt like taking the first flight to Florida to thank Chad in person. But she couldn't just barge in and interfere with his training. Or could she? Perhaps Elias had a better explanation of how a training base would take to visitors.

CHAPTER 21

Sitting on the chair by the desk in his bachelor-style house at the base, Chad stared at the blue diamond nestled in its red velvet box. Even the room's energy-conserving lighting couldn't keep the diamond from glittering.

Adrenaline surged through him. In the week since he'd left Pleasant View, he hadn't been able to talk to Tessa. But he could imagine her scent through the subtle detergent still lingering on his T-shirt.

Besides not having his phone charger, the number of tests he'd undergone upon arriving had kept him busy. They wanted to make sure he was stable before leading the IED division. He'd asked the sergeants in his quarters for a charger, but no one had his kind of phone. Until this evening, he hadn't had time to go into town to buy a charger or phone.

He'd intended to propose to Tessa before he left. Instead, her disappointment in him not sharing his decision had confirmed he was way ahead of himself in his expectations for their relationship—or was he way behind? He *had* decided without consulting her. Not something someone committed to a serious relationship should do.

She had every right to be hurt.

Still, her reaction caught him off guard. He'd expected Bettina to be the one giving him a hard time. Instead, she'd been understanding. After Tessa had stormed off on the trail, Chad had gone to the cabin, showered, and changed. Then he'd returned to the house to explain to Tessa why he accepted the task. Bettina had just returned from work, but Tessa wasn't home.

After Chad told Bettina he was leaving, she'd said there was no need for him to say goodbye if he was coming back. So he'd asked for paper to write a note explaining his reasons for leaving. He'd then decided against it and left with the paper.

He hadn't planned on leaving the next day until he got to the cabin and tossed and turned all night, battling emotions and imagining tears flowing from Tessa's eyes during their goodbye. So he'd saved both of them that agony.

He closed the ring box and set it aside. Tessa may not have liked a blue ring anyway. The blue diamond stood out among the other rings in the case, and the associate had talked it up as one of the rarest rings in the world. Her boss had won it in an auction in New York.

Elias had thought Chad was crazy to pay a fortune for a ring. Chad never spent money on anything for himself before, and Tessa was a lifetime investment. While he hadn't seen or noticed rings often, he'd never seen a blue diamond, and as rare as women like Tessa were, he liked having it as a symbol of the one-of-a-kind Tessa. His Tessa.

If she turned his proposal down, he'd take the ring back for a refund. His chest constricted at the possibility, and he glanced at the phone on the table, still charging from the socket.

Dusty's breathing filled the room from his kennel where he lay overly spent. It was only eight, but the dog had had a long day. It was the kind of day, Chad had brought Dusty onto the field while testing recruit candidates for their bomb suits. Over six students that day. Each had to run in eighty-plus-pound suits and perform other activities to prove they were fit for being EOD techs.

The days like yesterday when they'd disarmed the IEDs, Chad had left Dusty at home, but stopped by the house during his breaks to take the dog for his run and playtime.

He twisted his lips to one side and glanced at his new phone. If he was going to call tonight, he'd better call before Tessa went to bed. Reaching for the phone, he ignored the instructions he'd read earlier of letting the phone charge fully for the first time before turning it on.

After struggling to find a charger he could buy, he'd decided to buy a phone instead. Having kept his SIM card and phone number and transferred all his contacts, he found Tessa's number easily once he'd turned the phone on.

Something tight gripped his chest as he waited for the phone to connect. What if she was still mad at him for leaving and then not keeping in touch these days?

The moment he'd thought of calling Elias to go and tell Tessa about the properties, Chad's phone had been blinking a low-battery warning.

Now, Tessa answered at the first ring.

"Chad..." She was breathless as if she'd been eyeing her phone and waiting for him to call. "Don't hang up."

Relief swept through him, lifting a smile to his face, and he stood. "I'm not going to hang up." He'd bought and charged the phone just so he could talk to her.

"I've been trying to call you, but you left your charger." She spoke nonstop, barely pausing for breath as if afraid they'd lose the connection. "I'm so sorry I didn't support you."

He'd been more concerned not knowing how deeply his departure had affected her. He'd loved how she fussed over him so much. "I like that you worry about me."

"Oh my, Chad. Why did you waste all that money on me?"

"Oh, Tessa!" His muscles loosened, and he braced a hand against the windowsill, cradling the phone to his ear as he savored the warm astonishment in her tone. "It's our money and our soldier ministry."

He was a soldier after all.

Once he helped her set up her business and had it running, he'd apply for a job at the firehouse or join the local law enforcement, if they could use him in any department they saw fit.

"I miss you so much." Her sincere voice seemed to caress him, and he ached with a longing to see her.

He pushed from the window and sank onto the double bed, much smaller than the one he had at the cabin. "I miss you too."

"Tell me everything you've been up to since you got there."

He crossed his bare feet. "I had to pass some tests to prove I'm mentally stable before I taught the class."

"If you passed them, I'm guessing you're sleeping better, then?"

"Still a steady five hours." The flashbacks were less and less with Tessa occupying his mind and keeping him busy, then Elias sharing how he handled PTSD.

But more importantly, it came down to God giving Chad peace whenever he prayed or played a spiritual song on his harmonica. Yep, he played more spiritual songs these days than the sad ones he used to play to match his sad mood swings.

"What have you taught your students so far?"

Chad smiled. It had been thrilling two days ago to see the adrenaline coursing through the men he'd led. This had been his favorite division during training. "Two got to disarm an IED." He told Tessa about the cool tools the students had to learn to attach to the robot. "Then I had them putting on the bomb suits a million times."

"You sound happy."

Being here felt right. Instead of focusing on the failed last mission, he'd been focused on training candidates to learn to think on their own and going deep into physical aspects. Using mistakes he'd made in their place helped him emphasize the importance for students to follow directions. All that wasn't what he wanted to discuss with Tessa when he hadn't seen or heard from her in days. "What have you been up to?"

"I signed the leases this week. I've been overwhelmed by all the options of the exercise equipment on the website." She breathed out a thready whisper. "I don't even know how to thank you—"

"You already have." A warm feeling of comfort ran through him.

"Mom has been dying to reach you so she can thank you."

Unable to handle the praises, Chad asked how Bettina was doing. She needed to slow down or at least cut down her hours at the hardware store.

"She didn't work late today."

With the two-hour difference from Florida, it was probably six p.m. in Colorado. "That's unusual for her to get off at six."

"Mom hasn't taken on extra shifts. She's so relieved to have the property paid off. She even hosted friends for dinner twice in the last week. One of Dad's army friends is here right now."

It must be the veteran who visited before Chad left. "Is he still struggling to find a job?"

"Yes. He's here with two of his sons."

Chad's mind wandered where it shouldn't. "How old are the sons?"

"About my age—"

"Are they in the army?"

"Um... they're both in the Marines, I believe."

He cringed, bombarded by unease and jealousy as he lay down facing the ceiling. He braced an elbow behind his head. Was Bettina setting Tessa up with someone else? Did these Marines live in town? He closed his eyes, struggling to bounce back to his normal self.

"Are you still there, baby?"

Tessa's voice had him blow out a breath to compose himself. "Yeah..."

"My heart belongs to you," she said as if aware of his insecurities. "I'll be waiting when you come home."

He cleared his throat, finding his normal voice. He trusted Tessa. Otherwise, he wouldn't have gone off and bought a fancy ring. But would he always have that lingering fear driven by his ex?

"There's only four and a half weeks left." He said it more to himself than her.

"I love you. Remember that when you're dealing with bombs. Stay safe, baby."

"I love you too." He loved her so much that he felt weak by the way she affected him. Tessa only confirmed that he'd never been in love this much. And a love so strong could only end in one of two ways—a fairy-tale ending or a colossal heartbreak. What if she realized how special she was and decided to look for someone better? He wasn't naturally the jealous kind. The foreign emotion left him uncomfortable, and he didn't want it in his heart and head.

When they hung up, he fell back on the bed. Conflicted all over by his insecurities, he closed his eyes and asked God to help him gain confidence. Tessa had said to talk to God as a father and friend, so Chad spoke assuming God was right there listening.

"I don't want to be a jealous boyfriend. I hate worrying I'll lose Tessa."

As if God was reminding Chad that things were out of his control, memories of his virtual time with Tessa while he was on deployment resurfaced.

She was in love with him before they'd even met in person. She could've dated whoever she wanted—and still could—but she didn't. Why would she stop loving him now after they'd spent time together?

Even if Chad had been present with Nelly and available to her all the time, she probably had it in her heart to pursue someone else, or at least she may have at some point.

Deciding to surrender his relationship with Tessa into God's hands, Chad settled enough to sit up, rummage through his bag, and pull out his Bible. It was hard not to remember his evenings after dinner when he, Tessa, and Bettina prayed together before Tessa walked him to the cabin and they made out like reckless teenagers. When he prayed in the mornings and read his Bible, he thought of his time with Tessa during their morning devotions before his race. But four and a half weeks would pass before long.

Maybe the best way to quit worrying was to give Tessa extra space and not call her as often. The last thing he needed was to have her tire of him hovering.

FOR THE NEXT TWO DAYS, Chad continued his regimen. Today, he was grateful it was Friday and he'd almost made it through his second week.

In the expansive open field, the afternoon air was muggy, even as rain poured while Chad and Sergeant Malcom led a bomb-suit agility drill.

Due to the forecasted rain, he'd left Dusty in the house.

Performing tasks under duress conditions, the candidate they were training had the afternoon cut out for him. Besides wearing the suit that weighed over eighty pounds, he was also carrying fifty-pound weights in both hands. Chad and Malcom clapped while shouting instructions.

"Take two steps backward"—Malcom shouted over the clatter of pouring rain, then moved closer to the candidate—"two forward."

"Do six squats," Chad shouted, standing within feet of the candidate. Before the man was done with the squats, Malcom was ordering him to run toward the orange cones yards away. Chad wiped the rain from his face, the camouflage uniform weighing more when wet.

The candidate continued to prove his agility and sharpness as he responded to the commands under duress and uncomfortable weather conditions. Getting used to the catastrophic feeling was part of the test. Every tech had to be physically capable to make critical decisions while under pressure and still be able to disarm the explosives or perform any required tasks.

The final test Chad announced to the candidate was to run to where Leane sat on a chair strapped with wires and decoys around her chest. "She has a time bomb, and after I start the countdown, you have five seconds to save her life."

The man shook the water from his hands, clearly panicked, and Chad could relate. He'd feared he wouldn't recall everything he'd learned in the classes before the IED division.

"What if I cut the wrong wire!"

That would be the candidate's worst nightmare. Chad held his breath as he pulled out the timer from his chest pocket. One wrong wire cut, and all the man's hard work prior to this step would have been wasted. "You've got this. Go!"

"At this point, you should know what wire to cut!" Malcom shouted a response.

Uttering a silent prayer as the man fumbled behind the woman, Chad stared at the timer.

With only one second left, the candidate shouted, "I got it!"

The rain flowing on his face to his mouth tasted so sweet as Chad moved to high-five the man. "Congratulations on passing this division!"

The man beamed as he yanked off the vest. "I thought I was going to die."

"You've got what it takes." Malcom took the candidate's vest.

"If you get through the nuke division with this kind of perseverance"—Chad helped the candidate to ease out of his helmet—"you're on your way to being one of the best techs."

There were only two divisions left for the young man to train, and Chad had no doubt at this point he would make it. A candidate didn't make it this far without passing several tests, but passing a written test was always the hardest. Chad had passed because he was motivated to get to the IED division so he could get his hands on more explosives rather than memorizing all the foreign terms. Later, he'd learned the importance of memorization and how it played out in the real field while you were handling explosives on your own.

By the time they stored the equipment, the rain was slowing down, but Chad didn't see any reason to wait until the rain stopped. He was already wet.

As he walked out of the door, his captain was coming in.

"Sergeant Whitlock!" The captain's hand and wrists went straight, his elbow inclining forward in a crisp and fast salute.

"Captain." Standing still, Chad did the same immediate salute in recognition and respect to the man who'd instructed him in Virginia when Chad had had his basic training before advancing his training to Florida. The same man had been in Kuwait leading another unit when Chad was there on his tenth deployment. Their time in Kuwait was the reason Chad assumed the captain had recommended him for this current task.

"I can tell you belong here." The captain wiped the gentle drizzle from his forehead. "There's openings for contractors...." He continued relaying the base's need for instructors. "If you wanted flexibility, you could become a contractor instead of a full-time staff member."

Chad was only here for a purpose. "I have a job waiting for me." And a beautiful woman he wanted to spend each waking moment with. "But I'll keep that as a possibility if I change my mind." It was the right thing to say.

The captain nodded in response. Then, with a final salute, they continued their separate ways.

Needing to get back to Dusty, Chad jogged through the expansive facility alongside paved sidewalks and walkways between the lush grass.

He felt sticky, and oh, how he longed for the light Colorado air, the same air Tessa breathed. But he was not going to act like a needy boyfriend. He was busy, and so was she.

When he got to his place and opened the kennel, Dusty leaped for him, smearing Chad's face with his wet tongue.

"I missed you too, buddy." Chad patted the dog's head, his fur tickling Chad's palm. "Ready for your run?"

The dog marched to the door, and Chad stood, needing to change out of his wet clothes. He rummaged through the chest of drawers at the end of his bed and pulled out a T-shirt and shorts. He'd shower after their run.

As he slid his arms in his T-shirt, Chad couldn't help himself and walked to his phone on the table. The same way he'd done the last two days of deciding not to call Tessa. Deciding not to be jealous didn't mean he didn't want to hear her voice.

Tessa had called him yesterday and left a voicemail, but he hadn't called her back, trying to see how long he could give her space. When he touched the phone, it flashed the time of 3:56—and a text from Tessa.

Dusty scratched the door.

"Hold on, buddy." Chad kept his gaze on the screen, then swiped to read the message.

Tessa: I'll be at Tundell Steak House in Destin at six thirty. Any chance you can meet me there? I know you're busy, so if tonight is too short notice, I'll come back tomorrow too.

Destin? Chad frowned as he reread the text. As in Destin, Florida? That would only be thirteen miles away, but why was she in Florida?

His heart finding a new rhythm, he tapped out a response.

Chad: Where are you?

Tessa: Here in Florida.

Chad: I'll be there.

Tessa: Can't wait to see you.

He tossed the phone back on the table, reached for the ring box, and set it back down. Tessa was in town. A rush of warmth flooded him. Dusty moved from the door and back to Chad.

He'd better take the dog for a run first.

It was the most distracting run Chad had taken. His mind played out a visual of the restaurants he'd been to Destin, but it had been too long since he'd been there to remember where the steak house was located.

As soon as he returned, he left Dusty eating while Chad showered. He then changed into his gray pants and a navy T-shirt. Not fancy, but he didn't want to appear like he was going to church.

He reached for the ring box, the velvet soft in his palm. He felt warm, his shirt already damp, as he tried not to play out a strategy of how and what he was going to say. Then he turned to the dog, which was staring at Chad with sympathetic eyes as if he knew Chad's biggest problems at the moment.

"Will she say yes?" He lifted the ring to Dusty before pocketing it in his trousers.

It didn't hurt to have a ring, whether he worked up the nerve to ask her or not, though he intended to try before he said good night to her.

With Dusty in the truck's back seat, Chad drove using the directions on his phone.

The rain had stopped, and the sky had cleared by the time he pulled into the parking lot of a modern limestone restaurant with floor-to-ceiling windows. It was five forty-five, but he didn't mind being early. He needed to process whether he'd be bold enough to ask Tessa to marry him. With the parking lot half full, he easily found a spot at the end. When he stepped out, he opened the back door and patted Dusty who was hovering close to the door. "Wish me luck, buddy."

The dog licked his arm.

"I'll bring Tess to say hello afterward." Perhaps he would have popped the question by then. He'd proposed before, but he didn't remember being this overworked. Could be that he'd been young and fearless, too confident Nelly was going to say yes.

At least he arrived with forty-five minutes to spare. If he got them a table in the restaurant, he'd be less likely to act awkward by the time Tessa arrived.

After closing the door and pressing the key fob, he strode past cars to make his way to the sidewalk. When he glanced at the paved palm-tree-lined pathway, he stopped in his tracks. Tessa, with her handbag on her shoulder, was rushing from the entrance and toward the parking lot—toward *him*. She flashed her pearly whites, and her genuine smile warmed him to the core.

An onslaught of feelings too tangled to sort assailed him, and his entire body quickened, his palms sweaty. He forgot to swallow or breathe. He tried to take a step forward, but his legs went numb. Instead of sprinting to meet her, he stood there just staring and ignoring the movement of people crossing the lot toward the restaurant.

She'd arrived just as early, and here she was all the way from Colorado. As far as he knew, she didn't have a family member or friend in Florida.

Her floral-patterned white summer dress swayed over her slim hips and danced at her knees while the evening breeze lifted her glossy hair. Dark wisps of it kissed the sweet flush on her flawless cheeks and obscured the glow in her eyes. His fingers twitched to brush it away, to keep anything from hiding her from him—or touching her when he couldn't. She was so beautiful, and the sight of her left him nearly dizzy with longing.

"Chad!" She slowed when she was within reach. "I tried to wave at you when you pulled in, but you were so focused."

Her brown eyes, so full of promise, reflected the longing he felt. Her name rolled off his tongue, and in one moment, he closed the gap between them. He scooped her into his arms and swept her close. The purse brushed against his arm as he moved his hand to her cheek, her hair now tickling his fingers. Then he bent his head and kissed her with all the feeling imploding within him. The heady smell of rain and mountains all felt so familiar as she kissed him back. When he drew back, breathless, she tucked her head against his chest, unable to look at him at first and then finally doing so with eyes full of such love and appreciation it stole his breath again as he looked in her face. "I love you, Tess."

She touched his chest again, laying her hand over his heart as if to hold onto it forever—for surely, let go or not, she would hold it forever. No one else would ever hold it as she had. "I love you too, Chad." She'd said those words before, but they seemed to register more now. He had no doubt she was the woman he wanted to spend his entire life with, regardless of any unexpected circumstances that may be thrown at them.

His thumb trailed against her soft, velvety skin. "Why did you come all this way?"

Surely, she'd come for him.

"I didn't say goodbye." She stepped on tiptoes and brushed her lips against his neck, scorching his body with awareness.

"You did. On the phone." When they'd talked.

Her eyes danced in the golden evening light. And she whispered, "It's not the same."

"When did you arrive?"

"This morning."

"Where are you staying?"

"At a hotel here in Destin." The tender way she looked at him reminded him of the small box in his pants, but a parking lot wasn't an ideal place to propose. Thankfully, she eased back, looping her arms around his waist, her hair tickling his fingers on her back. "How's Dusty?"

"You wanna go say hello?"

She nodded, beaming, and Chad took her hand in his to turn back to the lot. As they wove in between the cars, she talked about her attempt to make an appointment so she could surprise him at the base, but the next available appointment for her to get into the base was a week away. Meanwhile, his mind was spinning, and his free hand thrusting into the pocket and brushing onto the box.

At the truck, he opened the door, Dusty all but leaped out, and Tessa squatted near the cab and wrapped her arms around the dog. She then slid her handbag off her shoulder and set it on the concrete as if it was in the way of her giving Dusty attention.

"Hey, big boy." With her smile spreading up her cheeks, she rubbed behind the dog's ears.

Forget all the reasons why he shouldn't propose in the parking lot. It was now or never. While Tessa loved on the dog, Chad ignored his panic, shoved his hand into his pocket, pulled out the box, and flipped it open. Concrete scraped through his pants when he knelt on one knee and cleared his throat.

Tessa turned to him, her eyes widening when she saw the glittering diamond he offered her. She moved her hands from the dog and tossed them to her chest.

"Tess. When my unit received a package with a note almost two years ago, I never expected writing back would be the beginning of an adventure with the love of my life." There were so many things he needed to express. He'd need a lifetime to tell Tessa all she meant to him and what a better man he'd become by having her in his life.

Tears glittered like diamonds in her eyes, and she let out a shuddered breath.

So Chad continued. "As you've noticed, I'm like a time bomb that could blow anytime. Still, you've not given up on me, but instead stuck with me even when you're unsure of where that would lead you or if I was serious about us."

"Oh, Chad..." Her lips quivered.

"I want to spend each waking moment with you. Will you marry me?"

Her hands crept to her mouth. "Yes," she whispered between her fingers, then laughed, and spoke louder. "Yes, I will marry you."

Dusty, as if sensing the emotion, moved between Chad and Tessa, then scooted to slurp Chad's cheek, since he was kneeling closer to the dog's height.

Chad slid the ring from its box, and his shaky hands let the box drop to the pavement while he took Tessa's hand. Dusty barked and retrieved the box, his eager tail thumping against Chad's side, and Tessa's warm tear hit his hand as he slid the ring onto her finger, amazed by how perfectly it fit.

"This is so beautiful. I love it." The diamond danced in the evening light. "How did you know my size?"

His chest rose, puffing with pride, and he reached for her hands and stood up with her. "I know you so well—everything about you and your heart and soul."

"You do?" She slid her hands onto his shoulders, her tone playful as she stepped on tiptoes and brushed against his lips. An invitation he couldn't refuse.

"I do." He spoke over her lips before anchoring his hands in her soft dark hair and kissing her long and deep, lingering.

When Chad stepped back, Dusty nudged his hand with the ring box, and Tessa laughed, scooping it from the dog's mouth.

"Thanks, buddy." Chad rubbed behind Dusty's ears, unable to take his gaze from Tessa and the future ahead of them.

While Tessa felt like a fantasy, she was his everyday reality, and Chad was willing to become the best version of himself by being unafraid to live out this dream. That was a choice he'd made the moment he fell in love with her. After all, love was not a feeling, but a decision based on how much he was willing to risk and how hard he was willing to work to avoid mistakes he'd made in his first marriage.

EPILOGUE

Almost three months later...

Gavin Kress wouldn't have guessed a winter wedding could be as magical as Chad and Tessa's. For the small ceremony, less than one hundred people gathered in a rustic barn glittering with lights strung across the lofty open-beamed ceilings and twining around the support posts. Now, with the winter festival atmosphere, everyone lingered after the ceremony while the photographer snapped photos of the bridal party.

But more beautiful than the ceremony's tasteful locale had been the couple's sentimental vows. Like half the people sniffling and reaching for tissues, Gavin had fought tears after listening to how Chad and Tessa had met—and he wasn't one to cry easily.

Gavin had met them at the Stone family reunion, through his friends. Besides Chad attending the bachelor party Bryce had hosted for Gavin, Gavin had been working with Chad to fix two of his buildings to suit Tessa's businesses. He also planned to help the couple find a perfect home when they were ready to buy, though, for now, they seemed happy staying with the bride's mom. Gavin had wasted no time in returning to work after his wedding hadn't gone as planned. Being a Realtor, a property manager, and an investor in their tourist town and the neighboring towns kept him busy throughout the year, which he'd welcomed these last few months.

When Chad told him about the wedding and extended an invitation, Gavin didn't hesitate in accepting. Just because his wedding hadn't worked out, it didn't mean he still didn't want to observe what couples in love looked like. He'd certainly thought he was in love with Lucky.

"I don't know. I think we're rushing things.... If anything, the sudden rain was an indicator we shouldn't get married...." He winced as her words echoed, still seared in his memory. When he'd left the altar and entered the adjoining room, she sat there sobbing as if their wedding day had caught her off guard. Three years together, and she selected their wedding day. Then she chose that day of all days to decide she was making a mistake. Gavin should've paid attention to the signs instead of moving things forward. If he had to do it over, he wouldn't go for a long courtship. But he was done with relationships.

Laughter from one of the merry tables rang over the soft music, and he shook his head, ridding himself of unpleasant memories.

As painful and sad as he should feel, he felt anything but as the happy couple moved from one table to another to interact with their guests.

Chad, dressed in formal military attire, had a protective hand on Tessa's shoulder as his green eyes shone beneath the sparkling lights. A warm feeling of comfort ran through Gavin at their obvious happiness.

Eric and Bryce, both Gavin's friends, shared his table. As bridesmaids, their wives had rejoined them as soon as they finished posing for photos. Now, Bryce held the little bundle in his arms, and Liberty squatted, smiling as she cooed to their newborn.

Being far from starting the family he so desired created a melancholy Gavin couldn't ignore.

Needing to find his normal self, he reached for his drink, sipped the sweet hot cider perfectly in keeping with the winter festival ambiance, and peered through the nearby French doors to the world beyond. Snow danced on the deck and shimmered in the air when a breeze blew it off the bare trees, but stars shone clear overhead. With the moon rising full and bright, the snowy fields appeared celestial, and snowcapped mountains cut stunning silhouettes against the sky.

"Ready for your upcoming trip?"

Eric's voice pulled Gavin's gaze back to the table.

The ladies had left, and so had Bryce.

Gavin's trip was only two weeks away. "I just need my malaria shots, and I'll be set."

"Let me know if you need any tips for your trip."

Gavin rubbed at his clean-shaven jaw. "Brady emailed me a massive booklet of what to know before leaving."

Brady, one of Eric's best friends and Gavin's longtime friend, had moved to Uganda. They'd met when Gavin worked in New York.

Eric and Bryce took it upon themselves to mentor Gavin after his nightmare wedding. Eric had suggested Gavin take some time off work and travel abroad. When Gavin mentioned it to Brady, he'd concocted a one-year trip to Uganda. With Gavin's business booming and three trusted managers in place, he needn't worry about running things. Helping people in need would take his mind off his heartache.

When Chad and Tessa approached the table, Gavin and Eric turned to greet the couple. Chad chatted with Eric, and Tessa leaned in to give Gavin a sideways hug. The lace on the arm of her gown stuck on his cufflinks.

"Sorry about that." She chuckled, her face as radiant as a bride's should be.

"Not a problem." Gavin carefully freed his button from the lace without ripping a dress that would surely be sentimental for her—not given away unworn and unloved as Lucky's had been. As he had felt.

"Chad and I are so overwhelmed by your gift."

Gavin dismissed Tessa with a wave. Honestly, he'd rather see someone enjoy the Caribbean cruise he'd purchased for him and Lucky. "Better than let it go to waste." Like his honeymoon had gone to waste. "I'm glad you could use it."

"I'm not sure I want Tessa to get used to cruises." Chad moved closer to his wife, wrapping his arm around her waist. "But, man, you're setting quite the bar."

Gavin smirked. "I like setting the bar."

Lucky had wanted to take a December cruise to escape the Colorado winter, and there was nothing that Gavin wouldn't have done to make Lucky happy.

AFTER THE WEDDING, Christmas and New Year's flew by. Now, Gavin was going through customs in Uganda. Following the long flight, the endless drive from the airport to the Nile dragged on. Reaching the facility at nine p.m. Ugandan time worn out, he needed to head to his cottage and collapse on a bed. Tomorrow, he'd investigate his new surroundings. For now, he was content with what he'd seen online of the three grass-thatched cottages, each with a private pool.

He trudged into the facility's lobby and yawned while the man's dark-skinned hands flew on the front desk's laptop keyboard after Gavin had given him his name and presented his ID. The place smelled of fried food, fresh-cut flowers, and a myriad of homey scents.

With his luggage next to him, he surveyed the half dozen tables in the small restaurant, its dimmed lighting soothing after the garish lights on the plane and the strobe of traffic.

A woman he couldn't see clearly spread out linen tablecloths, then added flowers to a vase on one of the tables. Her movements hypnotic, she crossed to another table, yanked off the linen, replaced it, and arranged the flowers. She adjusted the chairs before moving to the next table and doing the same.

Wow, she was fast.

"The restaurant only caters to our guests." The man's voice pulled Gavin's attention back as he continued in a heavy accent. "You can choose to have room service or come to the restaurant." He went through the list of what Gavin needed to know, but Gavin opened and closed his mouth. He'd be here for two weeks, plenty of time to learn what to expect and so forth.

"Here's your key." Three keys jiggled when the man handed them to Gavin. "Hope will show you to your cottage."

"If you give me the map, I can take myself."

"Hey, Hope!" the man bellowed, ignoring Gavin's response. "Come take this guest to the Sunrise Cottage."

Gavin followed the man's gaze to the woman setting the tables.

"One moment!" She spoke with a crisp almost-British accent. Then she expertly added two more flowers to the vase.

"When I call you, I don't expect to wait!"

Startled by the man's harsh tone, Gavin spun around and jerked back a step. He acted that way right in front of a customer?

"Come, now!"

"Yes, sir." The woman brushed her hands together and started toward them.

Gavin glanced from the rude boss to the woman striding their way with grace and confidence, her head poised as one would balance a crown. Dressed in a white blouse tucked into a black skirt, no doubt this pseudo princess was the waitress and did janitorial work. As she approached, the light from the counter illuminated her flawless brown face, casting a bronze gleam over the curves of her pixieish features and glowing in the biggest, most guileless eyes he'd ever seen.

Stopping a few feet away, she moved her gaze to Gavin, and something shifted in him. She held his gaze, not giving any indication of being bothered by her boss's degrading behavior, before clasping her hands together and bowing. "Good evening, sir."

She was mesmerizing! As time stood still, Gavin couldn't remember what he was supposed to say. He reached for his luggage.

But she darted to him and snatched it from his hand. "It's my job."

Her hand brushing against his arm quickened his heart in a most annoying manner. Confused, he stepped away, not daring to argue about who should and shouldn't hold the luggage.

Good grief! Like a docile puppy, he followed the beauty out the back door and onto a path through lush gardens. A floral scent drifted in the air, and with it, a dreamy hopefulness swirled in his head before he got a grip.

He ground his teeth. He was far from pursuing a relationship. So whatever reaction his heart and body conjured his mind could conquer. He *would* stay focused while exploring the Nile for the next two weeks. He was here to recharge his batteries before venturing to a remote village for an entire year, *not* to fall for an enchanting fantasy.

-THE END-

Check out all the other books in the Series on my Amazon Page.

Stay tuned for Eric's siblings in the spin off series-The Billionaires' Reunion.

Also Stone Enterprises Will be featured in The Office Heartthrobs.

If you would like to connect with me, join Rose's Facebook group[1] and connect with other readers as well. **Rose Fresquez's Reader Group.**

---

1. https://www.facebook.com/groups/243932449976110/?ref=pages_profile_groups_tab&source_id=435344610252020

Next in the Caregiver Series!
The Realtor's Attendant

She's escaping an arranged marriage. He's recovering from a disastrous breakup. When sparks fly between them, will they brave a second chance at love?

Touted as the ideal daughter, Hope Njeri chafes under her dad's strict rule and dreams of discovering who she is beyond his influence and traveling the world beyond his threshold. So, when he tries to pressure her into an arranged marriage, she flees Kenya for Uganda, determined to become the woman she's always kept hidden. Even if that means working around the clock as a hotel maid and putting up with her overly critical boss.

After being left at the altar, small-town Realtor Gavin Kress jumps at the opportunity to spend a year in Uganda doing charity work. Maybe some distance from his ex will help him heal. Dating is the last thing on his mind—until the beautiful Hope stumbles into his life and restarts his heart.

When he witnesses her boss verbally harass her, Gavin steps in to help—and gets her fired. With no other options, she accepts his offer to work with his charity organization. But as their feelings blossom, Hope and Gavin must decide how hard they're willing to fight for true love—especially when they travel back to his small town and his ex wants a second chance.

Gavin's let a woman walk away before, and Hope's always let everything get taken away from her. But this time, can Gavin trust the woman he loves isn't going to walk out? And if Hope fights for the love of her life, can she stand up to his parents who aren't fond of her?

A NOTE FROM THE AUTHOR

Thank you for reading *Soldier's Trainer*.

It's always a blessing to meet new readers. And to those who have read all my stories, thanks for giving me another chance and for your reviews and notes of encouragement.

I can never forget to thank God who enables me to create these stories. Thank you Lord!

You can connect with Rose on Facebook or email her at rjfresquez@gmail.com

ABOUT THE AUTHOR

Rose Fresquez is the author of the Buchanan -Firefighter series, Romance in the Rockies, The caregiver series, two short stories and two family devotionals. She also writes in a multi-author project: Chapel Cove Series.

Rose is married and is the proud mother of four amazing kids. She loves to sing praises to God. When she's not busy taking care of her family, she's writing.